Dear Reader,

I have always had strong dreams, a tendency I inherited
from my father. So it seemed right that this story should
begin with a woman dreaming.

Aurinia, regarded with suspicion because of her powers
as a healer, is isolated. Across the barrier of distance,
her dream connects her to another person, a warrior
on a battlefield, Macsen, perhaps the only person with
the power to understand the qualities that lead others
to shun her.

The significance of dreaming has long aroused fascination.
In the England of 876, people believed the soul traveled
widely without a person's conscious knowledge while
they slept.

By 876, the Celtic and the Anglo-Saxon heritages were
strongly mixed. Both cultures were enamored of dreams,
and in Celtic tales the tension between the dream world
and the real world was very strong. A favorite Celtic
legend told the story of a much earlier Maxen, who
dreamed of a British bride, and crossed land and water
to find her, before becoming emperor of Rome. Time
confused the connection to real historical figures,
but the point of the story is the power of the dream.

My next story, *Captured*, touches on that other fascinating
mystery of early times, the role of "luck," fate, *wyrd*—
the fortune that turns on the fall of a rune stone or a
pair of dice. Rosamund, trapped among the Vikings,
wins a chained prisoner in a game of chance. He is hers,
unsettling and dangerous, a tough fighter who takes
the hard way. She will need his help.

Helen Kirkman

Visit me at www.helenkirkman.com.

Praise for Helen Kirkman

"Dark Ages? In Helen Kirkman's hands, they shine."
—HQN BOOKS author Margaret Moore

A Fragile Trust

"Kirkman's lyrically descriptive prose sustains an unusual emotional intensity. This one generates that rare urge to read it straight through."
—*Romantic Times BOOKreviews*, Reviewer's Choice Award Winner

"*A Fragile Trust* tells the story of a love so powerful that readers will never forget it...absolutely awe-inspiring and sure to be one of the best historicals of 2005!"
—*Cataromance.com*

A Moment's Madness

"This debut novel is rich with textural details of an ancient time, retelling with flair the age-old story of love trumping vengeance."
—*Romantic Times BOOKreviews*

"*A Moment's Madness* is a mesmerizing tale and I was loath to put it down until the very last page was turned."
—*ARomanceReview.com*

Forbidden

"Very graphic and sensual, this tale is well-told and fast-paced from start to finish."
—*Old Book Barn Gazette*

"*Forbidden* will hold your attention from the vivid opening to the climax."
—*Romantic Times BOOKreviews*

Embers

"The lush backdrop and intrigue-laden plot make for good reading."
—*Romantic Times BOOKreviews*

HELEN KIRKMAN

UNTAMED

HQN™

HQN™

ISBN-13: 978-0-373-77165-3
ISBN-10:   0-373-77165-7

UNTAMED

www.HQNBooks.com

Printed in U.S.A.

To Ann, Lynn and Sarah—
for all the good times we've shared together.

Also by Helen Kirkman

Fearless
Destiny
A Fragile Trust
A Moment's Madness
Forbidden
Embers

And coming soon from HQN Books

Captured

N

Viking forces control
all of England north of
the River Thames

Saxon warriors fiercely
defend their king in
the last free land...
Wessex.

NORTHUMBRIA

THE WELSH

MERCIA

EAST
ANGLIA

Sutton Hoo•

River Thames

London

WESSEX

•Winchester

KENT

Wareham

CORNWALL

Wytch
Heath

England 876 AD

The Viking Armies have advanced westward to Wareham
and find themselves surrounded by King Alfred's men

CHAPTER

1

Wytch Heath, near Wareham, the South Coast of England,
AD 876

This time the dream of him was different. The dark
warrior that had invaded her dreams was closer. Aurinia
caught the sense of danger from him and her breath sharpened, even in the bands of a sleep that was at once real
and unreal.

She saw his face first, only that, the strong lines and the
night-black hair, the eyes dark as ripe sloe berries, and her
heart tightened on the familiar dizzying ache.

Light and shadow from her empty hall flickered over her
closed eyelids and the dream pulled her down, overmastering her senses, making them catch fire. He called to her, her
dark warrior with the costly armour and the eight strands
of gold at his neck. His presence and the potent sense of

his vitality overwhelmed her. But this time the shadowy bond was fierce, intensified by the danger. Pain.

She smelled the blood. It was all around him, terrifying and death-filled, like the shouting.

He saw her, had sensed her, five miles away on the battlefield.

The brilliant eyes locked for one burning instant with hers and the unspoken bond snapped tight, frightening and deep. Then the contact broke. She saw him swing round, the swift sudden movement of the leaf-bladed spear in his hand, its flight like lightning through the dark, a bright curving arc of terror.

Aurinia's fist clenched, hard against the patched linen of her dress. The shouts all around him were in Danish, Viking words. He was not Danish, with his dark eyes, fine high-bridged nose and his bronzed skin that spoke of southern climes.

Then even as she watched, caught in the dreaming, the sharp arrow points ripped through the air, a death rain hissing toward him, and the slighter, unarmoured figure next to him fell. The screaming voices, the fast feet of the Vikings, rushed forward like a wave.

He had kept his feet, but he would have to turn, run.

Run. Her heart spoke to him across distance and time that had no meaning, as though they were one, she and the dark warrior who fought so bitterly against odds that were desperate. As though he could feel the desperation in her own heart, as though his unmatched strength had the power to penetrate the frozen isolation that held her trapped in this empty hall, to shatter it with his heat. As though they could touch.

Run.... She watched him unsheathe the glittering line of a broad-bladed sword. She could smell death, death and wounds.

He did not turn back. He stepped in front of the fallen man. The wave broke over him.

And she— The desperation flooded her heart, terrible, matched by a raw will.

"Lady!"

The sharp sound of Huda's voice shocked through her, real, close. The grip of her steward's hand on her shoulder shook her awake in the quiet hall at Wytch Heath. His breath rasped with his fear.

She was shivering. The dream dissipated, lost like the hot vital grace of the dark-haired man.

"Lady Aurinia..." Huda's voice, anxious, demanding, cut through, breaking the sleep that had come over her as she'd sat beside the window. The only retainer who had remained faithful to her had come to tell her what she already knew. That the invading Vikings and the troops of King Alfred of Wessex were fighting at Wareham, not five miles from here.

"...there is a battle. Men fleeing from the army may force their way through here."

"They cannot." Aurinia sat up, forcing movement through her stiffened body, every muscle wound tight with tension. One thing in this world was certain. No stranger had ever reached the hall at Wytch Heath. The pure isolation of her home stood unbroken.

It had the strength of a curse—

"No Viking will get through."

"No," answered Huda, the heaviness deliberate. "Nor Saxon." He paused and then said, "Not even a king's man."

A king's man. Aurinia had glimpsed the stranger of her dream, in a hall greater than this, cloaked in shadow and rich light, the weight of the golden dragon pouring down his shoulder like fire. The Saxon king's sign.

"Are we not on the same side as the king's men?"

Huda's hand tightened for an instant on her shoulder. "No one is on our side."

She looked away. Huda was the nearest thing she had to a father. She had to protect him as she did herself. The isolation at Wytch Heath existed for a reason. Her fists were still clenched, as though the terrible life-and-death struggle of the stranger touched her even now.

No one ever found the path through treacherous ground to her hall. It was wolf-ridden.

Unless— She stood. The white cloth and the rune staves at her feet scattered. She had already read those angular shapes carved on wood, at once an ancient alphabet and signs filled with hidden meaning. She did not look at how they fell. She had seen the portents.

They had spoken of death.

The red glow of sunset filled the chamber, stinging her eyes, staining the pale cloth like the blood she had smelled, tasted. She could feel pain, heat, despair. How could she turn away from that? From *him.*

Sudden sound made her gasp, and Muninn's winged shape sliced through the sunlit air in a flurry of disturbed plumage. The raven perched on her windowsill. Muninn, bird of memory, sacred in the old days to Woden, chief of the sky gods. A raven was a messenger.

Huda crossed himself, even though every living creature who visited her was familiar to him. Ravens were double messengers; they might bring bliss, or they might come to feed on the battle-dead. The sun struck the bird's blue-shadowed wing as it settled. It was the same colour as the night-dark hair of the king's man.

She could feel the power of the man's will across the distance that separated them. It reached inside her. Her heart seemed to stop, suspended between one beat and the next.

He would bring the outside world and the scent of blood if he fought his way here. If she let him. If he lived.

Her life would change.

She did not meet Huda's eyes. Her decisions were her own. They always had been. She watched the raven.

He would come.

Wareham—The Vikings' Fortress

MACSEN STEADIED THE THIN, unconscious figure draped across the front of his saddle. He was careful not to touch the protruding arrow shafts. He was trapped. The river blocked the way to the king's encampment. It might have been possible for him to cross alone, even with the pursuit behind him, but not with the wounded man.

The shouts behind closed in, so near he could make out the Danish words. They wanted the helpless burden he carried. They wanted death.

He would not let them take it. The hot rage at what had

been done to the injured boy's body burst inside his head, its power fed by fury at the threat to someone helpless and by something darker that belonged to the past, his own unatoned blood guilt.

He wheeled the horse left, the movement abrupt and complete. The rest of the Saxon force had withdrawn and his pursuers were close. But they hesitated, even Earl Guthrum's guardsmen with their red shields and their burnished chain mail, because they understood which path he chose, toward the barren heath and the dark woods where no one lived. No one except the reputed sorceress, the Saxon *hell-rune*.

The Lady of Wytch Heath.

In his head, he could see her, standing alone in her hall, her beauty as strong as the sun breaking the clouds. The light streamed in through the open window, dazzling her eyes.

Five miles. The knowledge of the distance that separated them formed out of the air. As though the thought were hers. The awareness of her burned him, mind and flesh and harshly tightened skin.

Five miles. He moved and Du Moro, named for that other black stallion of legend, responded. He did not know whether luck would last long enough. Whether the wounded boy he held would survive. If the arcane reputation of Wytch Heath was enough to stop pursuit…

Two of the group of five pursuers followed him.

The luck gave out with the light. The empty heath vanished, and with it the eerie brilliance reflected off the autumn bracken, crimson-bright against the deep purple of ling and heather. The black woods closed out the dying sun. The thick undergrowth hid ground that was treacherous.

There was no other way. Macsen set spurs to the exhausted horse. The others, fresher, unencumbered, closed in. If he could not lose them, he would have to fight. It was unlikely he would win.

Even as the thought took shape in his head, the first sound came of a pursuit that was not human.

Du Moro, trained to battle, trained even to the smell of death, reared, hoofs sliding on the narrow moss-slick track, nearly unseating him. Macsen kicked his feet free of the stirrups. If the stallion fell back, it would kill him.

He sought for balance, to hold the helpless burden of the unconscious man. The bolt of fear that surged through the bunched sweating muscle beneath him was primeval. The same nameless fear was in his own blood, transmitted through the unearthly sound, through the touch of panicked flesh beneath him, into the dark place that existed in everyone far below the reach of reason. It was enough to blind him.

He fought it. The power in that moment dominated by primitive instinct came not from high courage but from the savage force of his anger. He controlled the war-stallion, fear-mad, nearly five times his weight, by the depth of that appalling power. This time, there would not be the death of someone hunted. He would stop it.

Anger gave him the power to force Du Moro forward. Anger let him keep the stallion moving so that it could not rear again. Tree branches whipped at his head. Behind him, he heard one of the pursuing horses go down. There was a raw scream that encapsulated all the primitive fear in the black air. He could not tell whether the sound was human or animal. Across it was the unearthly noise, the nightmare of every civilized creature, the howling of wolves.

The lone Viking bolted right, followed by the lithe flash of a grey shape, the movement of its muscles liquid in the dark. The blackness swallowed them.

The rest of the pack stayed with him.

The wolves would scent the injured boy's blood, the traces of his own. The stallion, weakened by exertion before they'd begun this journey, burdened by the double weight and haunted by instinctive terror, was vulnerable. They could bring it down.

The pack had driven one horse to stumble, working as one, injuring the rider in the process. Easy meat. But they did not stop to feed their hunger. They hunted him.

Their shapes moved in and out of the shadows, light and swift as wraiths, keeping pace with the laboured movements of the heavy horse hemmed in by trees. They could have outstripped it, circled ahead, closed in. But the howling stopped.

The grey shapes still shadowed through the darkness like smoke, their yellowed eyes points of light where none could exist. Only Du Moro's nervous reaction told him they were real. The tang of fear still choked his own throat, the destructive edge of pain and exhaustion. His grip on the motionless body slipped. The skin was cold. He could smell death, feel its greed.

Not now.

He settled his hold on the unconscious man, pushing on through the undergrowth, seeking the higher ground by instinct. *The valley feet are adder-ridden, boggy, treacher-ous*— The knowledge came to him out of the dark air, out of the skin-tingling awareness of the woman who waited beyond the reach of the trees, unmoving in the silent hall. The closeness of the wolves pushed him.

When the trees thinned, he saw her hall, the opened window shutters that had let in the sun and now framed the deepening night. He pulled rein by the doors thrown wide. The courtyard was deserted. Nothing moved, neither animal nor human. He slid down off Du Moro's trembling back, his hand resting soothingly for an instant on the thick sweating pelt. The pain of standing, of every movement, jarred through his back. He ignored it.

It was difficult moving someone who was unconscious, even a lightweight of seventeen. He caused more blood. The yellow eyes watched his every move from the black veil of the trees, but they did not move in, as though the hall yard marked the edge of their territory. Smoke rose in an indeterminate spiral from a roof whose heavy thatch had once been fine. The roof ridge still showed a twisting pattern. The elusive smoke was the only sign of life, of the presence of human beings. It melted against the first stars.

He walked up the five worn wooden steps. She had carved runes, those angular shapes so beloved of Saxons. He understood what they meant. He read the *dæg* rune placed above the doorway to stop harm from entering and beside it *ethel* that marked inherited property. The door frames themselves were studded with nails. He knew why the nails were there. They held the power of the *Is* rune, protection and changelessness. Or a bond. His scalp prickled. The doors were open because she knew that if he lived, he would come here.

Now.

After three weeks of something that was not real, of shared awareness that filled mind and body. There was no other preparation. Only the opened doors. He walked through.

She sat on a carved chair at the head of the hall. Light framed her white face, the deep gold of her hair, its wild feminine richness not hidden from his sight by a veil but falling over her shoulders in waves. The glow reflected off her skin, off the white gown that hugged the small subtle contours of her body, familiar and unknown in all their hidden intimacy.

Her deep grey eyes met his. The distance of ten paces across the empty hall vanished, as though he touched her. He felt the sudden shock of heat with sense that was not real. He saw her slight form tense, as though the same intensity struck through her. But she never moved.

As he took the first step across her threshold, his blinded senses became aware of whispering movement. The ancient hall was not deserted. Pools of gold light from the flaring torches flickered across carved and painted pillars and the air rustled with the stirring of living creatures, seen and unseen, the unquiet hounds at her feet, the fierce measured restlessness of the unhooded hawk.

The Lady who held Wytch Heath remained unmoving. Her gaze was fastened on him, on the bloodied wreck of the injured boy who had once set the walls of a far greater hall ringing with the sound of joy.

She stayed still, even though he believed she had seen all that he could not name.

Only one other occupant of the woman's hall was human. It did not lessen the threat. He was armed.

Light caught the fast gleam of an unsheathed sword. It was a snake blade. Her hounds fanned out to flank the armed man, flat-eared and low, hackles risen, obedient to their purpose.

Macsen set down the burden, the movement unhurried, careful. The agitated rustling sound in the hall increased, as though a score of unknown people like the armed warrior moved in the impenetrable shadows. The sound swelled, a black echo of the hidden threat in the forest, edged with the same primitive tang of fear, the fear that pushed men to fly from unseen horrors at their back. He did not turn.

He stood across the body and drew his sword.

"Stop." Aurinia's hands fisted. Now that the moment had come, her heart beat wildly, out of control. She stood up. Her eyes widened, her gaze fixed on the strong lithe body poised to strike, on the scarcely bound implacable power.

The familiar stranger ignored her voice.

The night shadow of his hair shrouded the stark lines of his face so that she saw only the power, harsh, turbulent, intensely male. A warrior's force that could deal death. The power of it shivered across her skin.

"Stop." She sprang off the two steps of the dais into the firelit body of the hall. Neither man drew back. Nothing changed in the deep raw intensity of the fighting challenge. They were closely matched. The stranger in full armour and bloodied. Huda untouched, older.

Sweat gathered at her spine. The air that had been so full of movement became still. The hounds dropped in obedience to her gaze, reluctant, wary. She tried to breathe.

Then she took the next step, the one that placed her small figure squarely in the burning space between the two warriors. She thought for one timeless harshly stretched instant that Huda would not draw back, that the volatile calling forth of masculine honour would drive him forward in spite of her words.

"You must stop."

The defence had been mad, vain and dangerous. Just as it had been vain to think that the kind of desperate threadbare trickery she had used would work. The mail-clad stranger, the molten power beside her, shifted. The danger of him reverberated off the flimsy inadequate walls of her hall. He would not turn and run, leaving the wounded man to her care. He had not abandoned the burden that had nearly killed him on the journey here. He would not abandon it now.

She had let him through Wytch Heath's defences and now it was too late.

Too late. Huda saw with a warrior's trained instinct. There was a moment without conscious breath, then her protector grounded the ancient sword.

The sword in the dark-haired warrior's gloved hand, equally old, snake-patterned, did not move.

She had begun this. She had seen that the stranger would fight his way here. The depths of her heart told her she had willed it because the alternative for him had been death, and now there was no turning back.

Aurinia stepped within the sword's range. The honed steel edge hovered above her neck, rock steady. It did not touch her but it did not move one inch further away from her skin. The chilled flesh along her nape prickled.

She had appeared to threaten his injured companion, someone who was helpless, and by that she had shattered every sacred custom of hospitality, stepped outside the boundaries of honour. He could kill her. Aurinia kept her spine straight.

She knelt down beside the wounded man, placing herself near the vulnerable head, the seat of the life force, so that the sense of him could reach her, even through the heavy shroud of unconsciousness—pain and fear and something else. Grief? The wounded man affected her with a power that was unexpected, with a clearness that had been over-shadowed by the greater presence of the warrior.

Her gaze fixed on the slackened form. He was very young. Her assessment was rapid, a matter of skill, super-ficial until she could examine the wounds more thoroughly, ease what he felt…discharge her duty of healing. She could not think further than that.

Her decision was made. No other was possible. Not because of the wounds that needed her skill, but because of *him,* the dark warrior. His presence cut through every defence she had, through flesh and blood and to the inmost core of her being. The dreamlike power of that awareness was familiar; the raw hot reality of it was not.

She kept her gaze on the injured man.

"I can help him."

The dark warrior did not speak. The only sound was the

whisper of a steel edge moving through the air of the hall. The hawk stirred on his perch. Somewhere behind her one of the hounds shifted in the rushes on the floor, the low rumbling sound of a growl starting as a vibration, then reaching the edge of human hearing. Bruna, the nervous one. Hunter, who was part wolf's kin, stayed silent. The wolves had not touched this man.

The sword stilled. The slight movement had been caused by pain. She sensed it, sharp and bitterly suppressed. It would not be enough to stop him from whatever he wanted to do. The sword was again held motionless, the deadly coldness of the steel an awareness beyond sense, but he did not strike.

Bruna's claws scratched the wooden floor. The man shifted, correcting balance, the small movement fluid, un-hurried, controlled despite the pain and the anger, such anger. Fury. She looked up, her eyes fastening on the alien being who had invaded her hall, and she was drawn by the very power that made her afraid.

Her gaze sought every detail, the heavy, darkly flexed foot in its fine leather shoe poised five inches from her thigh, the swell of his calf in the dark linen trousers, cross-gartered tight against the curving muscle with strips of painted leather, the straight knee and above it, where the thigh flared out, the richly braided hem of his tunic. Above that, the leather-bound edge of chain mail.

It sang with his slightest movement, almost with breath, a cold metallic rustling that froze her skin. The glittering steel was muddied. There was blood. He was hurt. She knew he had killed recently. He had had no choice. She stared at the hard, metal-clad body, the moving battle net, the richly decorated sword belt with its complicated arrangement of leather straps that kept the long leather-faced scabbard close at his thigh. She stared at the steel links spreading across his lean hips, at the heavy flaring line of his chest, the powerful upraised arm.

Gold glimmered from the cross guard of the sword. There was more gold at his strong neck, bright against the black fall of his hair. The thick curve of the eight stranded torc was not Saxon, just as he was not. Even that difference divided them, like the greater division of the opulently displayed wealth. Her gaze stopped at the twisted gold.

She took a breath that was unsteady. He watched it. She forced speech.

"I will help your companion."

She touched the injured man and the sense of pain washed over her with a force that was deep, as though the wounded boy were in some way bound to her. She pushed such disturbing echoes aside. It was not possible. The boy's fate was linked to the dark-haired man, the pain bound to his in some way she did not understand. They must be kin. It was the only thing that made sense.

She stood up, the movement so fast he had to spring back to avoid touching her with the blade in his hand. Huda pushed forward but it was over. Finished. Or just begun. It was as though the link between herself and the dark warrior had snapped tight, strong as one of the riveted steel rings that sang with power on his body.

She turned away. But her heart lurched, beating fast. She closed her eyes, but there was no darkness. She was achingly, burningly aware of the man at her back, the living force of him. Of the way he could touch her. If she let him.

"Huda, take the boy. Carry him to the empty chamber beside mine." Her dog, Bruna, moved, pushing closer, brushing in nervous circles round her feet. Bruna kept her eyes away from the hot unslaked force of the warrior.

So did she.

He had not spoken a single word.

HE FOLLOWED HER. HIS FOOTSTEPS made a whispering noise in the rushes covering the hall floor, harsh and deeply restless. He never hesitated. The solid feet in their finely made shoes kept effortless pace, unrelenting as a furious predator at her back. The heat burned between them.

Aurinia pushed the warped oak door of the healing chamber open, sparing a glance for the *ur* rune carved above, shaped like ox horns, sign of primal strength and of healing. That primal strength walked behind her now. She felt its spellbinding power, just as she felt the answering inexplicable, pent-up force inside herself.

She watched the heavy hands place their fragile burden carefully on the bed. It had not been Huda who had carried the patient. The bloodied warrior would let no one else touch him.

Huda shut the door. Bruna, of all her hounds the most retiring and elusive, had insinuated herself into the room. Hunter, who feared nothing, who was as relentless as a wolf's shadow, was content to stay back. A quick glance showed nothing else except a stray owl lodged in the rafters. That was all right. Owls were bringers of wisdom and healing. Bruna ignored the bird, coiling herself up near the bed, choosing shadow, only her anxious eyes visible and a glimpse of the glossy brown coat she was named for, her slender side vibrating with the faint nervous movement of her breathing.

Aurinia began to prepare herself, slipping the protective robe of white linen over her tunic and underdress, refastening the girdle over the top. He watched her, and under that hot, night-dark gaze, what she did became unbearably intimate, the touch of her fingers on her dress, the movement of the material against her body, even though it revealed nothing of her concealed figure. She added clothes rather than removed them.

But her hands poised at the curve of her waist, the drape of the light linen across her hips, took on an edge of bright tension, wholly unsettling.

Her hands suddenly fumbled, their unsteadiness beyond her control, as though she had not fastened and refastened the worn iron clasp a hundred times. The metal shapes of her girdle sang, their note different but as sharply clear in the still air as the rustle of his chain mail.

The movement of her fingers stopped. The metal shapes suspended from her belt were simply hangers for the implements a woman in charge of a household might carry—keys, a small pair of shears in a leather sheath, pretty trinkets. That was all people saw.

The dark eyes of the stranger saw past the obvious surface. He knew that the iron shapes beneath her hands were signs, the hidden forms of runes.

She made her fingers move, fasten the small buckle.

"Huda, will you—"

"Send him out." The sound of the stranger's voice startled her. It was liquid night, deep and composed, dark-shadowed underneath. She took an unsteady breath.

"I will need help." She knew what was to come as no one else did. She knew what would be required—

"I will provide whatever you need." The statement reverberated off the narrow walls, as though the ordinary chamber could not contain its significance. The words seemed to echo inside her skin, stirring the fast heat into disturbing life. Her gaze slid from the muscular body in its covering of steel to Huda's rigid face.

"It is all right, Huda." Her throat was dry. She hoped the only loyal retainer she had ever had would not notice. "Could you arrange for some hot water for me from the kitchens? I will need that more than anything and I cannot leave the injured man."

It was a weak compromise. Huda's eyes rested where hers had done, on the huge shadowed form standing beside the bed. She swallowed.

"And there is the warhorse outside. It will need care."

After a moment, Huda went.

She was left alone with the disturbing stranger and the man who might be dying.

"What is his name?"

"Bertred."

Sharp memory flicked at her, bitter and old. But it was a common enough name. She shook off the distracting thoughts, stepping forward with the assumed confidence that was all she had. "And...and yours?"

"Macsen."

Macsen. The overtones were British, belonging to the people who had come here long before hers. But the true origin of the name was Roman. It belonged to Magnus Maximus, whom the British called Macsen Wledig, the long-dead emperor who had dreamed so deeply of a woman he had determined to take her. Even though it had meant coming all the way to Britain, even though he had lost his throne in the end. Yet now people began to say he had not. That was how legends grew, out of the power of people's dreams.

Dreaming. Her skin turned ice cold, then flushed hot, aching. The disturbing awareness, the bright predatory anticipation, stood revealed for what it was, the primitive heat between man and woman. Her heart lurched. Darkness and dreams. She pushed them back, speaking.

"Will you make more light?"

Shadows flickered. He turned away.

Aurinia took a shaking breath and tried to steady her heart's savage beat, to find control, the sense of self that the stranger had ripped away from her without even touching her heated skin.

She had time while his attention was elsewhere. Time to make herself ready, while his competent fingers, bared of the leather gloves, used the strike-light, caught the sparks against the tinder. She forced her hands to work, setting out the herbs on the white cloth next to the clean and polished knife. But her head turned and she glanced at the stranger and she watched him, lost in fascination.

His left hand had been broken some time ago, and someone had made a competent attempt at setting it. But the damage deeply etched into the bones beneath that fine flesh was still there. It would always be. Her eyes narrowed. It was deep, as though there were something there unhealed.

He used the hand with that complete competence that was his, nothing spared. Sparks flared. The thin streak of red fire licked tentatively at the tinder held in his strong fingers, like a wild creature feeling its way. His careful breath kindled it into flame.

Her gaze followed the brilliant intensity of the fire, spell-caught. The flame broke the dark. She felt the rush of golden warmth through her body, its onset quick and bright and strangely overwhelming.

She was suddenly aware of how she had come to accept the empty deadness of exhaustion, not physical, but a thing of the spirit, the consequence of the struggle to survive. Now it was pushed back. She felt the hidden power of life quicken, striking heat out of nothingness. She tried to hold the warmth in her head and her fingers because she would need it. So that it might flow from her touch into the patient.

Her eyes fastened on the movement of the flame caught in Macsen's hand. She watched him lean over and take the lamp, light the wick in its bed of precious oil. The sudden glow reflected on his olive skin, in his dark liquid eyes. She closed her aching eyelids but she could still see with her mind. He lit the next lamp, each movement slow and careful. She thought that the slowness was perhaps foreign to his nature. But it was what she needed.

I will provide whatever you need. The golden light flared. The warmth was there, stronger than she had ever felt it, richer, and the sharp awareness pierced through her. An awareness that was different from the work of healing she did now. Its heat was raw, the kindling of it bright and dangerous. Carnal. She stumbled.

He caught her, his hand settling on her arm. It was the first time he had touched her.

2

Aurinia's breath choked in the dryness of her throat, the sound loud, harsh in the silent air of the sickroom. The stranger held her arm.

She stilled like someone snared. His powerful fingers reached all the way round the width of her forearm, so that the edge of his well-shaped thumb and the blunt tip of his middle finger touched. The warmth of his broad palm penetrated the thin double layer of her linen sleeves. She felt the heat of each separate finger and her heart leaped, the response violent and beyond her controlling. He sensed it.

He sensed the wanting in her that should not exist, that no one else had ever read. *Whatever you need.* She heard the small distinct sound of his indrawn breath, masculine, real, utterly different from dreams. The first crippling brush of panic stabbed through her belly.

"Let me go."

But he did not. Not straight away. He held her steady. Nothing more, until the rich golden warmth returned over the disorienting stab of coldness, so strong. That vital strength had echoed off the walls of her hall like spring thunder, physically so much greater than her own power.

It was offered to her.

She recognized a gift, one that was full and unreserved, though surely fleeting. There was no mistake. That measureless strength was hers to use however she wished.

She took a breath, the slight movement of her body pressing her flesh against his clear through the deadening layer of clothing, filling her lungs with his scent. He smelled of battle, of deep earth and deeper power, and there was blood. And hidden pain.

"It means so much to you that your companion should live."

It had been plain from the first moment. That was what the gift was for.

"He will need that strength."

"Then he has it." He did not ask what she meant, as any other man would.

She had seen it done, the transferring of life's potent force from one person to another. The price of it was high. She watched his eyes. They were filled with power, with the strength of will that had sustained him through battle and the confrontation in her hall.

She turned to the figure in the bed, to the two arrow wounds, to what had to be done. The youth moved.

Holy mother. Not now. She touched him. Her hand lit on his head, the seat of life. The rich warmth was in her fingers, the double strength that came from the strong-willed warrior. She hoped the drugging power of the warmth would drag the wounded man back under. But even that was not enough.

The pinched eyelids in the white face fluttered open.

"W-what—"

"It is all right," she said. "You are safe."

He had brown eyes, lighter in colour than Macsen's, and now bloodshot and clouded with pain. He was younger even than she had guessed. Seventeen winters? Rich brown hair flopped over his face.

"You are far enough from the battle. It is over. You are safe," she repeated, her gaze on his, her hand at his head. "I know healing. I will help you. All you have to do is let me."

"The battle—" he said again. She felt the tenseness catch in him, the mixture of pain and memory.

"It is over."

The strong brows drew together in the effort it took to concentrate even on such simple words. His restless glance took in the brightly lit room, its spare furnishings, the hound in the corner. His pained eyes softened and she knew why Bruna had come.

The confused gaze slid past, fastened elsewhere, drawn by the raw power beside her. The solid wall of muscle at her shoulder never moved. The patient's pain-filled eyes widened and the confusion lingered for a blind instant, then it was replaced by an abrupt flare of recognition.

"You," he said. "I know who—" he took a shallow breath through the mess of his chest "—who you are."

Surprise lanced through her, discernable perhaps even to

the boy, definitely to the man who was a stranger, little more than a stranger, it seemed, to both of them.

"You are the king's man." The clouded eyes turned brilliant. "A man of the dragon banner. Macsen." The tortured brown eyes turned briefly to her. Despite the pain, they were shining. "He is one of King Alfred's hearth companions."

"A thane, then." A nobleman. But what else could he be? She had seen the gold. But her mouth was suddenly dry. *A nobleman.* "Bertred…" She used his name, trying to soothe the hectic words, but the boy kept speaking.

"A British nobleman, with lands west of Selwood and not just—"

"Stay still—" she began, but it was the voice of the British thane that stopped him.

"Hush. I might have brought you out of the battle, but it was not to lose you to too much talking. Close your eyes."

Bertred did not want to. His gaze followed the thane's every movement, the way a child's gaze followed a hero come to life out of tales. He saw the arrow shafts.

She moved quickly, bending low over the bed, turning his head to face her, catching his gaze and trapping it with the power of hers.

"It is all right. I know what to do." Her voice held nothing but firmness. "You will be well."

In the part of her brain that assessed rationally, she did not know whether that last assurance was true. But the golden strength flowed through her fingers and after a moment the horror loosened its grip a little and he calmed. But it was the hero he turned to, part of the man's world he had just entered at such a cost.

She knew enough to let him go. The stranger called Macsen talked to him, low voiced, one solid hand resting lightly on the undamaged shoulder, answering the frightened, halting stream of questions—*Will you stay? What will happen...* and the question that was not spoken, *How will I bear it?*

The careful hand and the faultless answers achieved what she wanted, perhaps more than she herself could have achieved with all the force of healing. She moved away to make up the draught with sleep-herbs and poppy, and listened to the different spell cast by the night-black voice. At one point, the boy asked quite clearly, "Will I live?"

The jolt made her hand slip. She raised her head. It was not the arrow-shot boy she looked at. It was the dark stranger, Macsen.

His fierce, starkly etched face never changed. But she knew she was not wrong. The simple, bald question had had a meaning below the surface, touching on the edge of another dimension.

The brilliant thane's rejection of that unspoken dimension was instant, all the more forceful because it was not shown, neither in expression nor in words. She heard his voice answer, its pitch faultless, the words ordinary and re-assuring, utterly and carefully controlled. The strength underneath was brutal. She put the glass vessel down until she was no longer afraid her hands would drop it.

The boy noticed nothing. But the frown was back in his transparent eyes. He had wanted an answer that touched on the other unseen dimension. Expected it? Macsen's voice, the touch of his hand, which held the deep spellbinding power she had felt herself, drew him past it. The words flowed. The boy spoke of an uncle who had died in the same battle, a man he was proud of.

Macsen praised his kinsman, in that dark, calm voice. He used the example to praise the boy's courage, to foster his belief in his own strength that would be so necessary.

He said the name of the dead man, *Edwald*, and she realized who the boy was.

Her hand clenched tight on the smooth hardness of the beaker, surely with enough force to break the precious, fragile glass. She straightened her fingers.

She understood now. The wounded youth was important, worth saving. His usefulness must be the reason for such intense determination on the part of a desperate king's man. That was the hidden connection that she had taken for kinship.

Kinship.

It was not to the stranger, Macsen, that the bond of kinship belonged. Only then did she let shock of the words permeate her mind, only then did she let herself think it— *the father, who had so long been estranged from her, was dead.*

Edwald.

The sound of her breath was loud in the quiet room. The low murmur of voices paused, but after a moment began again. She did not turn round. She could not. The boy had no idea who she was and besides, even the shock of news such as that should not be able to touch her in her forced isolation. She should not care, *did* not.

She had hated her father. Hated him—

She stirred the draught in the glass beaker, careful with the dangerous herbs, with the lacing of wine to soothe him.

The boy was her cousin.

Light shivered across the moving liquid under her hands. He must have come here only recently because she had neither seen him nor heard of his presence. Brought here because her father was facing battle and had no heir. Because he knew he might die. She thought of the death-rune on the white cloth. She had been blind. Blind because she had wanted to be.

The shade of death had touched her father. She had not understood that, just as he, setting out for battle, would have taken no thought for her. He had seen her less than half a dozen times since she was born and that by mischance. Every time, he had looked away.

Across the room, the dark warrior stirred. The boy started talking again. Kinship made no difference. There was no point in his knowing who she was. If he did, it might only mean that he would not accept her help. She lived outside the bounds of his world. Like every other inhabitant on this strip of land, he would cross himself, or perhaps make the sign against evil, and turn his face. Or want her dead.

Macsen, the king's man, would feel the same.

She continued stirring the mixture in the glass vessel. It was as strong as she dared to make it for one so ill. It might hold him or it might not. If he surfaced from the drug, Macsen would have to hold him down. She turned her head. There was no need to say that. He knew. She watched as he undid the rich sword belt at his waist. He set the painted and embossed leather-covered scabbard on the wall bench. Then he drew the rustling net of hand-linked steel over his head. Light sparked briefly off hard metal and was just as quickly extinguished. But the power was still there, and his body in the light was like fire.

She lowered her eyes. Everything was ready. They waited for her skill, for her to try and pluck a miracle out of disaster. Life. Her hand was shaking on the fine glass vessel and for one bitter, mindless instant, she considered turning her back.

If she did, the boy would die as surely as the sun set at eventide. A quick enough end to pay for the drawn-out living death her mother had endured, for the undeserved despair. It would be like a wergild, the life-price required to avenge honour. She made herself hold the thought in her head.

But she could not do it. Something in her rebelled at the way guilt was communal, tainting the innocent as much as the offender because they shared kin ties. Nothing that had happened was the boy's fault. Besides, her decision was set. It had been fixed in the hall, with Macsen standing over the wounded body alone.

She watched her shaking hand. The unhealed anger burned inside her. She would never be free of that, or of the taint of what she was. The low voices stopped. The boy was fading. They needed her aid, the wounded oblivious boy and the king's man who burned her like fire. They would take whatever help she could give them. It was only afterward that they would reject her.

Both of them.

She turned. The boy stared at her. Macsen raised his head. The light made sable beauty out of his hair. A raven's wing. Bliss and the ruthlessness of the battlefield.

"Are you ready?"

"Yes." No way left but this.

She sat down beside the bed and Macsen's hand touched her.

The bright offering of strength had not been false. In the end, the absoluteness of it, the unreserved completeness, broke every defence Aurinia had.

She was trying for something that was nearly impossible, at the outside limit of her powers. There was no choice but to accept the help. The hot and dangerous strength of the stranger supported her at every turn, seemingly inexhaustible.

It was as though he were part of her. Her awareness of him penetrated through clear mind and sensitized body with an aching, almost fierce completeness. As though some inner barrier that held her apart from every other living creature had been ripped away and underneath was the self that she kept hidden. A self she did not even know.

The stranger saw it, touched it, and it seemed in the close confines of the lamplit chamber, locked together in another purpose that lay outside both of them, that there was a joining that had no explanation and needed none.

She would have found it hard to manage without his strength. Macsen wanted the boy's life and he fought for it, just as she did.

It was as though they moved together in the shared dream. But that world was as elusive and as fragile as the dream itself. When she touched him, it was like brushing past lightning, the potency sharp as fire.

As she worked, she stole a look at the fierce intentness in the stranger's face, at the familiar features that had invaded her dreams, her mind, yet were unknown to the touch of sight. The finely carved cheekbones were alien; the warm flush of blood beneath the skin spoke of a life unknown. The uncompromising lines and dark shadow of stubble already forming along the solid jawline were the physical sign of a masculine virility that was shockingly unfamiliar.

Yet he helped her.

The boy twisted against her hands. She held her breath, steadied her fingers. The heavily muscled arm with its gold-braided sleeve clamped tightly, but for the first time, the drugging hold of the opium and the herbs broke. Bertred tried to drag away. Macsen pushed him down and held, rock-steady, even when the boy fought him, the sound of his young voice raw and filled with horror. Somehow she managed to force the last drop of poppy down the choking throat while Macsen held him.

She would not dare give the boy more, whatever happened. But in the end, it was not needed. Bertred was too exhausted and the warrior's weight held the light body beneath his, immobile. All the time, he kept speaking, in that deep, dark-witched voice, as though the wounded creature could hear him.

WHEN IT WAS OVER, she was too afraid to try searching her unknown cousin's future with the runes. The impossible question of life over death hung like a shadow. She waited for the man called Macsen to ask it.

She was lying on the bed with the patient, curled up at his side. Her hand was on his head, which was how she had begun. The seat of the life force. It was faint, battered. But it had the resilience of one who was young and new.

The thane with his terrible strength stood up and walked

toward the open window that showed the black moonlit emptiness of the trees and the heath. She heard the rustle of his footsteps. He did not ask her the question, even though he bitterly wanted to know.

Why not? What lived in his head?

The dangerous stranger who had invaded her home looked away.

She heard the disturbed shiver of Muninn's wings.

HER RAVEN WATCHED HIM. Outside the window, Macsen glimpsed the yellow eyes of her wolves, low among the bracken against the dark bulk of the trees.

Beyond them was Earl Guthrum's Viking invasion army pinned down by the Saxon troops that belonged to the only kingdom not yet completely conquered. It was scarce five miles to Wareham where he and Bertred had fought against a party of Guthrum's men sent to forage for food. Two of those men had attempted to follow him here.

They might or might not now be dead.

He heard the rustle of the raven and a thin uncanny sound on the wind that could have come from the uneasy throat of a wolf. He should be at the army base at Fearnros where the king waited, not locked in this circle of shadow and light with a *hell-rune,* a woman who had tried to turn him away with a Saxon rune over her doorway and a hall peopled with noisy shadows, a fragile conjurer's trick to make him run.

Apart from a murderous war veteran of his father's generation, she was alone. Aloneness in these days meant death. She might have courage, but the layer of otherworldliness that was her protection had the potential to bring her down. He did not think she understood the ordinary world.

The ordinary world made no allowances for that.

He gripped the timber window frame harder. The wood was rotting. He could rip it out with one hand. The raven slid past him into the lamp-lit chamber, seeking its mistress. He did not turn round to see her. No need. He had seen her in his head for three weeks. He had only to think of her and her presence filled him.

Even now, at a distance of five paces, she touched him and his blood burned. She drew him as she drew the predatory wolves who roamed her treacherous heathland.

But that heathland had already been invaded. If there had been two Norsemen, there would be others. She would not be able to defend herself.

The knowledge filled him with blank fury, a need to set things right, to protect her from consequences she could not see. Behind that was a gut-wrenching possessiveness that he would not examine, as primitive as the wolves' instinct.

It was impossible for him to stay here. Just as it had now become impossible to leave her. He had set his foot on the path the moment he had turned toward Wytch Heath. Perhaps in the moment he had picked the injured boy from the field. The unreasoning side of his brain told him the actions were linked. That side was deadly.

He let go of the window. The movement shot pain through his shoulder and into his back. He shut his eyes against the crippling unexpected measure of it. He could not afford weakness. It was the reckless boy who was injured, perhaps fatally.

Macsen thought of the power of the wounds, of what had
to be done. The rank desperation of it still clung to him.
Battles were one kind of necessity but there was something
unclean about holding someone down while they suffered
pain, even if it was needed. He moved, body and mind
restless, still driven by the demands of fighting, the demands
of what had followed, the sickening drag of pain and exhaustion.

Bertred was too sick to be moved. He might still die
like— He cut off the thought. What was important was
now, Bertred. The Viking army.

The woman.

He heard her move, as though even now, after their
combined struggle for Bertred was over, his thoughts
touched her. He forced a painful breath. The danger of the
world outside swirled round her in waves. She had no idea,
in her deliberate isolation, and she was full of secrets.

He knew he should uncover them, but the shockingly
deep consciousness came to him that he did not care what
she had done or with whom. All that mattered was the fact
that he had found her.

She had tried to hold him off. It was too late for that.
Too late for both of them. They were trapped.

He turned round but he must have been too precipitate.
The double pain broke and this time he did not have the
strength to stop it. He pitched forward. The blackness of
it closed over his head, unquiet and filled with dreams.

Even in the blackness, he was aware of her nearness. She
touched him but there was nothing she would be able to
do. She could not move his weight. He tried to break out

of the dark but it was as though it was he who was drugged and not the boy.

In the black paths of his mind, she lay down with him in the rushes on the floor. He felt the touch of her body pressed to his, the small round fullness of her breasts, the smoothness of her thigh against his and the hidden curve of her hip. Time vanished. When he opened his eyes and the waiting pain scored through him, she was back with Bertred, curled up like a child on the bedcovers, watching him.

"Where?"

The guard called Ulf swallowed. "It was not clear, Jarl."

"It was not clear?" Earl Guthrum kept his voice impassive, as befitted the leader of a Viking army; even so, it echoed off the walls of the looted hall. The man swallowed again, as though bile rose in his throat. As it should.

Earl Guthrum's fist clenched. The English *thane* who had rallied his people around Wareham might be dead, but the heir had slipped through their fingers. Worse than that was the failure to take the grain and the cattle he needed. If Alfred the Saxon could stop him from taking the harvest, his army was lost in this godforsaken trap between two rivers. He had to break out.

Or negotiate. The other possibility had always existed, that the Saxon king would pay him to leave. His arm rings caught the torchlight. Gold. Gold and the power that could be bought with it. But it was not what he truly wanted. He wanted conquest.

"You have captured no supplies and you let a mere youth

escape you, even though you say he was wounded, and now you do not know where he is?"

Sweat glistened on Ulf's skin, on the chalk-white face. It was fear, fear of his Jarl's terrible and justified wrath. But there was something unnerving about that dead whiteness, unhealthful. If it was sickness— Anger lashed at him. He turned his mind to the only problem he could grapple with.

"Tell me where this thane's son is." The youth was valuable. Taking him would break the power of local loyalties away from a desperate king.

They knew something, something they were not saying. He could tell by the quality of the silence, the sudden shifting of hidden hands. They made the sign against enchantments. Guthrum's own fingers moved instinctively to the amulet suspended from his neck. Much use it had been.

"Well?" he yelled.

They fell back, but they answered him. "Lord, it had to be Wytch Heath. There is an enchantress there, a *vargamor*, a weaver of spells—"

"Enchantress." He spat it. A fear of magic was as useless and demeaning as any other fear. It had been fear of enchantments that had led to the loss of the golden sceptre of Wessex, taken from him by the Saxon king. Or the hand of the Saxon's god—

"Lord, two of the guards followed. They did not come back. The ground is treacherous. The valleys are infested with snakes and the *vargamor* has familiars, wolves who run for her. She—"

Sorceresses. A *vargamor*, a wise woman of the woods who commanded wild wolves. He stood.

"It would have been an ordinary man's hand who killed my men if they are dead, some Saxon with more guts than you have…."

They nearly fell over themselves at the insult. He did not care. He wanted answers, not bleating. Ulf's white face turned livid. He was sweating copiously. If it was the sickness, the scourge of that ran through his troops… He knew in his heart it had begun.

If it took hold, he was finished.

His mind blanked it off. It was unacceptable. The guardsmen kept talking, oblivious, justifying their own petty selves.

"He could not have done it without help—"

"There were two against one and he had the body of the wounded thane's son—"

"He was injured himself. Ulf did that much to him. But he was a king's man."

King's man. He stopped listening. He had heard enough of Alfred the king's men. They turned his own warriors into gibbering fools. It made him spit into the stale rushes.

Things should not have turned this way. He was dogged by ill luck and trapped. Halfdan, king of the conquered lands north of the River Humber, should have sent him help by now.

If Halfdan failed, the only way to get help was to try and buy it from those of Alfred's own subjects who were not Saxon but British. It would take time.

And this sickness…

"He took the thane's son to the *vargamor* because she knows healing," said Ulf.

A healer. The pattern of luck changed.

AURINIA SAW THE FIRST MOMENT he regained physical consciousness. She stayed still on the bed. He would know she
had already touched him, more intimately than she had
touched anyone. There was no barrier with him. The lamps
in the healing chamber flickered. Huda had come and gone.
The raven settled its feathers. She sat up.

She had to go to him.

She swung herself to the floor and stood. Bruna raised
her head from where it rested on the side of the boy's bed.
The edge of Aurinia's skirts brushed the curled up paws in
passing and the hound's head settled back, but the wide eyes
watched Macsen. Aurinia crossed the room. Her feet
crushed rushes strewn with the Nine Herbs to promote
healing and ward off enchantments.

But the enchantment was inside her chamber. The light
slid over his hair when he moved. He had got as far as
propping himself on one elbow, not the damaged side. She
watched him avoid it.

"Bertred?" That was the first thing he said.

"He is asleep. That is what he needs. There is nothing
else I can do at the moment." She did not say that there
would be fever, that in some ways the struggle to come
would be worse. He would know that.

Will he live? He still did not ask the question. Though
she could see he wanted to. She watched the shadowed line
of his jaw, his harsh mouth and the deep curve of it, and
the awareness between them stretched the air.

"God will watch him." It was as near as she could get to
an answer. People assumed she did not believe in God. She

had seen the cross on the gilded pommel of Macsen's sword. The British had been Christian far longer than the Saxons. His black gaze slid away from her.

"You are hurt," she said.

The sharp edge of his pain was growing beyond bounds. She would have to touch him, now, when he was conscious and aware and filled with vital power. There was no choice. She knelt down on the floor beside him and extended her hand, slowly, the way she would with a wild animal.

She felt the shock through her skin, the wildfire that had shimmered in her hall overwhelmed her, as though consciousness blanked out.

The bonds of time and place faded, became meaningless. The fire passed from his flesh into hers where they were joined, first through the smooth vital movement of his body, then through the dark unrestrained ardour of that harshly curved mouth on hers, through the bright heat of his skin. Through madness and intense, desperate pleasure, the deep unrestrained power of his heavy body filling hers.

She made a faint sound. At the other side of the room, Bruna stood, nails clicking on the floor. Her sight cleared with shocking abruptness. The vision faded. But not the awareness. Her flesh tingled as though it had been touched.

Her body was taut, physically aroused, tormented by a wanting that was new and at the same time achingly familiar. Her burning flesh, untouched by any man, was filled with knowing. Her overstimulated senses were inflamed by a wild desire called into being by his skillful, potent touch. But there was more. Other hidden things that belonged to lovers flowed past her in the air. They touched her as though they were part of her soul, held her.

No.

She leaned back. Nothing touched her in that way. It was a trap.

She took a breath of the clear air of Wytch Heath and the sights, the intense, disturbing feelings, faded. The air in her lungs was cool and familiar.

Empty.

She swallowed.

Nothing had happened. Nothing but the pressure of her hand on a fully clothed arm.

She did not see glimpses of the future in that way, with vivid, fully felt visions.

Sometimes she could interpret rune staves cast on a cloth. Always, she could guess things about people that they would rather keep hidden because she read the thousand small signs others were oblivious to. But she was a healer. There was no more.

The sight of the future had come from him.

Her hand still rested on his arm, on top of the fine linen sleeve, a touch that was modest and acceptable, chaste. She knew that he had seen all that she had, the way her body had moved under his, had surrounded and taken the fierce and complete invasion of his flesh inside hers. She was trembling. Deep inside. She ached with a terrible need.

He moved. The lamp-lit silence of the healing chamber snapped back into focus. There was only one course. She moved her hand, slow and slightly clumsy because of fatigue. She sought control.

She began to unlace the fastenings of the padded tunic made to fit under his chain mail. Behind her, Bruna subsided onto Bertred's bed. The owl fluttered in its corner of the room.

As she worked, her mind filled with the vision of their bodies entwined. Her senses ached with the intimate touch of his flesh. She watched her hand become unsteady.

It would not be now. Not in this room with the sick boy and the scent of pain. Surely… He was that much civilized.

But what of the terrible, tearing need he had shown her? How civilized, in the end, was she? If he touched her now in that way would she—

She no longer knew herself. Or she had discovered something that had been buried, covered over, ruthlessly lashed down because it was not for her, the terrible, hidden yearning for all that circumstances had denied her—human closeness, the touch of another person.

It was so fundamentally dangerous.

And she wanted it.

3

His tunic came undone.

Aurinia stopped. Her hands were resting against his skin. She knew she must be mad. Her fingers caught on the muddied edge of the padded linen, bloodstained from fighting.

"I have to touch the injury—" She stopped her voice. Why had she said *touch* instead of *examine* or *tend?* He would think— What? That she used witching? He had already felt the flow of golden warmth, the unexplainable side of healing. If he stayed, she might be able to hide nothing from him.

Chills stabbed through her.

Her fingers brushed the warm skin of his neck under the midnight fall of his hair. He moved to help her. Their hands met, joined. She touched the pads of his fingers. Even the small movement of his hand brought pain down his arm from his back. He had used his strength for the boy. The marks of the battle now clawed at him.

She eased the padded tunic over his head, then the linen shirt beneath, finely braided at the neck and the sleeves. She was very careful of the damage to his back. The shirt fell away and she let the bloodied white linen pool on the floor.

The glow of the oil lamps reflected on the deep olive colour of his skin. His beauty shocked her. It was not something she associated with men, with the few who had ever crossed her path, Huda with his ropy leanness, the stooped rough bodies of the fishermen and farmers, the blanked-off blond heaviness of the thane who had disowned her.

The sheer fascination of him held her, like inescapable spell-craft. Her heart beat too fast. Her fingers clenched in the fine linen, still warm from the touch of that brilliant, exotic flesh. The lamp glow revealed the stranger's fierce grace, the uncompromising toughness, blackly shadowed muscle.

He was intimidating. He made her blood leap and her eyes fasten on the stark mysteries of his half-naked body. The scattered body hair across the curving muscles of his chest was dark, the flat nipples brown.

She could not touch that fine skin, the fierce masculine shape. She could not turn away from him. She reached out. Her hand closed over his arm, her fingers lost on the solid swell of living muscle. She touched the arcane decoration, the dark blue of woad etched deeply into the warm flesh. The design spiraled in a flowing circle around that tight curve, exotic. British. Different from the mark on her own body, imbued with power.

Her hand covered the painted skin and the dangerous

heat flared straight through her, driven by a sharp inescapable force she did not recognize.

The burgeoning feeling was far greater than need. It was hunger. She was torn by it, hell-bound and tormented by all the terrible, unacceptable things she did not want to feel. Not now. Not here in this room, at this moment meant for other things. Not ever.

Her breath choked in the tightness of her throat. The unforgivable sound tore the quiet air of the room meant for healing.

He took her hand into his, the movement slow, measured. The heavy fingers curved round hers in quietness, rested there without threat. It was not a gesture she expected from a man who lived by the edge of his sword. Not the kind a man with braided clothes and a ransom in gold about his throat made to an outcast.

He covered her hands with both of his and she let her hands rest there while her breath calmed and the mad edge of all the hidden things abated. She was herself again, the woman of carefully ordered skill who had healed her own cousin.

She closed her eyes for a moment and the strength filled her, the way it always did.

He took his hands away and she let go of his arm.

"I will need to wash away the blood and the dirt. Huda brought water for a bath." It would be cooling already, the herbal tincture she had added losing its power. The wound to his back was hours old. She needed to act. The bruising was bad.

"What caused the wound?" A glancing blow not taken

at full force because he must have turned, but the weapon had been heavy. The steel links and the padding beneath had saved him.

"An axe?" She sat back, the action flawless and well-steadied like her voice, strong and filled with purpose.

"Perhaps." He chose to answer in kind, the fathoms-deep strength the only thing visible. "I have no idea."

The finely curved mouth suddenly quirked at the expression that must have been in her face. She caught the first thread of amusement and thought it would be devastating if a man as stern as he ever laughed. She took a single, dangerous, intoxicating breath and leaned over him.

"Did you not take the time to look, then?"

"I was looking. Just not in the right direction." The smile slipped further. He had fine teeth, white against the bronzed skin and the stubbled jaw.

He stood up, the movement too fast, as though his strength were still whole. She caught him when he stumbled, leaning her slighter weight into his. The warm heaviness of him and the supple skin pushed against her, then pulled back as he found balance.

"Well, you will know to do better next time."

He braced his hand against the wall until he could stand. "Aye."

The dark hair covered his face. She stayed close, touching.

"Perhaps the armour is no good." It was worth nearly as much as the neck-ring, thousands of separate links of steel wire riveted together and crafted by a master. It had protected him from most of the damage, but it had caused its own. The lacerations and the bruising came from the metal links driven by the blow through the padding and into the flesh below.

"I'll tell the smith."

"Do that," she said.

She helped him strip off the last of his clothes, looking away from him, from the long clear lines of his legs, the flaring muscle at his thigh, the taut line of his hip, the dark shadow of his sex.

She wanted to leave him, then, to cross the small compass of the room and take the excuse of busying herself with the herbs she would need. But she did not dare let go of the heavy warmth of his arm. She locked her arm more firmly under his. He did not pull away, but he turned his body, leaving only the oblique angle of fire and shadow, tight muscle, the hideous damage to his back.

Heat burned below the surface level of their touching. She forced herself to keep speaking, her voice light, covering all that lay beneath.

"Perhaps you need battle training? I hear the man who guts fish at Durlston Bay gives lessons in axe throwing on the side."

The curved mouth made a derisive movement as somehow he managed the bath, the harshly schooled movement of the muscular body without flaw.

"It might help you." She surprised an entire laugh from him, but it was sharp and bitter with the edge of pain.

"You should have gone to Durlston first." Her heart felt tight but her voice was as light and calm as ever.

"Next time, I'll take your axe thrower with me."

"Will you? Do you like the smell of fish, then?"

"Only cooked and served with pepper, or perhaps cumin."

Pepper, or an exotic spice like cumin for an ordinary meal. A nobleman's table. She helped him wash, the dense skin, the tight moving muscle, even the long disordered silk richness of his hair.

Afterward, he stretched out for her on the padded wall bench, facedown. She stared at the lithe, fascinating shape before her, supple and heavy limbed, motionless. Alive with power. Light and the last sparkling threads of water glittered on his olive skin. The linen sheet was draped across the compact line of his hips. The glow of the lamp light showed her the tight muscle beneath the thin material.

She took the step that brought her near. The soles of her shoes crushed the Nine Herbs of enchantment hidden among the floor rushes. Their scent reached her, mixed with something else on the edge of perception, warm skin. Man. She was leaning down, close over him.

Her gaze, intent, assessing, swept over the sleek lines, upward from the well-shaped feet, the strong calf muscle, the shadowed hollow at the back of the knee, then the swelling thigh and upward over taut curving muscle and to the edge of the linen sheet. The flaring line of his back and the dark marring of the wound.

Her fingers touched him. The injury was ugly, but perhaps less deep than she had first thought. The muscles across his back were thick, the flesh dense, but still vulnerable. The thought of battle chilled her. She had seen, in some small part, both what he had suffered and what he had done.

She locked it away in her mind, forced her thoughts to focus on now, on healing, and the golden warmth came. It flowed through her fingers as she anointed each break in the gleaming skin, each shadow of bruising. She knew he was aware of the bright tension in her touch. It would have shamed her, but he did not let it. It was as though the deeply dangerous, unexplored bond between them covered everything. He let her do as she willed.

She touched the damaged flesh, the strong lines of the body laid out before her. She spoke to him, talking to his mind, the bruised spirit, her voice as much a tool of healing as her hands. Eventually, the sound of her voice lapsed into charms. They were old, a mixture of words that were properly Christian and some that were more ancient and not comprehensible.

Nu ic wille thine helpan....

Now I will help you.... Her voice hummed low. Sometimes she thought the words hardly mattered, only the soothing sound of her voice. And with him, the fire and the strange, untamed, inexplicable sense of closeness.

She said the charms aloud and time slipped so that it was some minutes before she realized what she had spoken so heedlessly. There was a moment tense with fright, but he gave no sign.

He had used a different aspect of the same gift with the wounded boy, when he had spoken in his dark steady voice of more practical things, of the battle, of courage, of hoping.

Her skilled, careful fingers moved over the fine skin, supported by her voice, and the stranger, Macsen, bore every harsh grievous thing she had to do, the power of his will unrelenting.

"Amen," she said, at last. *"Fiat."* So be it.

She withdrew her hand from the clean linen strapping across his back, pulling the protection of the bedcovers across his skin. The unreal golden strength faded slowly from her fingers, as though it had a life beyond her knowing.

But the warmth died, leaving her doubly prey to the bitter exhaustion that followed such difficult healing. She felt cold, filled with isolation and loss that was both deadeningly familiar and frighteningly new.

She turned away and watched the boy's figure in the great bed.

ONLY WHEN THE STRANGER WAS intensely asleep, locked in the bands of exhaustion, did she lie down with him. She stretched out beside him on the coiled rope mattress covering the wall bench.

She lay still, silent, unmoving. The shadowed mass of his body was shrouded from her by the bedcovers. It made no difference to the intimacy of what she did.

The dark night closed in and the lamps he had lit guttered. The awareness of him pulsed through her. The intensity of it still shocked her. That unremitting power cut through her defences. Yet she was not a helpless, directionless girl. Her decisions were her own. Always. She had survived in this place for the span of twenty winters, most of her life spent watching while her mother died by each breath she took. She had lived the last five winters alone.

She had never known anything different. There had been no one who had penetrated her reserve, both because of the circumstances and through her own choice. It had simply been too dangerous, for herself and the few who depended on her like Huda. Most of all, it would be too dangerous for any rash man who might have sought to touch the barriers that surrounded her.

The stranger had changed everything. First by taking her dreams and now by taking her home, her thoughts, her ruthlessly guarded self-possession. If he touched the core of what she was, she would have nothing left. She did not know how she would survive the aloneness then.

Because he would not stay, her injured, gold-decked thane.

The enchanted, brutally fine shape rested against her. The darkness swallowed the first of the precious lamps. She heard the whirr of Muninn's wings.

The stranger in her embrace never moved. She held him. The fire of him was still discernible, even through wounds. She felt it.

She knew she would lie with him in truth, soon. *Wif-lac.* But she would not be his wife after it was over.

MACSEN FOUND THE FIRST BODY before the sun reached its zenith. Earl Guthrum's guard lay where he had been thrown from his mount, half concealed by the thorny undergrowth. The marks in the scuffed earth and the crushed branches where the horse had stumbled were already fading, as though panic and the mad flight of nightmare two nights ago had never existed.

But the corpse was real enough.

Macsen's hand moved in the sign of the cross, even though the man was pagan, even though the Viking had sought to kill him, to kill a wounded boy. Death was death.

He did not go nearer. The neck was broken. There was no mercy for such a fall. It could have been himself dead, not just left with a glancing wound that was already healing more quickly than seemed possible.

He urged his horse onward, letting the great beast pick its footing with care. The way was treacherous even in full daylight, far more than he had imagined. Two nights ago, the wolves had pushed him left into the trees. This time, he held right, forcing his way through the dying autumn growth.

It was as though the woodland itself resisted him, reluctant to give up whatever secrets it held. The densely grown bushes seemed to rustle the way the restless air itself had stirred against him in the lady's hall. The uncanny noise grew. A merlin shot out in front of him with a rush of disturbed wings. He pulled the stallion up short, his spine tingling.

The sudden slope had been almost invisible. If a horse had plunged onto that in the darkness it would have been impossible to stop. His instinct had been to keep to the higher ground on the left—then the wolves had pushed him to it.

That was not possible.

He looked down while the hot preternatural prickling of sweat on his skin cooled. He could see the second body, half submerged in slime and dark brackish water, trapped and held by the boggy earth. A quagmire.

He dismounted on the slippery, uneven ground. The sharp pain through his back was enough to make him lose focus for half an instant so that he only saw the movement obliquely, a sliding rush at his feet, an impression of speed, scaled skin, dark gray zigzagged with black.

The valley feet are adder-ridden.

Du Moro shifted with nerves, wanting to stamp on this new threat. Macsen tightened his grip on the reins, keeping the horse ruthlessly still on the unsteady edge, the charm against snakes unfurling inside his head. The thick sinuous body, two feet long, with its banded head and its coppery-red eyes, coiled back. The snake turned abruptly, vanishing down the slope where the dead Viking lay below, turned away by bad temper at the disturbance to its rest. Or by the enchantment.

The charm that had risen in his head was not British, but Saxon, the product of a few hundred years of coexistence, a natural progression. The results of that progression had seemed clear to him; the enemy who now threatened them all had to be faced as one. Though it was not what he had been taught, not what his father, the die-hard Celt, so passionately believed. But in some ways his father had seen more clearly. He had seen death, the death that Macsen had not stopped.

He led the war-stallion away from the dangerous slope. No further sign of poisonous snakes. *Hal westu.* He finished the words of the charm in his head. *May you be healthy.* It was doubtless something the Lady of Wytch Heath would know.

He had to get back to her. The two Vikings who had pursued him might be dead and unable to carry back tales, but even an enchanted heath could not keep out a Danish army.

MACSEN STABLED THE HORSE himself and walked toward the chamber that held Bertred. Her grey dog, Hunter, followed him, guard or companion, it was hard to tell. On the way, he surprised half a dozen squirrels, a drowsing crane and an irritated swan. He thought there were some field voles and another sleeping owl. Other people had hens, or perhaps geese.

The dog trailing his every step ignored such distractions, his disdain lofty, impersonal. It did nothing to disguise the predatory wolf's blood that looked out of the gold-edged eyes. They understood one another.

The lady's belligerent retainer was in the courtyard, cleaning Macsen's damaged chain-mail byrnie. The red-blond head raised the instant he came into view.

"What did you find?"

Macsen stopped. No point in disguise. The man shared the same background and experience that he did. Fighting.

"Two corpses."

It was a bastard of a job cleaning chain mail. He sat down on the wall bench and picked up a linen rag and the edge of a metal sleeve. He could see the man called Huda wanted to wrench it out of his hand.

But he also wanted information.

"They were Viking."

The war veteran grunted. The wolf-dog settled slowly at Macsen's feet.

"They tried to follow me here." He left it at that. Huda passed him the oil.

"Because you had a thane's heir across your saddle?"

The thwarted violence seemed directed at Bertred as much as at himself. The reaction that brought inside him was too deep, too sharp, anger that reached too far back.

"Bertred had no choice."

He had no desire to make an impossible enemy out of Huda, but the anger pushed the next words out of him, with a force he could not, would not, hold down. "The choice I made still holds—to protect him."

The flexible liquid flow of the rings caught in Huda's fingers.

"Besides," said Macsen more evenly, "to a Viking, either of us would make a target."

"I see." Huda recognized all there was to see, both surface words and underlying intent.

"Rich yourself then, are you?" asked Huda, animosity seemingly directed back where it should lie.

"Aye." The gold at his neck was an obvious enough sign.

"Really? You look foreign."

Saint Brannoc. Despite the unslaked edge of anger, the irony hit him. *Father, where are you now?*

"I was born west of Selwood," he said to the Saxon. "In Devon."

"That's foreign enough."

It was part of Wessex. But he supposed, if you had never passed the boundaries of the shire of Dorset, it might be foreign indeed. The oiled linen rag slid over the linked steel. It was already rusting because of the blood left on the metal. His first attempt at cleaning it had been inept. He could still hardly use his left arm. He tried beating down the simmering anger and made himself wait. He could persuade most people.

It was his advantage and his bane.

"The lady might not like it there," said Huda.

The sudden switch to directness cut through the volatile feelings held inside him and laid the problem bare. Huda had been prepared to drive a sword through him to protect the lady. It was not a matter for holding grudges about. In Huda's position, he would have done the same.

What mattered was what came next, the possibility of hammering out an understanding, or the disaster of open enmity. He drew the links steadily through his hand.

"She cannot stay here." Macsen looked up, the movement and the words as abrupt as Huda's.

Huda jerked back. Macsen simply held control. The other man's eyes narrowed.

"I thought you said the Vikings who followed you were dead." The defensive anger was what he expected, but it was underlain by something more, something that he did not yet know enough to fathom.

"What else have you brought here?" demanded Huda.

He had no time to spend on fathoming what was hidden. The only course open was to press on. The danger that hung over the lady drove him.

"I have brought the outside world." He spelled it out, knowing that directness was the only possible way with a fighter like Huda.

"The Viking army at Wareham and the men on the ships in Poole Harbour number several thousand. They are desperate for the food they need to live, for the riches that will make risking their lives worthwhile, for whatever or whoever they can find and use."

Somehow, they would come here, to this place that had been so well hidden. He knew it at the deepest level of his mind. If he did nothing, it would touch the lady. He had brought the outside world and he had become responsible for her. There was already danger. He could not live with the thought of more.

Huda was a war veteran. He would realize how things stood.

"The king's army holds the Viking force trapped for the moment. But there is little time—"

"The king's army. You…" The contempt, the disbelief, could have been his father's. He felt the hidden rage slip control, fought to behave reasonably.

"Yes." What was important was the woman and her vulnerability. The lady mattered to both of them, whether Huda could accept it or not.

"I cannot leave her and neither can she stay here. Not now." Some deeper instinct made him ask instead of ordering. "Can you see?"

The blue Saxon eyes flickered.

He thought the understanding was there, but even as it surfaced, the power of long-held beliefs made it shatter. The frightened, angry face closed off and with it the possibilities. Macsen recognized the look in the other man's eyes to the depths of his soul.

He could not persuade in this. He should have known.

"She lives here," Huda shouted. The wolf at their feet raised its head, poised. "She has me to look after her. I have been like a father to her. Do you think I cannot protect her?"

Macsen said nothing. But the truth did not alter. It was there, beyond either of them—the presence of an alien army strong enough to break not just the lives here, but a country. He saw Huda recognize it and there was nothing he could do to salvage either power or pride. Huda's anger flared.

"It is you," yelled Huda and the enmity set, unbreakable, a damaged force awaiting its chance. "It is you who will cause harm, not prevent it."

The accusation hit through him, keen as a sword fashioned with venom twigs. But there was no way back. He knew that as clearly as his own breath.

"The choice is the lady's," said Macsen.

"Aye." Huda straightened. The wolf watched, ears pricked. "But nothing can change the past, all she has lived through and still does, not even you. I know it. It is me who has been here, who stayed with her when she lost her kin, when she was abandoned by them."

"They abandoned her?" The black rage inside him snapped tighter, harshening his voice. He stood, the restless wolf mimicking his movements.

"She did not tell you." Huda watched him.

No. She had not. They had said little enough with words these last two days. For him, the time had simply blurred into pain, a test that had to be endured, everything focused and centred on Bertred, on the bitter fight for survival that had to be won. And now—

"It is her past," said Huda. "Not mine."

The past, whatever was in it, was unchangeable. No one knew that better than he did. The only thing that could be dealt with was now. He could not leave her to be alone with a Viking army five miles away.

He turned away, back toward the chamber where she waited. Huda made no attempt to follow him. The wolf paced after and then stopped.

"If she trusts you enough," said Huda, "she will tell

you." The voice crossed the sunlit yard, bitter and filled with conviction.

"She never will."

MACSEN FOUND HER IN BERTRED'S chamber. She slept, curled up on the end of Bertred's bed. The high sun from the open window pooled round her. She seemed to attract it by her nature. The heat of her touched him across the width of the room.

The boy's eyes opened. They were quite clear. Two nights of unrelenting struggle with fever, and now his eyes were clear. It was like a miracle, a triumph of life Macsen had never expected. He watched the transparent hand reach out to the other hound, the brown-coated thoroughbred with not an ounce of unacceptable wolf in its makeup.

"Will you go back to the king soon?" asked Bertred.

The likeness to a different impulsive youth was very strong, a likeness that had driven Macsen to take the unconscious boy out of the battle to somewhere he might have a chance of life. Here.

The clear eyes regarded him. The other youth had fought for the hard-pressed king, too. He had not survived.

"Yes. I will go back to the court." *Court.* It was a movable war council and had been for years. Everything hung in the balance, waited on the next move.

Bertred's thin fingers paused on the hound's head. Something unknown moved in the corner of the room.

"I think it is the raven. It seems to like her." The boy's gaze strayed, like his, toward the pool of light. He took a breath, still too light and shallow.

"I told her she could come back to my uncle's—to my hall after this."

Every muscle in Macsen's body tightened. Bertred was not a child. Three days ago on the battlefield, he had taken the step into manhood. He was not so much younger than the girl sleeping on his bed. She had healed him. The rich magic of her would have struck through him, just as it had fastened its inexorable hold on the man in the courtyard who was old enough to be her father. As it had fastened its hold on himself.

"I—I meant only—I was not trying to seduce her." The tone, unbearably young and blameless, faltered to a stop.

No. It seemed only *he* sought that. Bertred stared at him wide-eyed, though he had not made a move. The raw power of what was inside him, the intensity that Huda had reacted to, must roll from him in waves.

"Macsen?"

"It is all right." He was caught in lies. Nothing was right at all. The impossible choices spun out before him. His gaze fixed on the girl.

The lady had not stirred at the sound of their voices. The sunlight clung to her, gilding the long uncovered swathe of her hair, the smooth curve of her thigh outlined beneath the rumpled skirts. The slender lines of her body had touched him already. The touching had burned like fire, cutting through him and igniting flame.

She sought the sun's warmth. She might have been oblivious. She might have been aware of him even through sleep. The awareness that existed only with her and defied the bounds of an acceptable world.

"She said she would not come." Bertred's voice broke through his thoughts. "She said that she wanted to stay here." The man-boy still eyed him warily, shifting uncomfortably in the great bed.

Macsen stepped forward. Even if she did not choose to be with him, she would have to go to the safety of Fearnros. "She cannot."

"No."

The agreement was unexpected. Macsen glanced at the stiff face.

"She cannot stay," said the boy who had faced Guthrum's troops. "She will not listen to me. But…but you…"

The air of the sunlit room burned like consuming flame.

"I will speak to her."

He crossed the small distance to the bed. His shadow blotted out the light. The lady did not move. Small fragments of sun glittered off her hair, the edge of her naked foot. The sun had warmed her skin. Or perhaps she was always warm, filled with the strange radiant heat that had healed Bertred. The heat that had touched him and then changed, turning to flame.

He touched her and the flame caught life, raw and beyond denying. He was already bound. The knowledge came to him beyond reason, like something that had already happened. That kind of knowledge had the power to lead to hell. Coldness touched his skin like the winter frost of Sol-month.

But he did not stop.

The delicate curve of her body made no resistance. Even with the injury, he could take her weight easily. She was very small. Like pure light.

He picked her up.

Nothing changed in the room. If Bertred thought that was an odd way of beginning a conversation, he said naught.

Macsen did not know whether the girl woke. But she let him touch her. Her light weight, fine and infinitely vulnerable, fell against him, like the sign of trust that Huda, the bitter warrior, had said would never be his.

AURINIA COULD FEEL HIS HEART beating. The solid wall of his chest was pressed against her and under it the small intimate movement that betokened life. At first she thought it was part of the dream. Light and shadow crossed her closed eyelids and then he moved, and the awareness of him was too strong, crossing the boundary between the dream-world and the real.

She heard the small sound of his indrawn breath and the shadow engulfed her. He must have turned away from the sunlight. She was in his arms. He was actually holding her. She could feel the fine linen of his tunic under her face, beneath that, the hidden warmth of his flesh and the strong beat of his heart.

The moving air streamed over her, thin and cool in contrast to his heavy warmth. He was carrying her. She sensed the open door that led from Bertred's room, the light outside. Bertred— He was taking her away from the sick boy.

He did not speak.

The dream man might know she was awake. The real man might think that she was asleep, helpless, that he could do what he willed. The warrior who was dangerous. The two sides to him brought intolerable confusion. The first stab of alarm shot through her.

She should not allow him to touch her. She had to stay with Bertred who was so ill. That was her duty. She was a healer before everything. Yet she knew full well that it was now possible to leave her patient without harm. It had been her choice to stay in the isolated sanctuary of the sick chamber.

Just as she could choose to stop this.

The soft edge of his hair touched her face. Her head rested against the impossibly wide shoulder, the broad plane of his chest. She was mostly aware of his warmth, the firm grip of his hands on her thinner flesh, the sure way he held her. It was so competent, as though an action so profoundly shocking was unremarkable and possible to him.

No one had ever held her in her life.

The closeness involved stunned her. There had been no other living human being who had been so close to her. Even her beloved mother had simply faded before her eyes, too lost in a different world of pain to lavish care on a daughter, certainly never an embrace.

Aurinia had touched people when it was necessary in healing but no one had held her in their arms, not in her memory. And now this stranger did, as though nothing else existed beyond the warmth of touch and basic human sharing.

She did not stop him from carrying her out of Bertred's chamber. She was not capable of it. The door slammed shut.

The heavy muscle beneath her changed, coalesced, the movement at once fluid and harsh with power. She had witnessed at firsthand the appalling measure of his strength, and the warning stab of alarm deepened. But alongside that was the lash of her hunger and an unknown sense of dark excitement, of risk, of stepping out into a world that was not limited by caution, that was wholly and intoxicatingly new.

She allowed her body to touch his and the excitement grew. She leaned into him and she felt his breath quicken and the strange excitement crackled, like the tinder sparks, arcing between their separate bodies, man to woman.

Her heart skipped and each slight movement of his heated flesh kindled the flame. Its power gripped low in her belly, sharp, like pain, but filled with warmth. The heat radiated out through her blood into every inch of her flesh, so that her skin tingled with it and her heartbeat was racing, stealing breath.

His arms tightened round her as though he felt the deep uncontrolled reaction in her and welcomed it, understood in a way she did not. She felt the change in the sheet of muscle beneath her.

Her own heightened awareness became utterly focused on the hard masculine strength of his body, on his power, on the depth of his will and the alien thoughts in his head. Because despite the witchery of physical closeness, the dark inadmissible link of dreams, he was unknown to her.

She had touched him, held him in the darkness while he'd slept, and in three days, he had never even asked her name. He was a creature masked from the world, filled with fire below a surface that seemed impenetrable. He was infinitely and intensely dangerous, from the barbaric gold at his neck to the hard strength she touched, honed in the bitterness of battle.

The strength under her hands far eclipsed her own. His flesh burned her, as though traces of that inner fire leached through his skin. Ungoverned fire and carnal knowledge. She knew she was in far over her head. Everything about him should have made her draw back.

It was exactly what she wanted.

The vision of his naked body filled her mind.

CHAPTER

4

The familiar walls of her bower were unrecognizable as though the shapes Aurinia had known all her life had lost meaning. Embers glowed in the small hearth and the brilliant slash of the sun pierced straight through the narrow width of the chamber.

He laid her down on the bed. The familiar blue bedcovers and the patched linen sheets rustled under his weight. The sunlight behind him struck red fire out of his hair. The shadows veiled his face, giving only a glimpse of skin and the liquid brightness of his eyes, their black centres widely dilated.

The blood surged in her veins. His face was close to hers, and the solid wall of his body in its fine woolen tunic with the edgings of braid. Light glittered from the gold at his neck, a nobleman's symbol, everything her life had taught her to avoid, and she had helped him come here. Or his own harshly honed will and his own luck had wrought the necessary miracle. The black forest had parted for him. Even the wild beasts had let him pass and he was here, just as in her dream. But vividly, sense-quickeningly, real.

She felt the touch of his hand first, the warm glide of it across her skin, like a presage of what was to come. It was as though her heart stopped. She watched his shadowed face, her gaze caught by the intentness in the night-black eyes, by the hidden knowledge and the deeply sexual edge. Her head moved on the bolster and she leaned toward him. The hunger inside leaped.

Then she was so close she could no longer see. The trained warrior's body moved. She felt the soft whispering touch of his hair, then that harsh mouth. His mouth...

She thought she would die. His heat touched her, the fine, fiercely carved lips, the deep intimate warmth of another human being. The warmth flowed inside her in a single rush, intense, overwhelming, completely invasive. She had no defence against it.

She gasped, the small uneven sound of her breath lost against his mouth, the power of the kiss. Her world narrowed to heat and sensation, the movement of his lips, the tight suppressed measure of his breath. There was no hesitation in his kiss and no restraint, as though none had been possible from the moment they had touched in Bertred's room. The golden outpouring of desire from him had no limit.

Desire for her.

The stark realization thrilled her, filling her first with a tearing instant of wonder, of disbelief. And then the power of that disbelief was driven under by the mad strength of her hunger, the bewildering reality of his desire. The fierce untamed excitement of it possessed her.

Her hand reached out. Her fingers pushed under the dark silk-rich mass of his hair, beneath its weight and its shadow. Her fingertips slid across the tense arch of his neck, the smooth heat, the taut muscle. She reached higher to touch his face.

Her hand traced the uncompromising lines, the strength of the finely carved bones, the heat in his skin. Her fingers brushed the roughness at the edge of the solid jaw, the dark masculine shadow.

The kiss, the sense-shattering touch of his lips against hers only deepened and under the onslaught of passion, the first taste of its power, the pulsing drive of her own shocking need, thought was impossible.

He pulled her against his body. The feel of his arms around her overwhelmed everything, so that she was drowning in sensation, in the warmth of him. Most potent of all was the knowledge that at this moment he could not hold back his desire for her. That knowledge touched the desperately empty place inside her.

His body arched over her, a dense shadow against the fire-shot light of the sun, dark, dangerous, filled with unknown power.

Deeply and intensely arousing.

His body covered hers and she touched him. Her hand slid round, across the fine, tight muscle of his neck, under the heavy raven-black hair, cradling his head. She sensed his weight, the inexorable power, the first brush of his thigh against hers. The smooth pressure of that warm, darkly flexible mouth intensified.

Her heart was beating too fast, every sense heightened. His mouth slanted over hers. The urgency complete, so that her lips, softened and full and aching with his touch, opened to him. Her hand tightened against his head, as though she would draw him closer.

She felt the touch of his tongue. Reaction ripped through her. Her whole body moved convulsively against his, filled with shock, with wanting. Such wanting, for the hard feel of his body, the relentless exploration of her mouth, the feel of lips and tongue and ultimate passion.

The desire pierced her. Her fingers trembled unbearably against his skull and the sound of her breath was raw. She could not stop the sound or the unsteadiness of her fingers. Her whole body shook in his embrace.

He broke the kiss and rolled away from her. Even as her harshly inflamed senses struggled to take in what had happened, shame washed through her. Complete and mercilessly damning, and laced with the accusing threads of guilt.

Even then she could not turn her head. Her gaze locked on the deep exotic beauty in the harsh face, the tough body sprawled across her bed. Everything a trapped soul craved and could never have. She did not once look away.

Her fingers still tangled in his sleeve, just above the heavy tablet-woven braid. She could not force them to uncurl.

Nothing was said. She wanted to pull away, to show that she was in control the way she had been all of her life. She wanted to release him. She did not.

He turned. The controlled movement caused pain. She wanted to spare him that, so she spoke. But her voice made a sound that was wordless and unintelligible, as ungoverned as her feelings, out of place. He would leave her.

He had twisted round. His free hand reached out and covered hers. Memory stirred—the way he had held her hand when her unacceptable feelings had become obvious in Bertred's sickroom. He had taken her hand just like this.

She watched their tangled fingers. More gold glittered at his wrist, real and heavy. Thane's gold, a nobleman's. A thane's gesture. Her breath choked, the sound ugly.

His hand tightened. She looked away. She did not know what he meant by that, or what was in his head, but she thought she would never forget that split moment for the rest of her life.

She felt him take breath to speak, smooth and fine and flawless. The decorated metal at his wrist moved across her skin, richness such as she had never worn. She imagined it. Clothes that were not years old and patched, a fine table, a great hall. Not this one with its draughts and its rotting timbers and its complete isolation. The hall at Fearnros…

Her mind pictured herself there, accepted. In her rightful place. The bitter hunger clawed at her, but behind it was the familiar despair. This time the choked-off longing made no sound.

He held on to her hand, as though it meant something. The golden light poured over them together on her bed. There was no movement, no sound, as though the very air outside the wide-open window of her chamber waited. She heard the rustle of his head on her pillow.

Then he spoke, in his dark-witched voice, "I want you to come away from here. With me."

TEMPT ME WITH LOVING, *with all that I want more than life*…. Aurinia turned her face away. He did not know who she was, *what* she was, this golden thane, her dark warrior. He did not know how she lived.

"I cannot leave this place."

"You cannot stay—"

She felt the quick, sudden movement of his body, the fierce impatient power. He would let go of her hand. Her fingers gripped his. She was ashamed of the gesture, unable to stop it.

"It is not possible." She knew she had to let go. *Knew* it.

He began to speak, about the fighting outside her walls, about the Saxon king whom he served and the Vikings encamped at Wareham, about how safe she would be at Fearnros, about so many things, things of the world that did not reach her.

Her fingers twisted with his and she tried to listen, but the words could not touch her. What did touch her was the spellbinding sound of his voice and the way he breathed next to her, the slightest movement of his powerful body, the rustle of clothing. Sometimes she looked, at his eyes perhaps, or the tangled, spread-out fall of his hair, the solid length of his arm, a bent knee, his thigh. Mostly she kept her face turned away because he was beautiful and he had touched her and created magic.

She knew he would leave here. She knew why. She could not go with him, in that her mind was set, even though her hand, too warm and not quite steady, gripped his.

He stopped speaking. There was silence, of a quality she

had never known, not the empty silence of Wytch Heath but one filled with a burning, potent energy that came from the two of them. Expectancy. He watched their clasped hands. She was suddenly, utterly aware of that burning touch, of the feel of his skin against hers, the sight of her slender fingers entwined with his, the broad width of his palm.

"Will you come with me?"

The energy, the power, sparked like a presage to flame. Her breath caught and her body responded, the reaction fast and complete, deeply physical.

She would not go with him.

He turned her hand with his. Her finger slid over his warm flesh, over metal, hard, solid, not cold but warmed from the touch of his skin. Gold. It was unbelievably rich, twisted and decorated to match the eight torqued strands at his neck. *A British nobleman,* her cousin had said, *with lands west of Selwood.* Her cousin, who would never acknowledge her if he knew. A wealthy noble with responsibilities far away from here. *King's man,* Huda had said. King's man… She had seen it herself. Her fingertip brushed the gold, rested there. He watched. She forced the words.

"How could I go with you?"

"You know how, *why.*" The black gaze suddenly caught hers, trapped it, and all the things that she had seen of him without bodily eyes, were laid bare. Their shades filled the small shabby room, the shadow of an awareness that was rich beyond thought, that could be…shared. The familiar dreams and the familiar hunger rose, the longing.

"I will not abandon you." The grip of his hand tightened, the touch of his flesh against hers, warm and very strong.

Abandon. Such a word he chose to use. *Abandon.* He said he would not…. She swallowed, forced down memories, all the bitter sum of her twenty lonely winters. Her fingers were crushed against the gold. *I will provide whatever you need….* The words he had said in Bertred's chamber that first night, when he had forced Huda to leave the room. The way his voice had sounded—so sure.

A rich man's mistress.

A mistress was naught beyond a plaything, a man's toy. *No.*

His hand round hers opened but the touch did not break. The movement took away the harsh pressure of the gold, leaving only the warm sense of his flesh. His hand moved over hers, over the fine skin of her palm, across the delicate insides of her fingers, the exquisitely sensitive tips. Her breath tightened. The heat held inside her flamed.

His solid hand retraced its path, settled round the thin veined skin and the fragile bones of her wrist, engulfing her. The slowness of the gesture was blatantly sensual and at the same time possessively complete. Like a promise.

I will not abandon you.

"Can you not trust to that?"

She did not speak. She had to tell him to go. Her heart pounded and she closed her eyes. But she could still feel his touch, wildly and more deeply without sight. The hunger leaped. She had to say… She felt his closeness behind her in her bed and she could not move. She was trapped by his closeness, fighting for the necessary words. Nothing came through her lips. It would be he who would withdraw, leave her because she—

Already she felt him pulling away, letting her go. The word *abandon* coursed through her head. Her hand moved, like something forced beyond her will, beyond calling back. She touched him, her dream shadow, her real man. Her fingers reached back and closed over the heavily muscled mass of his forearm.

"I cannot…." *I cannot go with you.* But they were not the words in her mind, and in that broken instant, he touched her, with all the strong tough warmth of his body, the beauty. She made the mistake of saying his name. *Macsen.* Just that and then there was no separation. She felt the fine heat of his thickly muscled chest at her back, the dense curve of his hips, the long line of his thigh. The dark-shadowed body of her dreams and the real man. The hot vitality engulfed her, drove out the cold, the emptiness.

"I do not have a future." *Nothing that could match yours.* "I cannot see it." It was all she could say, just those words torn out of her, no more.

"No one can, truly. No one can see all that it means." The voice betrayed nothing but she felt the sharp reaction just as she had before. Something expertly suppressed, choked off before it took life. Hidden depths. All the things she did not know.

"Do you want me to stay with you?" asked her lover.

Yes. She did not even know whether the word was spoken. It did not matter. He would know it anyway.

His head bent to hers. She felt the whisper of his hair on her neck, the touch of his lips, brief and hot as a brand of fire. She could feel the fire in him, the driving flame of desire. But he still spoke.

"Tell me what you want." She felt the deep warmth of his breath on her skin, the touch of lips withheld. "Do you want this?"

This.

The hunger claimed her for its own and the vision that had come to her when she had first touched him—the sight of his body moving with such smooth power in the act of love, his flesh joined with hers, the bright heat of his naked skin, the madness and the intense, desperate pleasure.

She turned in his arms. Her eyes met his. He had seen all that she had. The shuttered glimpse of the future.

No one can see all that it means.

She shut her mind against what it might mean.

He would leave her for his own world, for his endangered king. She could not follow him, but for this moment out of time he was here, caught in her world, a creature of dreams and a man who desired her, who would take all the bitter need in her and not reject it. Who had already taken it.

"Stay with me." She watched his eyes, the desire in them, only that, nothing else, because it was not a request made with honour or decency. Her lips framed the words against his. "I want you to touch me."

Show me what it means to be loved.

She kissed him. Her mouth settled against his fine harshly carved lips, the source of warmth, the dark seduction she could not resist.

It was as though *she* were what he wanted. *Desired.* Even she who had no experience felt the swift reaction in his body. Her own excitement surged, intensified, driven far beyond the reach of reason or thought.

It was best that he was a stranger without any future beyond the stolen time in her chamber. She could touch a stranger.

Aurinia put her arms round him and he pulled her into the hard heat of his body as close as she wanted to be.

Her hands tightened on the dense muscle of his shoulders. Her action at first was instinctive, and then it became something more.

She felt the reaction in the dense flesh under her hand, the same pleasure. She slid her fingers across that intensively reactive flesh, upward to the bared line of his throat, feeling the tense curve, the strength, the intoxicating vibration through his skin. His hand moved round to cup her head through the fall of her unbound hair, holding her to the kiss.

Her tongue touched the moving flexible line of his lower lip.

A harshly suppressed sound ripped from his throat. The fiercely muscled body moved. She felt his weight bear her back against the bed. But she was not afraid.

His hands caressed her, at her waist, the curve of her hips, then upward again across her rib cage, higher. His fingers brushed the underside of her breast.

She gasped against his mouth. His hand curved round the soft swell of her breast. Her back arched, bringing her flesh into tighter contact through the thin barrier of her clothing. The heavy warmth of his palm maddened her senses. His fingers moved to undo the ties of her clothing.

The kiss broke and his lips touched her throat, lightly. His fingers moved, competent, careful. She watched him untie the lacing of her tunic, uncover the shape of her flesh. The look in his eyes was dark, almost predatory.

He stopped at the rune she had placed over her heart, the shape she had drawn with woad on her skin, *eolhx,* elk sedge, the protective rune. She did not know what was in his head, what he understood. Her heart was beating so fast it would choke her.

She watched him bend his head.

His blue-black hair spilled out across the exposed whiteness of her skin. He touched the rune first. The finely curved lips brushed the small shape, covered it.

She tried to stay still, but her body moved, pressing toward him as his mouth settled on her flesh. She was lost in sensation, lost in his closeness.

The muscled weight of his thigh moved between hers, pushing her disordered skirts aside, and then his hand…

He spoke to her, his voice no more than a dark whisper of sound. She hardly heard the words, only the question, the thing no one had ever asked of her, or wanted—closeness.

Her reply was said against his hair.

"Touch me…"

The step was taken, her decision made. His body would move to cover hers. She felt the touch of his hand. The solid, careful fingers sought her most intimate hidden flesh with the slow sensual caress he had used on the rest of her body. Her muscles tightened with shock.

The broad hand covered her, the base of his palm pressing lightly across aching flesh, rhythmically, until her breath tightened in small gasps and she could not move except to push against the source of that exquisite sense-maddening pleasure.

She felt his fingers move, exploring the heat-slickened folds of her sensitized flesh, the sensation unbearably intimate, but she could not draw away.

The tips of his fingers traced the hidden entrance to her body. Then he trailed the heated moisture across her skin until his fingers found the place that gathered all the mad longing, all the burning need and the joyful pleasure into one. She cried out, the sound savage. Her body arched, but he held her as the exquisite sensations pierced through her and shattered.

She was still touching him when full consciousness came back. It did not seem possible, but the awareness of his warmth, the feel of his solid body against hers, were the first things she knew. She imagined waking up in bed each morning with someone there, a lover, a man who was *wif-fæst,* bound in marriage. She shut her eyes. She ached from the tingling fullness of pleasure. She felt the roughness of his breathing, the deep well of untapped desire.

"I did not realize," she said.

She moved her head on the heated curve of his shoulder. He was watching her.

"No one has ever touched you before." The night-black eyes were narrowed, the finely arched brows drawn together.

She thought, *He cannot believe it,* and the familiar coldness, the bitter destructive emptiness, lashed at her, the stigma of what she was. But she would not lie.

"No."

Of course, she was not acceptable. She raised her head. Her gaze registered the disbelief and the desire. She was not a fool. She knew that desire held no future.

Yet it pulled at her, as nothing had in her life. Madness. She forced speech.

"No. No one has touched me. I—"

The thick gold at his neck caught the sun as he turned away. She thought that perhaps she had breached some code of honour, something she knew nothing about. But in this moment it felt like the most bitter of rejections. Like *abandonment*— She caught his arm.

"But this is what I want." The edge of madness gave her the courage to say it. "With you." The words left her mouth and she knew he could hear the hunger in them, that he would be able to see it in her eyes.

Do not turn from me. Right or wrong, stay.... The plea sprang from a far deeper need than the ache in her body.

"Let me touch you." She looked into the unfathomable depths of his eyes and wondered whether he could see beyond her words into the pain-filled abyss of her mind.

She thought he did and then she thought nothing because the powerful body moved and he was so close she could see nothing but him. He took hold of her hand and drew it against the fine restless strength of his body. She touched him and felt the raw power and unslaked need, the beat of his heart.

He allowed the first tentative brush of her hand, the play of her fingers across his shoulders, the breadth of his chest. Her fingertips caught the hidden edge of the linen bandage round his ribs, skipped across it, moved lower, to the taut flexible line of his abdomen, the leather belt at his hips.

She touched metal, the round-edged shape of a belt buckle. Her fingers traced over silver, intensely decorated by some master of artistry, then the round smoothness of a gem, all heated from the touch of his body. She stopped, the sudden sound of her breath loud in the quietness of the room.

She felt the touch of his fingers round hers and the rich buckle fell away. His body moved and he kept hold of her hand, guiding her fingers down to the braided edge of his tunic so that it was she who drew the finely woven wool across the brilliance of his skin and over his head.

She was leaning over him, her hand on his belly. Such fine skin. She watched the beauty of it. Her fingers moved and the supple muscular line tightened at her touch.

Her hand smoothed the flaring line of his side, higher, pushing inward across the subtly bronzed flesh above the stark white line of the linen bandage, tracing the tightly muscular curve, feeling the push of his breath and the shape of his body. The sensitive skin of her fingers brushed the flat hardened nipple and the harsh sound that cut the air was the deep, fierce sound of his voice. Her heart leaped and the heat inside her flared.

The faint catch in her own breath was lost against his mouth as she bent down to press her body against his. Her arms closed round him, avoiding the damage across his back. Her hands settled at the slight springing curve at the base of his spine. She felt his hips grind against hers and her mind dizzied with the vision she had seen, the virile hardness of his flesh inside hers.

Her hand slid lower, across the edge of his trousers, down to the taut curve, feeling the muscle contract. Her heart raced and she gasped. The kiss softened and she felt him pull back.

"Do not leave me." Her voice against his lips was harsh as her raven's voice. *Memory and thought.* "Do not…."

"No." His hand touched hers briefly.

"Show me what to do," she said.

5

Aurinia watched the stranger's dark eyes and she wanted him, someone who would touch her, in warmth if not in the infinite impossibility of love. It could not be love. But yet there was no turning from this. Her body pressed his. His strong fingers moved to the dark line of his trousers. Her breath tightened.

Her hand followed his and her heart beat quickened. It was she who removed the last of his clothing, with his hand to guide her. With his body spread out before her on the bed, she leaned over him and unwound the leather strips that held the cloth tight between ankle and knee. Her dress slid off her shoulders, her crushed skirts bunched up around her thighs.

Nothing in her life had prepared her for this, but her fingers moved with a strange sureness and her blood burned as she watched every movement he made.

Her hands grasped his hips, the taut shape beneath fine cloth. Then, her hands were in his, easing the dark cloth over the bronzed skin. Her gaze fixed on the potent fullness of his flesh.

There was a moment without thought or breath, and then he pulled her closer so that her body lay alongside his, touching. The curve of her breast against his chest, the bared flesh of her leg against his thigh. She felt his heat, the scent of arousal on his skin.

The light of the dying sun gleamed off the damp skin in the hollow at the base of his throat. She bent her head and tasted him, the hot moist skin and the scent of him against her mouth and tongue. His hands in her hair raised her head, moving until his mouth found hers.

The fierce knot of sensation deep in her belly tightened, all of her senses. Anticipation coursed through her veins.

"I want to touch you," she said.

Her breath came fast and her body burned. The hooded eyes were on her face and his hand round hers. Then her fingers were meshed with his and he was guiding her so that she touched him, the tight hardness and the smooth heat-slickened skin. Such smoothness…

Her whole body ached, tightened on a surge of desire like a dizzying wave.

Her fingers traced the burning flesh and she felt the sharp reaction as though it were in her own skin. She watched her slim fingers on his skin, felt him move, the hot slip of his flesh against her palm and her fingertips.

"Now…" she said, her desire a terrible hunger that tore at the roots of her soul.

"Now." The deep persuasive voice held a thousand things she could not name.

She closed her eyes, felt the whisper of his breath against her skin, the strong flex of warm muscle, the slow inexorable movement of his body over hers.

She thought she knew all that would follow. It was her skill and her cleverness to understand the physical realm.

She knew nothing.

She was drowning in sensation as his scarred hand and his careful fingers created the overwhelming magic that had blinded her before. Need clawed at her and she held him, her hands gripping dense lithe muscle, her hips tight against his touch.

Her fingers tightened on the thick curve of his shoulder and she felt the nudge of his sex against her body, the smooth glide of that silk hot hardness against flesh aching with need.

Awareness of Macsen filled every sense, the night-dark shadow of his hair, the faint sheen of sweat on his skin, the strongly carved shape of his face. The tensed muscle of his shoulders under her hands and the sleek lines of his body. The harshly tightened tendon at his neck.

She held herself still, feeling the controlled movement of his body, moments she never wanted to end.

Then his lips touched hers, the lightest brush of that harshly drawn mouth. She moved against his heat and her choked breath formed the sound of her hunger and the need driving her onward.

She felt the heated slide of his hips, the hardness penetrating her body, the intense shocking feeling of male flesh melding with hers, the utter, impossible closeness.

She gasped, feeling him still.

"You are what I want." Her voice whispered through the

shadows, scarcely lifting the heavy air. She sensed the sharp tension in his body, the fierceness of his control.

Her body moved experimentally against his. She heard the faint sound of his breath, felt the hot silk hardness inside her, the power. Her body was so tight round his. He pressed deeper, the penetration achingly slow, building the hunger until she was mad with it.

Her hands tightened on the sleek heavy muscle of his shoulders, her fingers digging into the thick flesh. She arched toward him, feeling the last constriction give way to the push of his body, the quick tear of pain, then her senses spinning, filled with his closeness and his heat. With all that she desired.

When he would have eased back, she held him.

"You are what I want." Her voice strengthened. The words latent with a promise she had no right to give to a stranger. Words born three weeks ago when she had first seen him in her mind.

Aurinia held him close, feeling him move inside her, the smooth power of his body, the urgent strength, the heat of his skin. Real, different from her vision in Bertred's chamber, a breathless moment filled with its own life, with meaning she did not know.

Everything was lost in the feel of the heavy body filling hers, filling the emptiness, creating everything that she had been able to imagine and things that she had not.

There was nothing beyond him and his closeness, the sudden impossible tenseness as he thrust deep inside her body, the faint harshly cut off sound of his voice, and then the control was no longer there.

You are what I want. The words were not said. They only formed in her mind.

She thought he heard them.

THE DANGER BROUGHT AURINIA out of the dream. Primitive fear burst at the back of her mind. She was lying in her own bed with her head jammed against an expanse of bare skin, her leg pinned under the swell of a naked thigh, a warm weight of heavy sated male muscle. She took a breath. It seared her throat, laced with shadows and the dark intimate scent of sex.

"What is it?" The lissom body in her bed moved, the reaction completed before she could form words.

"I do not know—"

Things unseen. Things I do not believe....

The disturbance became sound, borne on the evening breeze, a sound between a deep-throated bark and the wild wailing howl of a wolf. Hunter.

"Someone is coming." The disbelief still clawed through her mind. "Here."

The sound came again and behind it, unheard, were the voices of the forest wolves, the fast disturbed rustle of their feet.

"They are here." She stared at the naked man in her bed. *No one ever came here. No one could. No one before—* The fear burst like a blow, so strong she fell back under its force.

"What have you done?" Her question came out of disbelief, out of the bitter anger that was the other face of fear. The accusation hung, spoken and irretrievable. The black gaze held hers, like looking down into an abyss without limit.

"Macsen…" The use of the unknown man's name was

instinctive, the way she responded when she saw physical pain. But the heavy body moved past her, strength beyond reckoning.

He tossed her cloak at her.

"Dress." He pulled on his own clothes, the movement of hand and body fast, efficient. Perfectly in control.

Her fingers scrabbled to gather the fastenings of her dress. She found her shoes. He was already speaking, planning it out. Warrior's thoughts.

"Is there another way out for you, without being seen?"

"Yes, but—"

"Take it."

Just her. She watched him.

Her stiff fingers snagged in the fall of her skirts. He had the sword.

"No. This is my home. I will not leave it." *My home. Mine.* Her refuge. The only place she had ever been safe. No one ever came here— She stared at unsheathed steel that could maim.

"Bertred."

"You will not be able to help him. Not against more than one." His face was shut.

"You think the Vikings have come here, just as you said." Her heart caught. "Do you *know*…"

He understood what she meant by *know*. Something flickered in the dark eyes and then was gone. The gaze was rock steady. "No." Then he said, "Go. You cannot help Bertred."

She held the cloak against her body. "And you?"

The same flicker of his eyes and then nothing.

"Do not wait. Go to Fearnros."

He moved, herding her so that she was through the doorway before him. He pressed something into her fingers.

She caught the touch of his hand, as warm on her skin as when they had bedded. Her heart beat frantically. She wanted to hold on and never let go.

There was no place for such dreams. There was only disaster and whatever could be saved from her home. Her responsibilities. She felt him pause, but there was no time, so she forced the last question she had to ask.

"Huda—"

He let go, the smooth movement taking him forward.

"I will send him to you if I can."

He strode away and there was nothing left, no sound, scarcely the swirl of shadowed air.

She bowed her head, turning over what she held in her hand. It was a warrior's weapon, called in her language a *wæl-seax,* a slaughter-blade. Inside the tooled leather sheath was a fourteen-inch length of single-edged steel. The guard protruding above the sheath was decorated with silver and engraved with the dark edging of niello. The handgrip covered in fine leather was wound with silver wire.

She would not go to Fearnros. She would never go there if it were the last place that existed on Middle Earth.

He did not realize that.

She pulled the knife gently from its sheath.

HUNTER FOUND HER BEFORE SHE had gone twenty paces. He was quivering, his dense grey fur dark and matted with sweat as though he had been running. He showed teeth. She dropped to her knees beside him and touched the heaving flanks. He was not hurt. He let her handle him, but it was a wolf's eyes that looked back.

She buried her face for a moment against the tangled fur.

"What happened? What do you know? What is it?" *What is happening now?*

His distress was less than she had expected. She tried to read in his eyes and his tautly held body what she needed to know. But there was so little without words. She raised her face.

"Find Huda. Find him. Now."

She stood up, nudging the powerful shoulders and he moved off, obedient. No, not that. He simply walked and she followed reluctantly. His silent pacing led her away from the chamber that held Bertred. But they did not go far. The smoke-grey wraith in front of her stopped in deep shadow and she was looking out into her yard.

He had not found Huda.

She was watching a straight, finely balanced back, a fall of dark hair. He faced a troop of mounted warriors that must have numbered three sets of five. There were spears, slender leafed blades on pale ashwood shafts, the smooth curve of a ready bow. He stood in full sunlight, motionless, the sword held loosely in his hand.

Fine leather and silver wire bit into her fingers. She touched the ruff of Hunter's neck with her free hand. There was silence, broken by the jingle of someone's harness fittings as a horse fidgeted and was abruptly stilled.

The man who had shared her bed moved, walking toward the leader where he sat astride a huge grey horse, surrounded by spears, an oblong banner furled close in the windless air. The tasseled edges suddenly swung, showing the glint of gold, a dragon.

The thick-necked, sleekly muscled stallion danced. Moving light caught the rider, shone off him, off his silver mail riveted with the golden glow of bronze, off his deeper gold hair, off gems. Everything spoke the expected display of a *dryhten,* a war-leader. But there would have been no doubt of who he was if he had been dressed in rags.

She felt Huda's silent presence behind her. Hunter had not led her amiss after all. Or he had known what she truly wanted.

She could not face such a thought.

The grey horse was brought to stillness with an expert hand. Macsen stopped beside the silver stirrup, the booted foot, the bent knee, the long gold-stamped line of a scabbard. The dark head and strong graceful neck of her lover bent.

Huda's curse touched the exposed skin of her shoulder. "He will cause you harm."

Her flesh prickled. "They are not Viking. They are not—"

The shining leader said something. The sun struck from the sword hilt beside his hand. Macsen answered, the words indistinguishable.

"He would have made an escape for me. He thought I would go to Fearnros. He does not know. He—"

"He knows nothing." Huda's breath rasped against her ear and this time she caught the violence. At her feet, Hunter made a faint sound. Her hand tightened on thick fur.

"Huda..." Ten paces away across her yard, the shining man raised a hand with rings on the fingers. The tight circle behind him drew back. Macsen kept speaking.

"He said he would send you to me. That he would try—"

There was a general movement among the men, the bright flex of glittering bronze and steel as the leader dismounted. He was tall, with such energy. It radiated like lightning. Macsen turned, began to walk back toward them, toward her. Her skin prickled with a different kind of warning.

"Try what?" Huda shifted, the powerless anger palpable. The sword was still in his hand. It was useless against what was to come. He knew it as well as she did. "He has brought Fearnros to you."

There was nothing to say.

Aurinia watched her fate cross the sunlit yard. She fancied that the dark stranger's gaze pinned her, even at that distance, even though she stood in shadow black as night. His loose stride covered the distance. The man who could only be the ruler of the last free kingdom in Britain walked at his side. The royal bodyguard, the *gesiths,* hearth-companions who now lived at Fearnros, followed.

She stepped out.

"Don't. Aurinia..." Huda's hand caught her arm as though he could stop what would happen. It was too late. It had been too late from the moment her dark lover had crossed Wytch Heath. Her home was already invaded. She stopped, her hand on the nail-studded door post. *Is* runes, protection. She realized she was not wearing her girdle. She had left it in her haste, in the bed she had shared with her lover. There was no protection. She had no power—

"Lady. I owe you my thanks for saving the life of my thane Bertred," said Alfred, King of Wessex. He had eyes like a falcon's. The ground shifted.

"It is not I who deserves such gratitude. Lord." Her tongue tripped over the word. She remembered to bend her head. She could not look at Macsen but the awareness between them was like fire. "It is your companion who rescued him, who—"

The ringed hand stopped her words.

"Macsen has told me of your skill."

Macsen. She saw him move, the competent turn of his body, the gleam of gold. A thane's courtesy. The sunlit figure speaking to a king.

"Shall we go and see the result of your care?" The quick energy carried them onward. The pit opened up beneath her feet.

They found the healing chamber, followed by the royal bodyguard. The King of the West Saxons walked through the door signed with the ox rune. She did not think he noticed it. He did not need to. He had his own power that had naught to do with things unseen.

The familiar whispers had begun before they reached the chamber door. Hunter's tail switched her legs in anger. He stayed close, moving with a low menacing sinuousness that was all wolf. She made him sit. But she could not let go of his thick warm fur. Her gaze sought Huda, but he was parted from her by the crowd of armed men.

Macsen stood by her side.

Bertred's face was incandescent with joy.

She stood near the bed, isolated in the space that had

formed around her and the wolf-tainted hound and Macsen. The eager boy poured out his story to the greatest Christian warrior in Britain. The king encouraged him. Their voices almost drowned out the whispering. But nothing had ever done that. Bertred's carrying voice said, *miracle.* Her blood froze.

The boyish mouth was still rounded over the final sound of the word. The whispering stopped. But not completely. She heard *bastard,* then *Edwald,* her father's name.

The king's head turned at the sound of a name that would be familiar to him. The hawk's eyes surveyed a bodyguard turned suddenly silent. But it was Bertred's face that Aurinia watched, Bertred's flushed skin suddenly drained of every last trace of colour, Bertred's clear eyes as they reflected the first tentative, appalling connection.

"You are my uncle's—" He did not actually say *bastard.* The overwhelming king was two feet away from him and, anyway, it had already been heard.

She thought of denying it. She thought of what Bertred's horror-filled eyes would look like faced by a cousin who was, despite popular belief, legitimate.

She could feel the wash of pain from the slight body she had saved from death.

"You are the one he repudiated," said Bertred. "When he cast your mother off because she was…was a…" The familiar word trembled on the edge of existence—*hell-rune,* sorceress. If it was said, they might want to drown her or stone her to death. She watched the dread in her cousin's face.

"You…when you healed me and you—" *must have used enchantments.* He did not want to say it, but he would. All around her, hands moved in the sign that stood against evil, the reaction unstoppable. Even the king's ringed hand traced a cross because that was what he believed so deeply.

Aurinia stood with her spine straight, islanded in a sea of armed men. Bertred's mouth opened. Far to her right, she thought Huda pushed forward. She tried to pick him out, to tell him to stay still for his own safety, but the focus of attention in the crowded chamber shifted elsewhere.

"Bertred, if you wish to say anything to the lady beyond expressing your thanks, tell me." The dark-haired man beside her had moved, just slightly. There was nothing in his voice except bland invitation. And the force that had filled her hall from the first moment he had walked into it.

"Macsen…" From shock-white, Bertred's face took back the colour it had lost. "You…" His gaze moved from his rescuer, the hero of his idolatry, to herself and she was suddenly aware of her bed-tangled hair, her creased skirts and her loosened dress, of the bronzed skin that showed at Macsen's throat, the smoothly turned rise of his collarbone at the open neck of his tunic.

She knew that every eye in the chamber saw what Bertred saw, that every man's mind thought as he did—she had used one kind of enchantment on a thane's nephew and another and darker kind on the favoured warrior of a king. Sorceress and whore. She thought for the first time, *This will taint him with the same curse that holds me, inescapable.*

She tried to find words but his hand reached for her, deliberate and unhurried, the touch oddly warm in the bitter air of the chamber. She watched the movement of his smooth throat, the glitter of gold, the tilt of his head, that

spoke of several dozen generations of impeccable ancestors.

"It is my right."

She saw Huda shove forward in earnest. They would kill
him. The king made a small gesture of negation, but the
restless energy tightened. Hunter stood, hackles tight. The
warm hand clasped hers.

"It is my right because the lady is—"

Aurinia's breath choked. The hard palm and the strong
fingers tightened, the flash of warmth. *Rich man's mistress.*

"No—"

But his voice overrode hers. "The lady is my wife."

CHAPTER

6

"I will not wed you."

She was alone with the stranger. The ruler of Wessex had congratulated them and then announced that his men would take Bertred back to Fearnros. They were engaged in making a litter in which to carry him.

No one had killed Huda.

Her retainer had unsheathed his sword in the presence of his sovereign and it had been seen, by the king undoubtedly. Alfred of the West Saxons had chosen to feign blindness. One did not argue either with or in front of such a person. Aurinia was not used to arguing at all, or to being so intolerably public. There was no one here in her own chamber.

No one except—he expected her to go to Fearnros.

She sat down in her creased clothes with her hair spilled over her face, still disordered from where he had touched it, buried his hands in its tangled weight, smoothed her face and her throat with his fingertips and—

"No."

He did not touch her now, for which she was grateful. She had to speak, to give voice to desperation, to all the bitter things pressing on her heart. She was sitting on the edge of the bed. The covers were rumpled where the stranger, Macsen, had lain with her, as she had known he would from the start. He had taken her into a world where she did not belong. Taken—how easy to believe that. But it had been her own hunger and her own greed.

"I cannot do it."

"Why?"

She could feel the suppressed force that had confounded Bertred and a king's retinue. Her back stiffened.

"You saw why. I am not…acceptable. I do not belong in their world. In yours." She thought of his warmth, the feel of his arms around her, the heat and the dark invasive touch of his body and the moment that had existed between them, shared. "I will not ever belong."

"That is not true."

"You did not know who I was."

"No." Then he said, "Tell me your name."

Her name. He did not know it.

They had lain together in this chamber. They had shared…such things. He had not known so much as her name and she had not cared. Neither had he.

He had offered marriage.

"Aurinia."

The name of another reputed sorceress long ago and far

away in the land of her ancestors across the sea. Of course, he would not realize. He was not Saxon.

"The wisewoman." The fine British voice held her, the black eyes that could change lightning-fast, shadow-creature with concealed powers.

She took a breath, but the thane was still speaking.

"Is Bertred right?"

She blinked. No one had ever asked that. They simply accepted. *No. I am Edwald's legitimate daughter. I have a better claim to the lands Bertred now owns at Fearnros than he does.* But there was no proof. The story of illegitimacy was so firmly entrenched it could no longer be gainsaid. And she did not want to. The thought of setting foot in Fearnros made her physically sick.

Besides, she would not tarnish a helpless boy like Bertred for nothing. Her pride would not let her. So she simply said the worst of it and ignored the rest.

"Edwald repudiated both my mother and myself before I was born. My mother was unusual because she could heal people and sometimes she could effect cures for them that did not seem possible." She chose her words. "If a thing does not seem either possible or expected, it can be frightening."

Aurinia glanced at the solid figure beside her who had not been frightened by anything and who had brought his own kind of impossibility. He moved, pacing the small compass of her room as though he could not keep still, a blur of shadow and thane's gold.

"Edwald said my mother was a *hell-rune.* It is not possible for a man in a position of honour to live with an enchantress, particularly not one pregnant with a child he did not acknowledge." The words stumbled and he was suddenly very, very close. She forced the emotion from her voice. "An enchantress could only birth something unacceptable."

Not a child to be proud of, who might inherit, who might be…loved.

She suddenly realized that the hand that had touched her was clamped around a silver-wired hilt.

Not the sword, but that more blood-chilling weapon, the *wæl-seax*. The tooled leather sheath was back with its owner, the thin leather straps buckled to the jeweled belt. Such a weapon was worn suspended almost horizontally across the abdomen, weight off the cutting edge. She watched the whiteness of his knuckles.

He saw the direction of her gaze quite clearly. He did not unclench his hand.

"Tell me." The beautiful voice was steady, an utter contrast to that hard-knuckled hand.

She moistened her lips.

"He cast her out. My father cast my mother out and so she came to Wytch Heath." Her gaze fixed on the solid hand at his hip. "She had three servants and one retainer."

"Huda."

"Aye." Her gaze slid past the dangerous knife-wielder because there was something about Huda's loyalty to her mother that had reached beyond duty. Yet Huda had never spoken, and her mother had never seen it.

"The servants do not live here but in the village. They come and help when it is needed. No one else would live here. There is only this abandoned hall, supposedly cursed and definitely wolf-ridden. But my mother did not mind that. She wanted no one and she had no fear of wild animals. In the end she preferred their company to that of people. I was born here and I stayed here. My mother died five winters ago." *She was tired of living.*

"And that is how you lived? Here in this empty hall with only your mother and after that alone when you must have been, what? Fifteen?"

It would seem so wrong to him. It would bear no relation to how he lived in his glittering world among companions. She shrugged her shoulders, tipped her head back and said, "I had Huda."

He turned away, the movement uncontrollably abrupt, the force bleakly visible.

"No one ever came here," she said to his moving back. "No one—" She stopped before the next words, finally and unexpectedly caught on the edge of the abyss. *No one before you.*

The force that shimmered in the air, the suppressed emotion in both of them, caught flame. The fierce movement of his body brought him sharply near, so close it was like touching, so close because the barrier between them had been broken, here in this chamber, perhaps even before that in their minds.

Aurinia did not want to think of that, of a future with him, of that sharing. It was not possible. Nothing with a person like him was.

She wanted to move away, but there was no room. She held back in case he should touch her, in case she became lost in the sense-shattering warmth of him, the terrible longing.

"I do not belong in Bertred's world, nor in the king's world. Nor in yours. I used to think that I might once. I used to go into the outside world and I—" Her breath caught. What if he touched her and she gave in to the madness?

She thought of him in her cousin's chamber, surrounded by antagonism, for all that he was so rich and so proud and so favoured. She remembered what she was.

"Such a thing is not possible." There was determination and there was pride. If she let those go, she would have nothing. She had to face things, find the courage to do what was necessary.

Her fingers, hard with fury, grasped the neckline of her dress. It was already undone. She pulled it down over her shoulder, as he had done in the intimacy of her bed, but she dragged the material lower, wrenching her arm free of the sleeve. His dark gaze swept her face, her skin. Then he saw the purple line of the scar on her ribs.

She saw the change in his eyes, the sharp flick horror that had transfixed Bertred. She turned away, but she was not dealing with an overwhelmed boy. He caught her arm and she jerked round.

"What happened?"

She stared at his face. She could not see the horror now, only deep anger.

"I used to go out and help people when they were sick." Her lip curled. "But what I do is not…ordinary or easy to explain. Healing skills are learned like any other but they can take on an air of magic to someone who is ill, or whose loved one is in danger. Even the lore of plants is perhaps threatening to those who do not know. But sometimes there is more than that." She paused. "You have seen it."

"Yes."

That was it. All she got. A single word that covered a whole world that was hidden, a thousand things she did not yet know how to read. But he had not seemed afraid of what could so terrify others. Perhaps because of all the men she had met, he had the strongest power, not just physical, but of the mind. Perhaps it meant he could think differently.

Perhaps—

The gold at his neck caught the sun from some movement he made, blinding her.

"Sometimes when I heal people it is like giving energy." She kept her voice smooth, even. "Sometimes it succeeds in curing. That is what Bertred felt and what he now takes for sorcery."

Nothing changed in the brutally set face, nothing except a small flicker in the angry eyes. Most people would have missed that, but not her. She was clever at such things. She hated herself for it.

"Bertred also knows you saved his life—"

"Oh, yes." She took a breath and watched the expressive eyes. "It was not failure that defeated me, but success. That can frighten people as much as they fear death."

She expected to see disbelief, but there was only a bitter acceptance that replaced the anger. The very harshness of it was a relief. She dragged the dress over her skin.

"You frightened someone so much they turned on you."

"Just in the village…just…" Her voice was not quite so steady now. It was filled with memory that still had the power to shock.

"*Who?*"

That was when she realized the acceptance had not replaced the anger at all. It had intensified it.

"Tell me."

"But—why?" It was over. Nothing could now be changed.

"Because when I find him he will know what he has done wrong."

"You?"

"What do you think I would do, leave you unprotected with no one to avenge your hurts?"

She did not say it. She would swear she did not say it, but the unspoken word filled the tense air between them. *Yes.* She watched the anger burst its bonds.

"You thought I would walk away."

"I—" What did she say to something so unexpected? "I have always taken my own decisions. I—" She stopped because she saw more deeply.

"That is what you thought."

She had struck something unseen. Honour? Some code she did not understand in her blank isolation?

His hand was still round her arm. "I said I would not abandon you."

"But I did not understand that you would—"

"I asked if you would be with me. We lay with each other in this room. I took your first blood. We were together."

She watched his scarred hand on her arm, felt the touch of his flesh.

"That is still what I want." The deft hand moved, the

suppressed vibration of power, the dark vitality and, locked inside, so many things she did not know. The warmth she had lain with.

"You cannot…" The sense of his nearness was dragging her down like a deep whirlpool. She tried to force speech. "It is not right." *All we shared, all the mad passion that held the edge of joy.* "You did not know then what I am."

"No."

She watched the big hand move. She felt his touch and the intimate heat, and the yearning tore at her, not slaked by what they had shared in this bed, but inflamed by it, as though the longing for him would never die but always be renewed, each time stronger.

She would rather die now than be faced again with the glimpse of a life she could never have. She turned, the movement sharply savage, vicious with the need to end what should never start, with the depthless brutal longing for it.

He did not let her go. He did not understand. Her fingers dragged at his so that she could free herself.

"You did not know what—"

"I do not care."

Her heart stood still.

"But you—"

"I do not care."

It was a lie, bravado, stung pride. She understood the lash of that, none better. He did not, could not, mean what he said.

"Listen to me," he said in the voice that wrought enchantments, *galdor-cræft*. "I do not care."

Her hand stayed, touching him.

"We were together. We are now. We were together before we even met."

She moved into his arms. The heat and the fire of his presence enfolded her and it was all that she craved in her heart.

She lay with him on the wildly disordered bed, caught in the power of his embrace, attuned only to him. She could sense the pure strength of his body, the fierce beat of his heart, the faint push of his ribs as he spoke.

"I have seen your face each night when I have dreamed. Since the first moment I came to Fearnros with the king's army, you have filled my thoughts."

Part of her wanted to say *no* because the enchantment did not seem possible. But in the end, she would have been lying. His hand touched her face.

"You were so close to me that even in the midst of battle I only had to think of you and you were there."

There was a moment of silence in her empty chamber, the memory of red sunlight on a white cloth. Her body twined with the supple strength of his. Her heart was beating just as fiercely.

"You saw me."

"Yes."

She touched him then, her fingers tracing the line of his upper arm, the solid muscular curve, the straight shoulder. She swallowed with a throat gone dry.

"I knew you would come here. I knew that neither the woods nor the heathland would stop you and that even the wolves themselves would let you pass. I think I knew from the moment you walked into the hall that you would not turn back and that you would not give up Bertred."

"He had to live."

It was an odd turn of phrase. Especially from someone who chose words for their most subtle shades of meaning. She felt the bitter echo of unhealed pain. Something that touched in an unseen way on the cousin who regarded her with such horror.

"Macsen…" She used his name, but then his arms closed tighter, drawing her closer into the enchantment of that different world.

"That is how things are," said her lover.

How things are, not how they were or would be, but how things are, a moment stretching out beyond the power of time either backward or forward, the different world that existed beyond this one. His hand touched her face.

"Will you come with me?"

"But the future—"

"It is already there."

This time she had been allowed to see his thoughts and she caught the bolt of pain full on.

She sat up.

"You mean because you see it? The future?"

"No." The denial was instant, savage. It made no sense. They had each seen the unspoken power in the other and neither was particularly afraid of it. The air shivered with the unknown force like the fast passage of a bird's flight. She looked up. Muninn, the black raven, was perched on her window ledge. Bird of memory.

Her hand moved, tangling with a smooth metallic shape half-hidden in the bed, forgotten. Her girdle, loosened by his hands when he had bedded a girl who was still a virgin.

Hidden signs ran through her fingers. The power was not gone. It was still there, a woman's power. The shapes hummed under her fingertips.

This stranger who offered so much might have come to her isolated hall like an enchanter, a warrior, perhaps the only man in Middle Earth who would sacrifice his world for hers, but she had her own power, her own abilities. She had been born to heal.

She saw the task given to her out of a world of bitter emptiness.

The girdle slid through her hand. A woman's task.

"I will come with you." There was no other answer. There never had been.

But she was not a seer like him. For her, the future was impenetrable.

His lips touched her and she let him draw her down into the fire. But the moment of flame was brief. The king waited, the dangerous outside world and the future and the task.

She did not know whether she could accomplish it.

BRYSE, OWNER OF HALF A DOZEN estates west of Selwood, of which this tumbledown waste was the least, glared at the terrified gate-warden.

The gate-warden shifted his feet and dripped rainwater. But he waited. With more loyalty than Bryse got from his own blood-kin.

"Lord?"

Bryse forced himself to listen, look. Something glittered in the man's outstretched hand, a token. It was a ravening bird of prey.

"Will you receive them, Lord?"

Bryse considered the number of bowmen on the walls, the fact that bowstrings would be wet. The number of competent swords that could be mustered at less than five minutes' notice. The tally was not great. This was the easternmost reach of his land. The estate had been neglected. It had once belonged to his son, the first in a line of many and greater gifts.

But Gorei was dead.

"Lord?"

"Admit them." It would be churlish, after all, to leave twenty armed Vikings out in the autumn rain.

The gatekeeper's mouth opened and shut. Bryse got to his feet, moving away already.

He never wasted time over decisions.

"I will receive him, the messenger who bears this token, in my own chamber. The rest will be entertained in the hall."

The hall was a small one, easy enough to surround in a short time, even in near darkness.

"Give the messenger the best wine before you fetch him to me."

That would give enough time. He walked out and gave orders.

Earl Guthrum's messenger, the bringer of the small, silver-gilt token came promptly. Rain still dripped off his rich furs. The light of the flickering oil lamps caught an impressive weight of silver jewelry. It was obvious by the design that the wealth had once been English. Looted. Bryse had no objection to that.

He smiled. He knew what the message would be before it was delivered. He had calculated the potential force behind it. That was less likely to sway him.

British support against the beleaguered Saxon King, Alfred of Wessex, would be welcome to the Viking Jarl Guthrum and it would be suitably rewarded.

Of course, the earl had now lost an ally, his fellow Viking leader in the north. King Halfdan had sailed away to Ireland. The messenger did not seem to know that. Bryse doubted anyone knew yet, least of all the Saxons at Fearnros. They were not part of the Celtic world, after all.

Bryse decided to offer the messenger a helpful hint. Once the man got over the shock, it would raise the price promised for assistance.

In the end, it came out as a fair offer if you overlooked who it came from.

The bitterness rose in his throat, choking him, the terrible truth that he actually wanted to take it.

The west wind of autumn blew through the cracks in the walls making the once-fine tapestries swing. The building should have been repaired months ago, long before the beginnings of another winter. The other estates were pristine, imbued with a stylish luxury that harked back to that far-distant golden age between the withdrawal of the empire of Rome and the coming of the Saxon barbarians—the barbarians now under threat from the Viking scourge of the North.

A drop of rain mixed with soot dripped from the crumbling thatch in the roof. Bryse glanced at it with distaste. Why the devil had he come so far east? Why the devil was he here where everything reminded him of Gorei and the decay of all that should have been?

A man whose favoured son had died unavenged must be the most contemptible creature on God's earth.

"…Wareham…" said Earl Guthrum's man.

The blackened raindrops began to drip steadily. Wareham. Anywhere was better than here.

"…the Jarl would…"

"I will go there."

The messenger stopped in mid sentence, staring at him.

"In due course," added Bryse with a smile at its most guileless.

Wareham, fought over by opposing armies of barbarians. Where else? He could visit his living son, his only heir.

Two birds with one stone. The eagle token glistened in the lamp light as though cold metal had the power of movement, as though the despoiler of battlefields scented its prey. Shivers crossed his skin like a bitter presage. But he was not given to dangerous fancies.

That was his son Macsen's gift.

He turned for the door.

FEARNROS WAS AN ALIEN WORLD.

Aurinia's hands tightened on the reins of her borrowed horse as the walls of fire-hardened wooden stakes closed round her. She had expected unlaid ghosts, the lingering presence of that arrogant, belligerent creature who had been her father, an outraged fury that would reach from beyond its burial. It was not there.

Fearnros was not a great nobleman's hall filled by a thane's ghost, or even by the fine uncertain imprint of an eager boy on the threshold of manhood. It was a military headquarters alive with bustling movement, noise, tension, a grim sense of purpose that was focused outward, to where the king's army lay encamped before the defensive ditches and the walls of Wareham. The fierce purpose, the energy were Alfred's. The same qualities lived in her husband. She watched him.

He slid down from Du Moro's back, graceful as ever. The swirling mass of people closed round him immediately. A tall man with deep gold hair like the king's spoke to him. She could not hear the words; the noise and the movement and the press of people broke between them like a wave. Macsen turned toward her but then something the fair man said caught his attention, held it. The alien world took him.

There were warriors, expensive men like Macsen weaponed with swords. There were also army levies, the men who should have been farming or gathering the harvest, and were now facing an army of professional marauders. Servants pushed through the throng with food and buckets and pitchers, their expressions harassed, leading horses, carrying firewood.

The chaotic noise assaulted her ears, the ring of hammer on iron from the smithy, the squawks of geese herded by small boys, the strident voice of someone trying to sell something. A woman's laugh. She saw the painted face, a slender arm glowing in the gathering dark, a man with her...

Someone argued, shouting. She felt the precise moment they noticed her, the sudden familiar change in awareness, the small island of space that formed round her in the yard full of people, the first movement of someone's hand caught out of the corner of her eye. The whisper that ran through the crowd. How it started— Memory surfaced and every instinct of mind and body gripped with the urge to run, the primitive need for the haven of Wytch Heath, the only safety she had ever known. For silence.

Her rapid gaze caught the dark-haired figure turned away from her, the most expensive of warriors—the broad back, the sword belt, the finely angled head. Her husband. She made her gaze fix there.

She dismounted.

Macsen turned his head. His face changed, the alteration of expression in those stark, perfect features almost imperceptible. It was right, like the first step on the path. She closed the distance between them, her feet precisely placed on the slippery stone flags, her heart thudding. No one in the shouting, hissing mass touched her. Macsen's sword clinked. He held out his hand.

"This is Garrulf, the king's kinsman…."

She could feel Huda move behind her. She took Macsen's hand. The blond man inclined his head. The handsome face, so like the king's, was impassive. He had brought bad news. She did not know what.

Macsen was still talking to her, in that steady persuasive way, different things about Fearnros, everyday things about what she should expect. The weight of the ill-tidings, the sense of hidden danger, was almost palpable. Her gaze flew back to his face. He would not tell her. Not now.

Perhaps never?

"Shall we go inside?"

Perhaps it was not done for husbands to discuss dangerous matters with their wives. She had no way of knowing
if that were so. She went with him. They stopped in the
shadow of a doorway. The golden-haired thane called
Garrulf waited for Macsen.

He would leave her to be alone, here in this madhouse
full of people. The suppressed panic coiled like a striking
snake. She kept her face as impassive as his.

"You have to go."

"With Garrulf, now."

She could feel the tension like a bowstring pulled taut.
The black eyes caught hers. "Will you wed me tonight?"

Her breath choked her. Macsen kept speaking.

"I had thought there would be more time for you to settle
here— I can make all the arrangements but it is your choice.
As you wish."

The press of people surged past them, the shouting. She
could smell the danger. She watched the turn of his head,
the shape and the darkness of his eyes, black fire, and for
an instant it was as though only the two of them existed.

"Yes."

Garrulf moved. Someone cursed. Huda pushed past and
the moment broke. She watched the turn of Macsen's shoulders, the harsh line of his jaw, the dark splashes of mud on
his sleeve. She let go of his scarred hand. Her fingers left
small white indentations in his flesh.

THOSE WHO WERE BLOOD-SWORN to the dragon had the use
of one of the king's chambers. Macsen sat down on the
bench. Tapestries glowed in the firelight. They were Alfred's,

not the boy Bertred's. Depictions of Cerdic the first West Saxon king stepping ashore. Invaders. There was a book left open on the table, soliloquies in Latin. Who else but Alfred? *Ignorance,* thundered the king's spiky handwriting, like an eternal accusation. *Nothing worse.*

He stood up. A shadow followed his movement.

"What is that?" Garrulf, the king's cousin, crossed his booted feet in front of the hearth-fire.

"A dog." The shadow was six foot long, gray and possessed of considerable teeth.

"Well-grown for his age."

Macsen grinned when he really wanted to curse. The wolf banged past his thigh. The animal probably had enough muscular weight to knock him off his feet. The furred skin above Hunter's nose wrinkled, drawing back the dark upper lip, for all the world like a man's sneer. It exposed solid gums and an unlikely number of teeth. Fangs. The perfect response to insult.

"The lady's gift?"

"In a way." The gift, or possibly jailer, eyed him unblinkingly.

"Quick courtship," observed Garrulf. "Three days?"

There were several answers to that, some of which involved violence. But Garrulf knew him, so he said the truth. "It was not three days."

Garrulf did not cross himself, or invoke saints' names, or make the older sign against enchantment. They were past that, oath-sworn to the king's purpose. They followed the golden dragon and they were bound closer than blood brothers.

"I see," said the king's cousin.

And that was that. Nothing else to say. Macsen moved away. "So who gave you the information about Guthrum's men?"

"Grimm. He said just before he had to leave."

Grimm, the masked one, the best of Alfred's spies. The message was true then.

"Another foraging party from Wareham," said Garrulf. "Tomorrow."

Tomorrow. He crossed the small chamber, suddenly and intensely restless. Somewhere behind him, he heard Garrulf sit up.

"My cousin does not expect you to ride out tomorrow with his troop. You were injured."

My cousin the king, offering him the perfect excuse to stay back, the same generosity that had offered him support over an unexpectedly dangerous marriage.

He wanted to take it.

The knowledge shocked him. Macsen stopped by the window, seeking the narrow gap between the window shutters. The air poured over him in a cold black wave. He felt each muscle tighten. He had never wanted out of a fight in his life.

The ceaseless movement that was Alfred's headquarters filled his sight, the flare of torchlight in the dark, the sound of muted voices. The king's command, when on campaign, did not sleep. It could not afford to.

He thought of the oath he and Garrulf and half a dozen others had sworn five years ago, at a coronation held in a fortress two hours after a funeral. Alfred was the last of five brothers. The royal kindred had a tendency to die in battle.

He said what he thought.

"I am glad I do not speak British," said Garrulf, who did, impeccably. Just like his cousin.

But the barefaced lie made him laugh, the release of hard-held tension unexpected. "Bastard," he said in the same language.

"I can only assume that last word was an undeserved insult to the royal kindred." There was a pause. "So what does your own kindred say to your upcoming marriage?"

His kindred. The familiar pain slammed through him like an axe blow. His hand tightened on the window frame. *Never underestimate the subtle mind of one of King Athelwulf's descendents.*

But the fault was his, not Garrulf's.

"I have sent someone to tell my father at Lydnan," he said in the voice that concealed everything. He dropped his hand to a suddenly tightened mass of wolf's muscle pushing against him. "My father will send back his congratulations." It was the way they worked, politeness on either side, something quite different underneath. The hound-wolf slowly uncoiled under his hand.

"Maybe your father will come here."

"Here?" He forced calm. "How much have you drunk? Bryse is as likely to come here as Guthrum is to go back to Denmark—" He turned his head to find Garrulf of the subtle mind watching him.

"Bryse might do it. Ealdorman Odda says there are strange things happening in Devon, much traveling. Some people say they have even seen Vikings." Garrulf's blue eyes held him. "Foolish perhaps?"

The ealdorman who held Devon for Alfred was not a
fool. He was loyal. Macsen straightened out his hand. It was
Bryse, his father, who had the hot head. But—

"No." The sureness of his answer was not based on any
foreknowledge of the future but on impossibility. If the
barrier of death lay between himself and his father, then it
also lay between his father and a Dane. There was no connection possible between his father and Guthrum.

The wolfskin shivered under his touch and the oppres-
sion was like lead in his chest, stopping breath, death-cold.
He pushed it down, forced clear thought. "The strangeness
is at Wareham."

Garrulf's heavy shoulders moved. "They are getting
hungry. In two weeks, they will be eating shoe leather.
Enough to make anyone flighty."

"Maybe. But they can still hold out and they know the
king cannot keep an army this size in the field forever, or
no one will be reaping the harvest. There is something else,
something even more urgent. You saw how they fought the
day they killed Bertred's uncle."

"Aye." Garrulf recrossed his feet. "That death has left a
gap."

The slowness of the words was deliberate. That *gap* had
to be filled by a nervous boy thrust into a responsibility he
could not yet match, a boy who did not know what to do
or which way to turn.

"You saved his life," said Garrulf with a force that had to
do with friendship. It seemed like another burden Macsen
could not requite.

"I played rescuer and then I gave him a shock." They

both had, he and the lady, the two people a terrified boy had trusted through a baptism of fire.

Garrulf watched him. "Bertred has to get over it." The fair head turned back toward the flames in the hearth and it was the king's cousin who spoke. "He has responsibilities."

They all had. Macsen thought that one day it was going to kill the lot of them. The gift of the king's support was not straightforward. Alfred could not afford Bertred's loyalty to be alienated. The balance of power at Wareham hung on a knife's edge.

Perhaps tomorrow would hold the answers.

"I will ride out." There was no other decision he could make. His blood ran cold.

He turned for the door. He had to find the girl who had agreed to be his wife.

7

"It does not fit."

"We will make a tuck in the back, then. Thread the needle."

The crowds were mercifully distant outside. Aurinia was in a fine and secluded chamber, in the grip of a pair of Valkyries, warrior-women. The chief one had possession of the needle. Aurinia looked down at a borrowed gown with silk trimmings that was too long and hung off her bosom. A wedding dress.

"Pull it," said the Valkyrie called Judith. She had been born a princess of East Anglia. Her brother, absent on the king's business, was Macsen's friend. Judith was good at sewing. "Mildred!"

Mildred, lady attendant, pulled.

"Not that hard. Athelbert's bones. It is less trouble getting ready for a battle."

"Don't start." The lady attendant rolled her eyes. The fine

material loosened. "She has been known to fight," said Mildred apologetically. "I do not suppose that you…"

"No," said Aurinia. "I try and put the pieces together afterward." But they already knew that. A small silence followed during which the neck of her gown was carefully realigned. Then Judith looked up.

"I sometimes think that is more difficult." Judith was beautiful without exactly seeming to know it. She had excessively clear eyes. For the first time since she had come here, Aurinia almost smiled.

"I am glad Macsen found you," said the princess. She must have been the only person at Fearnros to think that. She seemed to see nothing reprehensible in a marriage arranged after three days spent with a sorceress. Apparently she had her own turbulent love affair involving a foreign sea-pirate. Or perhaps she was simply immune to scandal having been well born.

"So what will he give you for your morning gift?" asked Mildred.

"I have this."

Aurinia moved her arm. The bracelet was of gold, decorated with an unbroken pattern of twisting lines that had neither end nor beginning. Her new husband had left it for her.

The thickness, the solidity of it, confounded her.

The three of them stared at the ruddy flicker of light.

"Handsome," ventured the lady attendant.

It was nerve-racking.

"Perhaps," added Mildred, recovering, "he might also give you one of his estates?"

"I…" A thane had an estate, like the luxury of Fearnros if he was lucky. But… "He has more than one?"

"Oh, yes. So a gift like that would only be proper. Did you not know? Did he not say what— And his father is—"

"Stop talking, Mildred, and sew. Is that hem finished yet?" demanded Judith.

Mildred subsided and stitched. Aurinia thought about the gold neck-ring, about the way people jumped to obey her husband's orders instantly, about how much she did not know about how the outside world worked, about *him*—

"I did not ask. I did not…I did not think." Because she lived in isolation and expected nothing else, while he…

"It does not matter," said the princess stoutly. "Besides, I doubt that what really concerns Macsen has anything to do with wealth."

What really concerned him. This rich stranger that she was marrying. "Then what do you think that he…?" She, of all people, was supposed to know. She kept her gaze fixed on the wall and said stonily, "I know little of men."

Judith rolled her eyes. "Do not ask me about men. Mildred?"

Mildred preened. "Well, in my case, there were two. Husbands," she added with a belated attempt at primness. "If you ask me, men might claim to be straightforward, but whatever they really need is the thing they find it the hardest to ask for."

"I see," said Aurinia. "Or perhaps not." She kept her voice light, ironic.

"You have already made a good start," said Judith. She was kind, despite being a princess. Anyone could tell that, and out of all this bustling crowd of strangers, she seemed to mean well. Aurinia kept her gaze on the tapestried wall.

"Marrying after three days," said Judith. "If you ask me, what Macsen needs is someone to have faith in him."

She might mean well, but it made no obvious sense. Macsen lacked nothing. He was a man of undisputed rank. He had the king's favour. Aurinia was slowly coming to realize to what extent.

Her husband wanted for nothing, for no worldly honour that could be bestowed. And it was not just the dizzying inherited wealth. She had seen the foundation below those worldly honours, the courage and the toughness and the lightning decisiveness that made up his nature. She could not see—

There was a small disturbance at the half-open shutters, a change in the air. She turned her head. Birds—not the raven. Owls. Birds of wisdom, several, beating their wings like white ghosts. They spoke, their voices unearthly.

Mildred dropped the needle.

"Owls never fly together," said Judith.

The swooping voices melded, like a message her troubled mind could not quite grasp. *Trust.* The fluttering feathers cleaved the air as though the birds had hands to reach out. The comfort of familiar things.

"They miss me." They had all watched her go, the birds of all kinds, the animals, even the wolves. They had been there, even though Alfred's men had not seen them.

"You mean those birds are from *Wytch Heath?*" said Mildred. She looked ready to swoon. The seeming friend-

liness had led Aurinia to speak without thinking. She had—
From the opened doorway, someone screamed.

"Well," said Judith. "That was a waste of good mead."

A broken pitcher rolled at their feet and a pool of golden liquid spread across the floor, sweet-smelling, over-rich ale fortified with honey meant for a wedding. The sound of the maidservant's light footsteps faded into the darkness, running.

"The maids," observed Judith bitterly, "are useless here. For one thing there are not enough of them and for another thing, they take no care with their duties because in a place like this they can earn more lying on their backs—"

"It is true," said Mildred in a kind of agonized squeak.

But Aurinia had seen the maid's figure in the doorway bearing refreshments, the look of horror in the painted eyes fixed first on the half-open window and then on herself— the *hell-rune* with her familiar spirits.

"If I had got my hands on that half-brained wench…" said Judith. But it could not matter. The tale would be all over the camp by now, in all its exaggerations.

A single white owl hung precariously off the window frame. The rest of the birds had gone. The door of the chamber was wide open. Macsen walked in.

NOT MACSEN. ANOTHER FACE OF the stranger.

Aurinia had thought him out of the ordinary before. Even with the marks of battle he had carried brilliance and she had been dazzled by the fine clothes and the fierce will. But this was a prince.

The spoiled honey-moon ale seeped through the rushes on

the floor. He stepped over it. The booted feet moved, the
swelling thigh muscle beneath the braided tunic nudged the
leather-faced scabbard with its gilded fittings. The sword,
half-hidden by the swirl of a fine-woven cloak, made a faint
sound.

"You are too early," said Judith.

"Not if you have started the festivities without me."

Aurinia stood in her borrowed gown with the cracked
pitcher at her feet. He turned his head toward her. The eight
strands of gold glistened round his throat. He had seen the
fleeing maidservant. He must have.

He took another step. Gems glittered at his waist on the
buckled and knotted belt, the end of the leather strap heavy
with carved gold. The prince was not going to say anything
about the disaster. She watched him with a kind of despair.

The pitcher rolled at her feet and she bent to pick it up
but the sudden fast movement of his body forestalled her,
the strength of his hand.

"Leave that."

The owl flew past them in a slow circle and then dived
from the window into the night. She straightened her head.
He was down on one knee beside her in the rushes. The
dark cloak pooled about him. It was embroidered. Gold
flowed down his left shoulder like flames, the fire-snake, the
golden dragon. The king's sign. She had seen him so in
dreams.

"Are you ready?"

She realized there were other people at the doorway now,
Huda, the king's cousin, heaven knew who else. Macsen's
hand touched hers. She remembered how her fingers

had clasped his in the crowded courtyard, what he had asked her.

"Yes."

But she did not know whether she had done the right thing.

They went outside. They moved like a procession, covered in torchlight, and every step of the way she did not know whether she did more harm being with him than not. She kept glancing at him, and Judith's words filled her mind. *What really concerns Macsen… What he needs…*

The tough, self-contained face beside her was unreadable. *What?*

"This is not the way to the hall." Aurinia came out of a kind of trance. The torchlight was gone. There was night and the blessed sense of being out of doors, in a world filled with the sound of trees and the unseen presence not of people, but of other creatures who were wild. She breathed the air. But she could not stay.

"They will be waiting for us. Inside."

"Yes."

"All the people. The king…"

"There are things that have to be said first."

It was very dark, nothing but the voice and the heavy body of the man beside her. She was fully and intensely aware of him, of their aloneness, of the moving, breathing power in him, the bated strength.

"Are you afraid?"

He was so close, the black shadow of her dreams and the living prince.

"Aurinia?"

"No…" It was a lie. Half a lie. She was not afraid of the

black shadow, not even any longer of the killing strength.
But she was mortally afraid of the prince. She took a breath
of silence filled with the glide of a bird's wings high above.
A night-hunter. She heard its voice in her head, the thin
screech of an owl.

"No," she said without the slightest idea of why she was
lying, only that it had to be done. He took her hand. Her
blood leaped and she wanted to lean into him in the gently
shifting air, feel the purely physical warmth of him, taste it,
taste of him and his dark power and the intoxicating heat
he had shown her.

But he moved away. The fine cloak swirled, the gold
caught starlight and was then extinguished. It was cold. It
was autumn.

"I have to ride out tomorrow."

"Tomorrow?"

"That is what Garrulf came to tell me. Guthrum's men."

The ill-tidings. That was it, but there was more, some
other disturbance hidden behind.

"If we marry tonight, you will always be provided for. You
will have wealth—"

"Wealth?" she said, distracted, trying to find the meaning
that was hidden. "You have already given me more than I
need. The bracelet. I never had chance to thank you for that.
I did not seek—"

The sudden movement stopped her, the sense of things
hidden. "Let me say what I must."

She almost stepped back at the force of his words, but
deeper instinct made her keep her ground. She waited for
him to reveal some fragment of what was in his mind.

"The settlement is made, including your morning gift. There are two estates which are yours alone. I have had the book made up. No one will dispute it. It has the king's witness and Garrulf's."

Bookland. Land given by a signed charter. It would be hers to do with as she willed, even if he left her, or she left him. Even if he died. Tomorrow…

A proper morning gift, said Mildred's voice in her head. The wind blew her hair, the fine line of his cloak so that the golden dragon rippled, pale in the starlight.

I do not want it. She took breath over the words but he was still speaking, the compelling voice strangely urgent, fixed in its purpose.

"There are six hides of land not so far from here and another ten further west. You can go to whichever is safest. There is also money."

The money Judith had told her was not the deepest thing he cared about, the money she did not want. She did not say it, trying to listen for what else was there.

"There is also enough wealth to restore and maintain the hall at Wytch Heath if you want to. If it is ever possible."

Wytch Heath. It might survive. Depending on what Guthrum the Viking did, on whether the king won an impossible war. The pressure of the outside world would kill her. That world held her husband.

She touched him. Her fingers brushed the embroidered folds of his cloak, gold, skin.

"Aurinia, you have to understand how things are. That land, the money, is yours, whatever happens. Even if one day you leave me…"

Her hand tightened, the reaction instinctive and faster than the mind's reach. Her thoughts scrambled to catch up, to form words. "I would n—"

"Remember that," he said, as though she had not spoken. The press of his body was suddenly very close, filling mind and thought and sense. Her hand was round the solid thickness of his arm, above the twisted gold arm-ring, her fingers beneath the braided sleeve edge, on his skin.

She suddenly, desperately, wanted to feel the nearness of his body, and its solid warmth, the scorching heat of his mouth.

He pressed closer. "I will not willingly leave you." The finely curved lips covered hers.

The kiss was like nothing she had known. His arms closed round her, slowly, like finding fire after wandering forever in the snow of winter. Its first brush was as intense as pain and then melted into pleasure so full that it had no discernible moment of beginning. It felt as though it could have no end.

His body was pressed against her and his mouth moulded hers, and she was lost in the movement of lips and tongue, in the dark heat and the sinful touch of pleasure.

She held him close, her hands seeking the animal heat of his body under the dazzling cloak, pressing closer.

When he let her go, it was like waking out of a spell. She had been aware of nothing but the intense touching, the weight of his body, his hot mouth. Her limbs were twined with his, her arms round his shoulders high above the hidden line of the bandage, her fingers twisted in his hair.

His lips brushed her cheekbone and her skin shivered from the almost imperceptible touch. The sweet biting ache of arousal was still there inside her, the burning aftermath of the intense exquisite kiss. Waiting. Like a promise.

THERE WAS TROUBLE JUST OUT of sight.

Aurinia walked round the hall that had once belonged to her father and was now Bertred's, lent to the West Saxon king. She passed the place where her mother must have sat in the great chair at the richly appointed table before her husband had thrown her out.

But it was not past distress that clutched at her with urgent hands. It was present.

The noise of feasting washed over her, ceaseless as the beat of the waves against a rock. It was so overwhelming it made her desperate. Her wedding feast. The guests were polite to her. She thought it was because of the formidable king. But it was also on account of her gold-decked husband.

She was a married woman. His. She watched him speaking to someone, the turn of his head, the solid line of his shoulders and the exquisite curve of his neck. Her feet in borrowed wedding shoes took her closer without her even willing it, like someone drawn on an invisible thread. She heard the sound of his voice, the sudden laughter from the man he spoke to. He did not turn. She was standing near the opened doors and suddenly the distress caught her.

She could not fathom it from here. The noise and the movement bewildered her, the press of people. She had to get outside.

She stepped through the door into the night.

Fearnros had transformed with the king's coming into a small town, a complex of different buildings large and small, permanent and temporary, connected and separate. The spaces and small passages in between were as complex as the tunnelings in a badger's set, lit even now by brands and torches, and there were people, always people.

She passed the bower where Bertred slept. Something on four legs stirred in the shadows. She dropped to her knees.

"Bruna." The glossy coat was warm under her hands. The dog whined, restless. "What are you doing here?"

But the answer was obvious. She stared at the heavy oak door. Shut. Her fingers moved over the dense fur. Bruna's head buried itself for a moment in her hand and she got a perfunctory lick. She looked at the barred door. Even the dog, for pity's sake.

"I am sorry," she said against the restless warmth. But there was little she could do. Her cousin refused to see her. The king's physician had asked her not to attempt it because it caused the patient too much anguish.

Someone, one of the kitchen servants, perhaps, had left meat bones. Untouched. She sensed the distress but it was not the same urgency that had called her outside.

"All right. You can stay here tonight. But tomorrow…" Tomorrow, what? Nothing would change. She got to her feet. Bruna's unwanted affections would have to be detached, but not now, not yet.

She moved away. Something small scurried at her feet. A mouse.

The stables.

She found Du Moro first. Her husband's fierce war-stallion, named for the magical black horse of Moro Battle Leader, butted her shoulder. She reached out and touched the thick-muscled neck. Nothing wrong, only a whisper of unease about…something.

She moved on. Voices, the flickering glare of torchlight, people gathered in a tight circle, something on the ground…

She stepped forward. The light and the noise surrounded her.

HIS WIFE OF LESS THAN TWO hours was missing. Macsen stood. The sudden tightening in his gut was unnecessary. She was quite safe at Fearnros.

He crossed the noisy hall where the king still sat at the high table even though he had forty thousand other things on his mind. It was almost impossible to move in Bertred's hall. There might be no host but every other man was there who had ever crossed Macsen's path or owed him service, or wished for a favour.

She was safe, outside the hall or in. Anyone who touched the woman he had married was dead, and their kindred would not be asking for the compensation price of a wergild. That was plain.

Someone offered congratulations. He replied.

She was entitled to go away, even from her own wedding feast, even if it was not much more than an hour after the priest had finished speaking and he could not bear one enforced moment without her. There was nothing wrong. He strode for the door.

The grey shape loomed in front of him, like mist, even the torchlight could not give it colour. He thought of its blood brothers spread out around him in the treacherous woods near her home.

"Where?"

Hunter's yellowish eyes watched his slightest movement. He was so maddened by now that he had not the slightest doubt the creature knew exactly where its mistress was. Everything in him wanted to plunge out into the torchlit dark. Now.

"Wait."

He stepped back inside the hall to collect the rest of her retinue. The difficult bastard was hers just as much as the wolfhound was. Take one, take them all. Huda followed him.

He discovered the Lady of Wytch Heath in the stables with a six-month-old colt on the ground next to her. It was lying on its side motionless. It looked as though it ought to be dead, but it was breathing. Aurinia was kneeling over it in the straw in her wedding dress. She was making crooning noises.

She had her hand on its head.

Surrounding her was a moderately sized crowd in various stages of alarm bordering on panic. Only the king's groom was smiling.

He remembered what she had said about people who got frightened when faced with a sorceress. In his mind he could see the marks on her skin. She had had no one to protect her then. She did now.

The surge of aggression was primitive. He watched his wife. She said something, so low he could not catch it, her attention focused on the colt.

He forced breath through his lungs.

At least he had had the sense to leave the shadow-wolf outside. Something moved behind him.

"Fetch some of the best ale from the feast." The words came out under his breath.

"What?" said Huda, crowding him.

Huda shoved forward. The wolf trod on his heels. Macsen efficiently blocked the way through the stable door and reversed an elbow with some force. There was an indistinct sound. Huda's hand dropped from his sword hilt.

"Do you want to get her out of this or not?" Luckily, Huda had no breath left for a reply. "Then do it. And you, wait." His other belligerent companion stared at him and showed fangs.

"You have a bad reputation." *The haunter of the wasteland, the wolf with bloody jaws at the feast.* "Out."

The amber eyes blinked. "I will call you if I need you." God help him. The last proof of insanity. But there was not time to think about it. He moved into the stable just as the foal staggered to its feet.

Success.

He caught the sound of a dozen indrawn breaths, a kind of convulsive movement from the crowd. Someone shouted something.

Huda had gone. The wolf was invisible. He stepped out into the pool of torchlight, left shoulder well forward, deliberately letting the cloak catch the light. Alfred's gold flamed. The shout was cut off.

He walked forward, taking his time, making sure the sword was clearly visible. He deliberately did not look at the small vulnerable figure kneeling on the floor. His blood was too high, on the edge of the carnage he had prevented Huda from. The combined attention left the kneeling woman and fastened on him. Torch fire reflected off the exposed pommel of the sword.

He kept his hand away from the hilt. He could talk anyone into anything. They stared at him, slack-jawed.

When he left, they were halfway down the ale barrel and singing. They had drunk the lady's health and that of the colt. It was now feeding and did not appear to notice. He kept his hand round Aurinia's arm. Huda elected to stay. They had not spoken. Nothing as deep-seated as what Huda felt was changed in a single day. If, indeed, it was changeable.

She was cold. He could feel it through the thin fineness of the dress. He felt the shivering movement when she took a breath.

"I…I had to—"

"Later." There were people in the yard. He kept his new wife in the shadows and fielded congratulations and the occasional amazed stare without stopping. Hunter followed them at a distance, less visible than smoke.

He realized he was walking too fast when her feet stumbled.

"I am sorry."

She said nothing.

He slowed down, but he did not stop until they reached the room that had been set aside as a bridal chamber and the door thudded shut. The wolf was outside it like a wraith. He managed to let go of her. When he turned from casting more wood on the fire, she was standing in the middle of the bower staring at him. The fine dress Berg's sister had made was ruined.

He realized that after persuading a potentially lethal crowd that all was perfectly ordinary in the best possible of worlds, he had no idea what to say to her.

"I will get you a bath." He went out and found Judith

to help her, ruthlessly detaching Mildred, who was inclined to become agitated. Judith, Berg's sister, was fortunately made of sterner stuff.

When he came back, after giving her time, Aurinia was in bed. Judith had had the tact to take herself off. The room was still warm. He took off the cloak with the king's insignia and the sword belt. Aurinia watched his every movement.

"Are you angry?"

8

Angry did not begin to describe what Macsen felt. He folded the cloak into small pieces.

His wife watched him from the bed.

"If one of those men had touched you I would have killed him."

He sat down on the edge of the canopied bed, not because he wanted to sit but because he had to be that physically close to her. The battle-rage was still in his blood as though he had in fact fought. He thought it must be visible. He forced stillness into every tight muscle.

She neither moved nor glanced away. She watched him, her eyes grave, as though seeking to understand, much as she regarded Hunter when he displayed the side of his ancestry that was sheer wolf. The firelight gilded the thin skin of her bare arms with colour, the taut line of her throat, the bright unfettered abundance of her hair. Her gaze was utterly fixed on his.

"The colt would have died," she said. "I knew it was in trouble. It had difficulty breathing, you see…."

He did see. Was it possible for her to have been involved in a clearer appearance of uncanny influence?

"And so I knew," she said, "that—"

She stopped speaking. He would swear he had not made the slightest move. He sought for calm breath.

"How did you know?"

Her gaze slid away from him.

The words were hardly loaded with accusation, not from someone like him. But he had to know, if they were ever to make any progress through a life that was now to be shared. She looked away and the small coldness between them settled like ice on his overheated skin.

He forced himself to stay still, to hold everything back, to betray nothing, do nothing that might break whatever trust existed between them.

"Aurinia—"

She looked up and he knew he would not get the answer. "I had to go there."

He assessed the clearness of her eyes and the fine tilt of her head. There was no fear. Her gaze held defiance, as though she thought he would not understand. His heart beat out of time, the cold prickling on his skin like a mindless response to danger.

I have to go there. It might have been his own voice speaking five years ago, his feet set on the path that had led to unatoned death. Memory. It was not the future that rode him with the spectre of disaster, but the past.

He stood up, the movement more abrupt than he could possibly stop, the force in it savage, with no control, no restraint, none of the things he had wanted to show her, none of the understanding that she needed or should expect from a husband on her wedding night.

The slight sound came to him, the movement of her small light figure in the bed, tense, fast. He did stop the uncontrolled movement, but he knew he was too late.

She caught his arm.

Her fingers fastened on the tight, harshly corded muscle of his forearm and stayed there. "Do not go."

Go. The coldness stabbed straight through and found its place in that broken and inadmissible part of him where there was no light. He forced the crippling power of it aside. Something to be dealt with later.

He made himself hold still in her grip, turning his head toward her. She thought he would have walked out on her. *I would not go.* He could not get the right words out, the ones he wanted to say. They choked him, lost in the power of the past and what he had once done to someone who had trusted him.

"We are married," he said instead, as though it were some sort of spell-word, as though the brief public ceremony they had gone through not three hours ago could possibly encompass the vow he had tried to make in his mind.

Her hand was tight on his arm, as though the contact were vital to her and the bond touched her as it touched him.

He was intensely aware of the closeness of her body, of the barrier that had been broken at Wytch Heath, of everything that had been shared.

"I am your husband."

She raised her head and the thread of fire that smoldered between them, beneath each word, beneath the most ordinary of actions, caught flame, the primitive reaction in blood and heated flesh complete, leaving him instantly hard, the control wire-thin.

"You came to find me," she said. "You came to look for me."

He watched her curved lips forming the exact words he wanted to hear and it was as though his heart stopped. The disbelief in her fine voice sent him over the edge, plunging into the lightless place that had no escape.

He made no movement. She was touching him but she could not have sensed the dark, or seen it, because she leaned into him, the soft fall of her body weightless.

"I am glad you found me."

The control shattered.

She came into his embrace so easily, as though it was what she wanted, as though the impossible trust were truly there.

His mouth took hers.

Her slender arms twined round his body and he pulled her down into the bed, the stab of pain across the back of his ribs ignored, the sharpness of it so much less than the driving need for her.

Time ceased to exist, only the smoothness of her skin under his hands beneath her shift, the erotic curve of her breast, the line of her side, the discreet fullness of her thigh, the way she pressed against him. And then the scorching inner softness of her, the dark moist slip of her heated flesh against his fingers, the way her body twisted and pressed against his, the soft cry of her voice and the desire.

The awareness of her desire pushed him and his touch quickened. She tightened, her body writhing against him, her fingers digging into his shoulders.

He felt the moment her body tensed against the light-fast movement of his hand. His mouth covered hers, taking the soft vulnerable warmth and the deep passion, the near scream that ripped from her throat.

She clung to him afterward, her lips smoothed under his, then pressed closer, soft and hot with arousal. The un-guarded movement of his body was a response beyond control. The madness in him was tight in his skin, in each tense aching muscle of his body, the hot fullness of his sex.

Yet the madness was most truly in the impossible need for her that he had no way to express except through this, the shared fire. It drove him so that the kiss deepened, seeking the response in her that he needed more than life's breath.

She gave what he wished, warmth out of the black freezing dark, the match of desire for desire, as though she were as desperate for its fulfillment again as he was.

Her body moved to the caress of his hands, her fingers locked at his neck, fisted in his hair, drawing his head closer. Her mouth opened to the heated invasion of his tongue. And when he slid her thigh over his, opening her body, and touched her, she was as hot as before, already restless with the sharp edge of desire. The knowledge broke the last threads of sanity.

He moved to position himself over her. She clung to

him, her hands raking down his body, her touch half blocked by the barrier of clothing he had not removed, as though he were some churl out in the fields, graceless and lust-crazed.

He held back for one instant, his gaze seeking her face, the dark pools of her eyes, seeking to know what was in her mind. Her wide gaze met his, straight, as if there were trust.

"Touch me…." His mouth caught the words as though they were physical, as though their desire and their meaning could be taken inside him. Then he drew his head back so that he could watch her face, his hand reaching between them to caress her heated flesh, feeling the heat of her tense against the play of his fingers, the moment when the desire climaxed.

He saw it in her face, felt her hands tighten on his body. His body covered hers and she moved with him, accepting him, the full aching hardness of his flesh, all the desire and the madness and the depthless need, and the feelings that had no name. Her body opened for him, moist and hot and ready from the pleasuring but still so tight that he fought to hold back, but she met him, the movement pure and need-driven.

The madness and the need for her had fused and he was falling, the slightest thrust of his body feeding the desire until it broke, endless, and there was nothing but the black intensity of it and her body round him. Her hands holding him and the impossible sensation of being one.

AURINIA'S EYES CLOSED as though she were blinded, the only sense touch, the feel of her lover's body, power, and the sightless edge of dreams. She would not open her eyes or move or breathe in case the moment broke. If she lay just so, filled with his power and touching him, the moment would be there, eternal.

She knew that was mad, foolish. Selfish. She opened her eyes to the dark sheen of his hair, blue-black like Muninn's wing, the heavy shadow of his body. The log in the hearth cracked. Light flared and died from the wood he had placed on the fire to warm her because—

Her mind shied away from the scene in the stables and what she had done…but the silent, heated awareness had already changed. Her lover's warm, heavy body shifted. She wanted to speak, to stop him. But she had already cried after him once not to leave her as though she were some pathetic child, a burden.

She had always faced life on her own. So she said nothing but let him ease away from her, let the vital touch of his body leave hers.

She noticed there was still blood, not much, just the faintest smear. She had not been aware of that. She sensed the sudden arrested movement of his strong body before she could react, heard him swear.

"I hurt you—"

"No!" She caught his arm, just as she had before. She had not sensed pain, only the fierce terrible edge of her own need for him, the pleasure of feeling his body fill hers. She had been mad with it, possessed. Nothing else mattered.

"It is nothing…."

But the dark eyes had pinned her and she was caught, with her clever knowledge of everything in theory, and nothing as it really was.

"It means nothing," she said stubbornly.

"It does to me." Something leaped in the black gaze and then was gone. She watched the careful control reassert itself. It seemed like a wall. "I am sorry. It was not what I intended."

Her heart lurched. "It was what I wanted."

It was the truth. She had wanted all of it, the madness and the fierce completeness and the lack of control. But she knew nothing. She watched his fine profile and his fine rumpled clothes and the glitter of gold.

Perhaps it had not been what a thane wanted from a bride. He did not look at her. His eyes saw something far distant and she felt the force of the barriers both visible and invisible that separated her from the world.

But such things had changed. The stubbornness in her clung to the thought. She tried to find the strength inside that had sustained her for twenty winters, that had been channelled so painfully into the creation of a healer. She was married, to a good husband who had done everything a man could, who had offered her more wealth than she could think of, who had spoken an oath on the hilt of his sword. She was lying in bed with him, her hand touching him, holding his arm. He turned his head abruptly.

"I wanted something better for you on your wedding night."

She shook her head. "I did not."

She did not know whether he believed her, or in truth whether that was what he wanted from her. There was so little to guide her. But she held his gaze, the full intense force of it; and then she could no longer see it because she was in his arms, held against the vital warmth and the strong hard beat of his heart. *It is the next step,* she thought, *the next step on the path. It must be.* Her breath was shallow.

"I am sorry about what happened in the stables," she said.

He shrugged. She felt the smooth glide of solid muscle.

"It made for an interesting wedding."

There was nothing to be read from his voice. She thought of Beowulf, the legendary hero, the warrior who had hidden everything beneath understated words. His hand touched her hair. She scarcely dared allow breath.

"And, of course, about the owls at Judith's window," she said in the same careless voice as his, deceptively smooth.

"Owls are nothing." His hand stayed touching her, like a miracle. "It is that wolf of yours that will be the death of me."

"The—" Hunter was outside the door even now, she knew it. A controlled breath. "It is a dog."

"A dog. Aye. Just well-grown for his age." He made a sound like laughter.

It was the last thing she expected, but the rich sound filled the empty chamber, like the sense of his power. His hand was coiled in the wild length of her hair and he was holding her more tightly, too tight. She came into his arms, rolling with the movement, the length of her body spilling over the thick heavy warmth of his, the fierce power.

He stayed with her and her hands fastened on the solid flesh in its fine clothing, the tight strength and the sleek muscle. She tried to hold back the unacceptable need that had made her behave so madly before. The hunger was not appeased. It never would be with him. She felt vulnerable, terrified by it.

"I know you miss your home," he said.

Her body jerked, as though it had taken a blow. She tried to hide the reaction, to speak, but she was mute, her breath bundled up in one hot mass in her throat. She thought of Wytch Heath, the safety and the silence. She had been in control there, not lost and drifting from one mistake to the next. But her safety had also been her prison.

She tried to recapture the sense of sureness that had somehow become lost in the press and disturbance of the king's headquarters at Fearnros. She had her task, a living task that breathed under her hand.

She moved her fingers across the linen-clad muscle beneath her.

"So much is unfamiliar to me here, that is all. I am not used to the world's ways."

Her fingers touched the edge of hard metal, the bright torc at his neck, eight strands of twisted gold, each separate strand made from eight wires. In her world, eight was a number of wholeness and symmetry. In his? Her fingertips slid across the solid weight warmed through from the touch of his skin.

"What about your home?" she said.

The reaction was instant, much more ruthlessly disguised in him. But she was a master at reading hidden signs. She knew it was as deep in its own way as the shock that had scored through her. The unexpected intensity stunned her.

She kept still, utterly quiet, touching him.

"I have not seen my home for a long time. I have been with the king."

Duty, more than that, an oath she was sure had been freely given. Yet even that seemed shadowed. She did not

know why. For all her trained senses and her sharp awareness, she knew nothing of the man she had married. She
had ignored that fact, buoyed up on the invisible connection she had felt to him. But now the lack struck her with
force. It was like seeking the way in the dark, blinded.

Did the difficulty lie with the demands of the king's
service or was it something with a deeper cause? How did
she choose? What if she stepped on the wrong path?

Her fingers rested on the carved, looped ends of the torc,
beside the shadowed hollow at the base of his throat. A man
so rich he could give two of his estates away at will.

"What about your family?" she said.

There was no reaction. None. False step.

"My father lives west of Selwood, at Lydnan. My mother
died a long time ago and…there are uncles and aunts and
a limitless number of cousins."

"I cannot imagine that." A family, a large kindred. Of
course, it was what everyone had and he took it so much
for granted. Where could there be shadows in that?

"Tell me about your father." Remembered words clicked
into place.

And his father is—

Stop talking, Mildred…. And the quality of the silence
that had followed. She had been too caught up in her fears
to heed it then.

"Will he know of your marriage?" asked Aurinia.

"Of course," said the smooth voice. "I have sent a messenger to tell him."

Deceptively smooth. The foreign gold was hard under
her fingers, heavy.

"And what will he say?"

"He will send congratulations."

It was the right answer. Perfect.

"He will send word to you," she said, feeling her way across the slippery path in the blind dark. "And you cannot leave the king, not now." Her throat was dry. "So will he come here?"

The beating of her heart stifled her. But it was his breath that came in the harshest of movements like someone drowning. She could feel it.

She waited for what he would say. Outside in the night of Alfred's encampment someone shouted. There was no rest in this place and no peace. Her hand touched lightly on solid gold. Such wealth. Her fingers traced intricate carving and the shape of a hollow-sided triangle filled with decoration.

"That is the maker's mark."

Her fingertip stopped on the angular shape. He would not answer. The right path or the wrong? A way cut off.

"I did not know," she said cautiously. "I know nothing of work that is so fine and…"

"British?"

She digested this. "I was going to say *rich*." She turned her head, just slightly, and watched the fine line of his throat, the braided tunic edge, all the careless refinements of a world she had never entered. She said it. "That seems the greatest thing to me."

He moved. Her hand slipped and she was no longer touching hard gold but warm skin under a thin layer of linen. She felt shallow breath.

"Because if you go outside and look around your home, there is not much difference between someone who was born British and someone who was born Saxon? Because half the time we share kindred and can no longer even tell?"

Her hand rested on the deep flexible heat. "Yes."

"But I am different. My ancestors were the Dumnonii, and not the ones who lived in the wooded valleys of Devon in the way you lived at Wytch Heath. My ancestors lived in cold stone palaces with coloured tiles on the floor and spoke in Latin.

"There are grave markers on our estates in scripts that no one can read, that might come from past the Middle Sea, as far east as Byzantium. But in the mind of my family, we come solely from Rome and Britain."

The fine thread of tension in the thick muscle beneath her fingers vibrated, like something deeply buried.

"You can tell by my name."

"Macsen Wledig," she said. "The British emperor Maximus who ruled Rome."

"A book of history will tell you that Maximus came from the land beyond the mountains south of Francia, that he ruled part of the empire for five years and then they killed him."

She shut her mouth. She had never seen a book. All the knowledge she possessed had come from her mother, or from what other people said, or from what her mind told her by looking at things and working it out.

"The songs people like to sing say that Macsen married a British princess, that it was the Britons who made him emperor and that he ruled forever as a Briton. My father believes that implicitly. Consider what he called me."

The tension in the warm flesh under her hand caught, hard as stone.

"Macsen the Briton ruled the world. As my father would tell you, there were no Saxon settlers in Britain then, no Saxon kings. He thinks it was a golden time."

She considered the words, the trappings of wealth worn by a man used to exercising power, the unknown depths of his mind. The sheer strength in the muscle under her hand.

"And what do you think?"

"Do I think of a golden age?"

"Aye." She raised her head, seeking the night-dark gaze but it was elsewhere, far beyond the neat wooden chamber at Fearnros, on all the things she could scarcely imagine, that existed for her only in the half-comprehended wonder of a bard's tale, but to him were real. The opened eyes were unfocused, their centers wide and black, and she knew the answer.

Yes. He had thought of that golden time, had seen it and felt it intensely. The echoes of it lingered in the brilliant eyes, the taut power under her hand.

Outside the bower, the sound of voices writhed on the night wind, distorted and indistinct, but still full of purpose. The man beside her heard them. The thick dark lashes flickered, a glimpse of fire, and then everything shut off:

"It makes no difference," said the man who could move through the veils that enclosed this world into the other that surrounded it, who felt dreams. "There are enough problems in the here and now. They are what has to be dealt with."

You have to leave your home even if you do not want to because the Vikings are close. The emotional attachment had not mattered in the face of a practical reality. She thought of the warrior who had walked into her hall with the blood of battle still on his body and the marks of it still in his mind, the man who had forced what had to be done. That person was as much a part of him as the dreamer.

"So you would fight for the king, even a Saxon one?"

The gold glittered with the fast movement of his breath. "I have given the king my oath."

It was so absolute. But the deeper feelings ran below, shadowed, complex, hidden and hard to reach.

"The king must deal with the problems that face him now," said the sworn warrior. "If the king fails there will be nothing, neither English nor British."

He stopped speaking. The flames in the hearth flared. The dark eyes stared into them. Then the firm mouth formed the words.

"I cannot leave him."

He did not say *will not.* He said *cannot.* She watched the strong profile and all that lay hidden beneath.

"But it is not your father's choice," she said. Not for a son named Macsen. "He does not approve of a Saxon king or of your oath to him."

"No." There was no movement in the strong body, no change in the harsh face. "He cannot." The selfsame word. She watched the stone-carved profile. *Holy saints.*

"My father will never come here to Fearnros," said Macsen.

He had answered her question.

She thought of her own father, of the corroding pain of

being sundered, even from someone she did not know. She could feel the trapped power under her hand like flame behind stone. He would feel anger—but it was something else, locked behind the impenetrable wall.

She tried the next step on a path whose beginning and end she could not see.

"He—did he cast you off?"

"No."

No. There was no guide in her own experience and she would never find the way through.

"Gorei, my brother, died five years ago. He has no other son," said Macsen.

The uncompromising statement belonged to a world she did not know, a world of kin ties.

"You are his flesh and blood." Acknowledged still, and despite a disputed allegiance, a source of pride surely. Of love? The deep feelings thrummed, hidden, out of reach.

"You are his heir," said Aurinia. A rich man needed a proper heir. She thought of Fearnros, of Bertred.

Bertred who had repudiated a kinswoman who was not acknowledged, not a source of pride but an embarrassment who shamed him, like a monster spawned from the race of Cain, a *hell-rune.* And a Saxon—

She sat up. "I do not belong in your world." *I cannot.* The terrible thought uncoiled in her head like a serpent that had been waiting in the dark, forcing words out of her mouth.

"Do you regret marrying me?"

CHAPTER 9

T he terrible question took shape in a kind of excruciating stillness. There was no movement, no sound. Yet the words reverberated in Aurinia's head.

Do you regret marrying me?

Such a question was weak and despicable. Wholly unfair.

Fatal, because a man like Macsen could not answer it. For all her long-held distrust of thanes, she knew this man was different. He was nothing like her father. He had not only been brought up to honour, he believed it.

We are married, he had said from the start, like a declaration, a commitment made that now had to be seen through, like anything he did, and he had done all that a wife could want. He had given a thousand times more. It was only her heart that was so hungry, so destructive in its greed.

I am sorry. Do not answer me.

There was the moment of appalling silence, quite short,

just the gap of time between one breath and the next. Yet time enough for a bright intense pain to take root somewhere deep. It was stupid. She had managed without love all her life. She hardly knew what it was. She could not miss it now.

She and the brilliant stranger had something more, a bond which had to be nurtured, a marriage which had to be made to work, a life together. She had a task to help him.

"No," he said. "I do not regret it."

She swallowed. "I wish I was…was acceptable. I—" She stared at the wall, at the hearth, at the wall bench with the gold-hilted sword laid across it.

He moved to take her in his arms. It was kind, as strong as anything he did. She felt his warmth. It made her body respond because the sharp desire that had lived in her since the first moment, since before then, was still there, so deep and full and rich that she shook with the force of it.

"You are my wife." His breath touched her hair, her tight, hot skin. She shut her eyes. "It will all work out. Aurinia."

Her hands were digging into his shoulders, seeking the blinding warmth beneath the linen, the fierce beguiling feel of him.

"Listen to me. Whatever argument I have with my father lies only between us. It will not affect you." His hands touched her hair. "You have a family now."

A kindred, the thing she wanted.

"Bryse is…the meaning of that name in British has a lot to do with hastiness, but he is an honourable man. If you ever need help, he will give it. If I am not there, for any reason, remember that."

She did not believe it.

If I am not there for any reason. Her hands on his back caught the edge of the hidden bandaging. She thought about wounds and pain, about the battle she had seen her own terrible glimpse of, about tomorrow and the fighting that had to be endured, survived. If fate willed. He wanted her to believe all that he did. His deep voice touched her.

"Remember that."

"Yes."

The word was a lie, so it was impossible to look at his face. But she said it. She would do whatever would ease his mind now, whatever she could. She sensed the hidden physical pain mixed with the tension in him, everything buried under the force of that impossible will. She reached up to touch his head, the seat of the life force.

Her fingers brushed his face, the harsh rise of his cheekbone, the roughness at his jaw, and the heat burned her. It kindled inside her as though their bedding had never been, as though it were the first time, as though the need would not die. Like him. *Please heaven.*

She watched the quick primitive flare in his eyes and the very tip of her finger touched the fine uncivilized heat of his lips, traced that maddening curve even as he moved, as the strong body covered hers and she was lost, drowned in the power and the hunger and the dark dizzying wave of passion.

Every intimate, sinful touch was slow. As though each movement and each breath were laced with meaning, every shared sensation to be known to the full, to be experienced now with stretched, highly attuned senses, to be held deep inside and remembered always. *Do not die tomorrow. I could not bear it.*

She touched him, her hands gliding over his face, the fine skin of his throat, finding the warm arch of his neck beneath the heavy, shadowed fall of his hair, the tense muscle and the deep flesh, full of the power of a man who was *unfæg*, as yet undoomed. But fate turned in the instant it took for someone to unsheathe a blade and use it.

She was caught in the spell, in the sheer blood-quickening excitement as he stripped off his clothes. She watched the brilliant naked lines, the stark symmetry of his body, all the power in him burning through that glowing skin.

Her breath tightened and he moved, slowly, like a beautiful hunter.

Her heart thudded, all of her senses tingling with need. It was so great, she burned with it, so great that her body jerked at the first brush of his fingertips, so great that she let him pull the linen shift from her body, let the night-dark eyes see her as she was, let the competent hands draw her near. She came to him and her body fitted to his, aligned to all that fierce strength.

It was the first time she had lain with him completely unclothed, skin to skin. The unrestricted touch robbed her breath. The deep voice told her she was beautiful and in that enchanted moment she listened. The broken hand slid easily over the protective shape of the *eolhx* rune drawn on her skin, over the scar on her side. Nothing else existed, but his voice and his touch and the wild beat of her blood in her veins.

Her body turned for him, her back arching as his mouth took the achingly sensitive peak of her breast. She made a sound, fierce and desperate. His mouth moved to follow the path his hand had taken. His lips traced the misaligned, distorted edge of scaring. Her body tensed. But the hot mouth, the pure fire, never faltered.

His lips moved lower, across the vulnerable sensitive line of her belly, the edge of her hip, her thigh. The fierce sound broke from her throat again. She watched the deep lethal weight of his shoulders, the feral gleaming line of his body in the firelight, the smooth curve of his head. The darkness of his hair spread across her skin.

There was a moment of complete stillness, of that heady, highly charged awareness and the anticipation of what he would do next and the mysterious hidden nature of it.

He waited. He would stop if she wanted him to. The ingrained protective urge to avoid intimacy suddenly flared. It drove her to pull back, but the bewitchment drew her on. *He* did.

She touched the rich fall of his hair. Her body ached, with the edge of fear, with arousal, with the deep, endless need of him. The heavy head under her hand moved.

She made her body stay still, her thighs drawn back. His lips touched her most intimate flesh, that harsh, austere, maddeningly sensual mouth. She cried out, desperate now with how much she wanted him. She was lost in pleasure, so that her body reacted without restraint to the touch of lips and tongue.

His hands cradled her hips, holding her against the pure heat of his mouth and her body lifted, arching against him.

Afterward, she clung to him, locked in his arms, her body alive in a way she had never known. Her hands caressed the rich olive skin, traced the shape of the mysterious blue design on his arm, moved to his chest. She felt the harsh, fast beat of his heart.

Love me. The words formed in her head out of nowhere. She thrust the thought aside, back into the dark madness where it belonged. She could not even see beyond tomorrow and the shadow of death.

It was not something she could ask of him.

Her fingers touched the edge of the linen bandage she had placed there herself. Hidden wounds. She felt the deep tension. It reached inside her as though it were part of her.

"Let me touch you," she said, instead of the mad words that still gathered in her mind. Her hands moved, just lightly, tracing the heavy muscle, but even so, the tension wound higher, lethal, the control over it wire-thin.

The fierce body moved. Her breath caught and her senses came alight, her sight fascinated by the matchless strength, the strength she had shared so intimately.

"Will you—" She did not even how to say it, the kind of words someone like him would use. His black gaze met hers and the fire leaped, wordless.

"No. I could only hurt you." The words were uncompromising, as though their bleak meaning lay elsewhere.

The mad part of her wanted to say that it did not matter, but she did not know how to speak such impossible thoughts.

He drew her down, hard against him, so that she was so close. Her body was wrapped with his and she could smell the clean hot scent of his skin. Her arms were round him, her touch on his body low. Her fingers grazed the edge of one tight hip bone.

She remembered touching him in her chamber at Fearnros, the big male hardness and the sense of power, the hot smooth skin, his hand guiding her. Her heart kicked against her ribs.

Her fingers moved experimentally, testing the shape of his body, the taut masculine line of his hip, then the hard, smooth, powerful, blood-quickening shape of his sex.

She felt his hands tighten round her as she touched him, her fingers exploring the shape, the heated, blood-gorged skin. Her senses were filled with him, fixed on him, on what might give him the deep, overwhelming release of pleasure he had given her. She caressed him, spellbound.

His body moved, pressed close. His hand tangled briefly with hers, showing her the rhythm. Then his arms closed round her, his hands on her naked skin, making her heart beat faster. She touched him and touched him until the pleasure broke, the strong body moved, the last moment far beyond the reach of that fiercely held control and she felt the hot burst of his seed against her hand.

SLEEP COULD NOT HOLD HIM. Macsen woke. There was nothing wrong in the warm room. The fire in the hearth and the darkness told him it was less than an hour since he had slept, but the shadows had already changed. Tomorrow stole in with the dark.

Weariness coupled with pain clawed at him. But the waking was complete and he knew that he had to move.

He left the bed, careful not to disturb Aurinia. His wife. She slept, outlined in the red glow of the banked fire. She lay facing the wall with its single shuttered window, curled

up in the smallest space at the edge of the bed. As far away
from him as it was possible to get. Her pale hair spread
across the bolster like moonlight. He remembered touching
it in the act of bedding with her, how it had felt. How she
had felt. So impossibly vulnerable.

Yet she had turned to him, as though the bond between
them had meaning, a marriage founded on three days and
the treacherous unreality of dreams. And he—he had acted
like someone crazed, just as he had from the moment he
had seen her. From before that.

He turned restlessly in the small confines of the bower.

He had acted as though the dreams in his head were real.

He had done that only once before and it had ended
in disaster.

Things would not end so for her. The force of what he felt
stole his breath. He had lived on, past the last disaster, even
though it had taken its place inside him. If the same disaster
took her, he would not.

He absorbed the knowledge, forcing the breath back
through his lungs.

He watched his sleeping wife. Her slender body was lost
under the bedcovers. But he did not need sight. He knew
her intimately, so clearly and so deeply that his body stirred
even now from that hidden knowledge. He knew her intimately and not at all. There were so many things she had
not told him and now there was no time.

Tomorrow.

He did not know why it weighed so heavily. The future,
even the treacherous, incomprehensible glimpses that came
to him, was closed from his sight.

Aurinia.

She did not stir or wake or look at him, or even turn toward him in sleep. But she was his. His responsibility. He had to provide whatever it was her heart wanted.

I wish I was… What had she called it? *Acceptable.* She had not given herself to a husband who was acceptable. But if the wealth and the power he had could provide what she wanted, he would do it.

He had taken the first step with the elaborate, hastily arranged wedding feast. As for what had happened afterward, there was only one way round that. Tomorrow, before dawn, there would be a priest to shrive those who rode out to fight.

Tomorrow—

The coldness settled on his naked skin. He moved, the force inside abruptly unbearable. He found his clothes. He made no sound. She did not even know when he left.

The wolf lying across the threshold eyed him.

"Stay," he said, as though the despoiler of the battle-slain were a trained lapdog. The great head sank. *Look after her.* The skin on his neck prickled like warning, but he could see nothing. Even the wolf with its finely tuned senses did not stir.

There were few enough people about; Alfred's headquarters was as quiet as it ever got. Despite the hour, lamps glowed from the chamber where the king was. He knew Garrulf would be there, the two dangerous subtle-minded offspring of Athelwulf planning the next move.

He knew what they were discussing—how to force Earl Guthrum to negotiate, keep him isolated from outside help…. Garrulf's pointless words stabbed through his mind, about Vikings seen in Devon, about Bryse, his father, coming this far east.

Garrulf never said anything that was pointless.

He turned away, for the first time since he had given his oath at Alfred's crowning, an oath sworn on saints' bones that he had believed was absolute.

The darkness swallowed him, dense outside the light that spilled from the king's chamber.

His father giving British help to Earl Guthrum.

It was impossible. It would also be impossible to steer through. Worse than that, there would be no point in everything he had done. There would be no safety wrested out of the chaos for those he loved, all the bitter fighting wasted, tomorrow wasted before it had begun. Tomorrow—

Something else caught his attention. More light striking through the dark where he had expected none. He strode toward it. There was a dark huddled shape at the closed door. It was her dog, the thoroughbred, Bruna.

"GET OUT," YELLED BERTRED.

His uncle Edwald's men, *his* men, knew better than to come back in here. Surely? The debilitating uncertainty struck through him, the unforgiving necessity to appear in control when all he wanted to do was throw up with the pain, forget the appalling events of the day, in fact everything that had happened since he had come to Fearnros.

Since the battle they had tried to keep him out of because he was too young, that he had rushed into anyway, to spite them, to prove himself, so heedlessly he had not even gone back to get his armour.

Nothing could be worse at this moment than facing his uncle's retainers, all twice as old and experienced as him.

The door shoved open with a kind of unstoppable finality. He had hauled himself partly upright on his elbows. "Get—" a gust of night air made the lamps gutter "—out…"

It was Macsen. He had the witch's dog with him.

"You." He felt his grip on the edge of the bed slipping. His palms were sweaty. "I did not think you would come." He sounded about six winters old. He choked the words off. Macsen watched him do it.

"I don't want anyone here." *I don't need anyone, least of all you.*

"Not even this?" Macsen's hand moved. The brilliant hound at his side looked at him out of its brilliant eyes. He thought of the creature curling up on his bed at Wytch Heath like a trusted friend, trusted like—like *her.*

"Take it out."

"You would vent your anger on a witless dog and let it pine to death outside your door?"

"She stayed outside the door? I did not know—"

Bruna was not witless. Damn it to hell. He looked at the shivering body pressed close to Macsen's leg, ears and tail down. She was shy, that was all, a fault any man could train her out of. *Damn it.* It was no wonder the hound was like that, trapped in a place like Wytch Heath, seeing no one except the female *hell-rune.*

The witch had doubtless enchanted the creature the way she enchanted everything she saw, *touched.* The way she had enchanted a king's thane like Macsen, who was looking at him as though he had committed kin-slaying. As if he had even the strength to get out of bed, as if…

"Since this is your wedding night, should you not be in your new wife's bed? How can you drag yourself away from the kind of bewitchment someone like her offers? Should you not be—" Thank the living heavens he did not say the rest. It would have involved words beside which *fornication* sounded polite.

Macsen did not move. At least, not yet. But everyone knew that the king's men could break people using the fingers of one hand. He lost his sweating grip on the side of the bed and he was falling.

The jolt shot pain through him that had no measure, so that he could not breathe or see beyond indistinct shapes. He thought that perhaps Macsen did move then, like a great black shadow. Like seeing your own death, worse than the battlefield. He actually yelled. Then there was a moment when he lost consciousness.

"Why are you still here?" He knew Macsen was still in the chamber because someone had moved him. He was not hanging headfirst out of the bed with his nose stuffed in the rushes but lying face up on the pillows, looking at the bed canopy and, beyond that, the thin layer of hearth smoke drifting below the roof.

"The answer to that depends on you."

Macsen wanted to kill him. But Bertred was in the right. Everyone thought so. His supposed cousin, Macsen's *wife*, was a *hell-rune*, a sharer in hell's secrets. The most generous interpretation was that she had enchanted Macsen. The worst was what he had so nearly said. He clenched his fist in the messed-up bedcovers. He wanted to scream. He could not hold it back much longer. *Just go.*

"What did the physician give you for the pain?"

Nothing I need. He wanted to say the proud-sounding words, but he was too weak, so instead he said, "On the table. In the flask." He could feel the shame of asking like fire behind his eyes. "Will you…will you get it for me?"

After what he had said— But Macsen poured from the flask, held the cup so that he could drink. Then he started talking. Nothing about the sickening words they had just said. Just ordinary things about the king's physician, Brother Luke, and practical things he did not have to answer. He swallowed the liquid.

"No more or you will not be able to keep it down."

"It will not be enough." Beren's bones. He was so weak.

"Yes, it will." The assurance was complete, and he was back with the king's favoured thane who had rescued him out of battle, pulled him through another ordeal like this, like her— He cut off his thought.

"You should have drunk this before. Where was Brother Luke?"

"He thought I was asleep. He left the flask for me, but then I sent the servants and the other men away."

"Why?" The question, this time, was edged.

"I was shamed." The words burst out of him. "They think I am useless already. That I am no good as a leader."

"You have already chosen the right course. Your men know that and they will follow it, follow you. The king knows you have a loyal heart."

"That is exactly it. People expect me to know what is

right, to do what is right, and now they think I have a…a sorceress for a cousin." He tried to hold back the worst of it from the dark bulk next to him, but he had to say something. It had all changed for the worse after the battle, after *her*. "Can you not see what she has done? They say she has bespelled you. You know what she did at Wytch Heath."

"Yes, I do. Aurinia saved your life."

Aurinia. "It was you who did that. You—"

"Get one thing straight if you want to be a competent leader. You have to understand what is possible and what is not."

"But—"

"You cannot lead anyone correctly if you do not know limits. All I did was carry you out of the battle with two arrows stuck through you. But I could not get you back here. I took you to Wytch Heath and if my pursuers were mysteriously lost on the journey, I feel nothing but grateful."

The black, fire-filled eyes held him, hard and utterly unflinching. No one had ever questioned Macsen's courage. They could not. But it was not the answer he expected.

"Understand how things were," said Macsen. "It was not a foregone conclusion that I could have defeated two unwounded men in the state I was in and with you slung across my saddle. At Wytch Heath, I could not have dealt with wounds as serious as yours. Only Aurinia knew how, and she chose to do so."

Chose to. The sense of betrayal drew tight inside him. He thought about trusting her, about…admiring her, just wanting her to so much as look at him with those slanting grey eyes.

"My *cousin* knew what she was doing. She knew who I was all the time, all the time she did things that…" *She watched me, talked to me as though she cared, walked round in that impossible beauty without even a decent veil over her hair. Slept on my bed…*

"She knew who I was and how rich I was, and she knew exactly the same about you." He glared at Macsen who was everything he did not know how to be. "I even asked her if she would come here."

"And she did not want to leave her home, to go out into a world where she had received nothing but misunderstanding and hostility and violence."

Violence? He had not known that. "What—"

"She still does not want to be here."

"But she does, she wants you." Something penetrated through his pain-fuddled, drug-fuddled brain. Macsen's stillness.

"I do not think either of us knows what she truly wants. But it is not riches, or even a name, mine or yours."

That was not true.

"If you want to be a leader," said Macsen, the king's thane, the cleverest at the king's counsel because of his foresight, "you have to look beyond the surface of things. Just think of that. Think of it before you say or do something you will always regret."

"I—" It was all very well for a man who had the power of a prince, who had neither done nor suffered anything that caused regret— He held the words back. Something else rose in the aching confusion of his brain, some rumour about Macsen's past…a dead brother? He was too new here to know the story. But suppose it was there, beneath the impenetrable surface? *Think.*

He watched as the king's best fighter, his "cousin's" husband, got up to leave. Macsen sent him Brother Luke.

And he left the dog.

THE NOISE WOKE AURINIA. It was just on the edge of her straining senses. But she, so used to aloneness, came out of sleep.

She watched her husband buckle his sword belt.

"You are going." Her voice, thick with the aftermath of unquiet sleep, was not quite under her control. The words, raw and unsteady, hung in the half dark like an accusation.

The competent hand paused on the gilded metal, a pale blur at the shadowed line of his hip. *Do not go.* She held the words back, as she would have recalled the others if she could.

But her heart was full of foreboding.

"It will be light soon." That was all he said. His hand moved. The red glow from the remade fire in the hearth flickered over the fine shape with its broken knuckles, resting on the sword hilt. Her heart felt tight in the constricted mass of her chest and her mind filled with memory, the way that hand had touched her flesh and created magic, how he had lain with her so intimately. Her whole life had changed, so much that her old self was lost. One day of marriage. Four days of knowing him.

"I know you must go."

She had not thought it would even be possible to sleep with someone else in her bed but she had wanted to touch him, even as he slept.

Such madness and greed. She had made herself turn away and now there was this.

She watched him adjust the straps that held the scabbard with long-practiced skill. Chain mail flickered in the light. "You are the king's man."

She sat up with the bedclothes caught round her, trying to say the right thing.

"I know that is how things must be." Shivers passed over her skin, born out of nowhere. Just the chill of dawn.

Aurinia got out of bed, heedless of the cold, snatching at her cloak to cover herself. She caught his arm, below the edge of the chain-mail sleeve, where she could touch his flesh through the heavy tunic.

He did not see her.

10

$\mathbf{M}$acsen did not know she was there.

Aurinia's hand tightened on the heavy forearm. The healer's reaction was instinctive, intensified by a fierce protectiveness that ran through her with the force of shock.

He did not know. She thought at first it was illness because of the wound, but it was something different. She sensed distance, something like brute shock and then an awakening that was hard and abrupt. Then ordinary things, the warmth of his skin even through the thick tunic, the rhythm of his breath.

He did not look at her. "It is nothing."

She watched the dark head and the glittering gold. He would not say. But let an Anglo-Saxon sense a meaning that was hidden below the surface like a riddle and they would never let go until they found it. A British prince ought to learn that.

"It was not nothing."

The dark head started to turn.

Her throat closed. She could leave it or she could not. She might never see him again.

"You saw something that does not have a place in this world." She raised an eyebrow, quite steady. "Or at least, not yet."

He did not say anything at all and she was suddenly aware of the heavy size of him in his war gear. Of the way she leaned toward him and the thin sheath of wool sliding off the exposed skin of her shoulder, of her nakedness beneath the cloak, and of him watching her. She was intensely aware of the way she touched him.

The dark gaze held her, dense and still half-full of dreams. The fire struck through her fingers where she held him, penetrating her skin to the very core of her body so that she burned despite the coldness.

She must have made some movement because the loose folds of wool slipped across her bare flesh. She wanted to cover herself. But she did not. She held his gaze for a moment and then he turned away, breaking her hold.

He swore viciously. Firelight glittered off a thousand links of steel as he moved. He ripped the covers down the bed. She felt him hold her, a fast dizzying weightlessness that took her breath, and then she was lying with him on the bed, wrapped in the bedcovers, caught tight against him, living muscle, the hard metal of body armour, male heat.

She buried her head against the warmth of his neck and said, "Tell me what you saw."

"Tell you what? Ignorance and madness and disaster?" His hands touched her bare flesh. She sensed the way his heart beat, even under the padding and the steel.

"Yes," she said simply. "If you have to."

She felt the sharp exhale of his breath. She touched his face and his hands tightened round her body.

"It was the wolves."

"At Wytch Heath." She took great care not to let it sound like a question.

"Yes. And your wolf."

Hunter. "My dog," she corrected, because she was frightened by the beating of his heart.

"Aye. Your six-foot-long lapdog." The further release of his breath brought a slight relaxation in the tight muscle. She simply pressed closer.

"I felt the same yesterday, like a shadow. Only now it is stronger."

She touched the taut skin of his face and neck and thought of the warmth of summer, golden and lazy like sunlight. She could feel the blessed relaxing power of it flowing into her veins, through her skin. Into his.

Please heaven.

"And?"

"I do not know." The beating of his heart was calmer. "I cannot see. And even if I could—"

Aye. Then what? How was it possible to direct *wyrd's* working? Fate.

"It might make no difference," she said.

He became utterly still. "I do not know."

But she was sure. She concentrated on the warmth, the

tenuous sense of something shared, new and unfamiliar and fragile. Outside in Alfred's camp, where it was still dark, there were already voices, the restless movement that never stopped. She tried to block it out. She said his name, her hands on his skin, her body pressed against his. She concentrated on the warmth, her gift.

He would not be afraid of its strangeness like Bertred. He would understand because of his own power. He was the only person in the world who would understand.

"The gift you have," she began.

"It is not a gift. A misplaced power like that is a curse. It brings destruction. If I could choose to throw it away, I would."

She could not stop her body going rigid in his hold. Her mind numbed, and there was a silence while the shock of what he had said seeped through her. *A misplaced power,* something wrong and unwelcome, that he would rather not have but was caught in. Like a curse. Beyond the firelit chamber, someone called out and was answered. The ordinary world.

The connection broke. He moved and she was no longer lying in his arms, no longer close.

"I must go."

She swallowed everything. "Yes."

He turned away. The gold-decorated scabbard nudged his thigh. *No. I do not want you to go.* She held it back because it would have been a scream. He got ready to leave. She saw the focus shift, the edge of concentration that blocked everything else out until he became the warrior and the prince, the leader of men, the ruthless fighter who had invaded her hall. The man who had walked out into the sunlight of her courtyard to speak to a king.

"Macsen—"

Light sheeted off gold, off highly polished steel. He looked up. His face was closed and there was not anything to say.

He crossed the room toward her. "Stay here."

At Fearnros.

"I—"

"I do not want you to go near Wytch Heath." The words were harsh, as though ripped from him. She stared at the relentless warrior's face, trying to find words, but they were lost under his. He moved.

"Huda will stay with you," he said, as though the direction of her only companion belonged to him. It probably did. He adjusted the *seax* blade that hung beside the sword slung at his hip. The chain mail rustled on his body.

"And there are those of my men who will remain behind." A commander's arrangements. He kept speaking. "You know what the arrangements are for yourself." The money and the estates, the thane's overwhelming gift. Her eyes narrowed.

The arrangements were for if he did not come back.

She touched his hand. The gesture took him completely by surprise. She sensed the reaction. The silence that followed was intense, made only the deeper by the noise and the movement outside.

His mouth took hers. The fire ignited and overwhelmed her and there was nothing held back.

He kissed her with his mouth and his hands on her bare flesh beneath the cloak so that her body sang, at once desperate and heated, and terrifyingly alive. Her mouth cleaved to his; her hands fisted in his black hair and the flame burned, so bright it would annihilate her.

He let her go.

He was the king's man. No other possibility existed. She watched him leave.

The six-foot-long dog, the wolf, came into her room.

"HE IS WELL, NOW."

The half-grown colt snuffled at Aurinia's gown. He was, indeed, well. She twitched her worn skirts out of the way of interested teeth, and was glad she had not dressed in the finer clothes Judith had lent her. The colt sighed reproachfully and tried to sidle closer.

"Seems to have taken to you." The stable hand eyed her doubtfully, his gaze running over the plain gown and the glaring addition of the gold bracelet. "Princess," he added. No one had called her *princess* in her life.

"It's a wonder," he said and the word seemed to echo from those gathered round. The interested group included at least three young men of higher status, warriors. One had only to look at their stance, the way they stared. Perhaps she should not have come here, even after last night when Macsen had made everything right. Her thoughts shied away.

She did not belong here. Nothing was truly right. It never would be. She turned away stiffly. Huda followed, like her shadow. He would not leave her. The crowd had already moved back, even the young warriors, but it was not for her.

She saw a tonsured head, a monk. He was small, spare, tired. He worked too much. She made the assessment without thinking. The other heads round him were bowed with respect. He had a large cross made of beaten silver set with beautifully coloured glass. A man of consequence.

She stepped back, too. But he smiled at her and she knew without being told that he was a healer.

"Brother Luke," he said. "The king's physician."

He began to speak to her about the colt, about healing, not as though she were some kind of dangerous mystic, but like a fellow practitioner, a holder of knowledge but at the same time someone perfectly ordinary. The crowd round them grew.

Perhaps he did not realize who she was. She said as little as she could, a defensive reaction, and then she forgot that; she even forgot the growing, whispering crowd. She forgot that she did not belong. Time and mistrust of the outside world vanished.

When the interruption came, the abruptness of it shocked through her.

There was shouting. People were making way for someone outside, a troop of horsemen, important—her heart leaped, even though it was too soon, even though it could not be.

She pushed toward the door with the rest. The monk would have taken her arm, leading her out of the press, but she could not stop. Even though she was horrified of crowds, she let this one carry her along, Huda beside her, swearing.

People actually tried to step back for her out of politeness, as though they had respect. But her gown and her hair got tousled in the scrambling good-natured crush. Then the three young warriors decided to come to her rescue. They looked no older than Bertred, laughing and elbowing each other out of the way like boys. She got to the front.

It was not the king's troop returning from fighting. The

mounted men were strangers, brilliantly equipped. Sunlight glinted off silver-plated harness fittings, off decorated sword hilts, off the bright tips of spears. Stable hands leaped out of the way.

The huge bay war-stallion in front plunged to a halt, snorting its irritation, a hair's breadth from being out of control. The leader, she thought, Beowulf of the legends chasing the Frisians. No. Attila the Hun about to sack Rome. The scourge of God.

He dismounted. She had never in her life seen anyone so angry. She could feel Huda's hand go to his sword hilt, even though they could not be enemies, so readily admitted to the king's camp still bearing their weapons.

The reins were thrown to a frightened stable boy. "Take my horse."

The scourge of God had an accent, as though he were not used to speaking English, as though it infuriated him, like everything around him. He was handsome, more than forty winters, but vigorous, energy wound tight. His dark-hued gaze touched her. Her skin prickled. She thought *Holy Mother, someone has hurt you past bearing.*

His eyes took in the poor clothes, the state of her dress. The contempt for all he saw tightened. His gaze swept on, past the open-mouthed young men at her side, rested an instant longer on Huda with sword ready to hand, dismissed him. People scurried round him. He turned away. She exhaled without having been aware that she had held her breath, or of the sharp tension in her belly. But then he turned back and the narrowed eyes fixed on her.

"What is your name?"

The turn of the question was offensive, even she with her limited experience of how the world acted knew that. The aggression was hardly held back, vibrating like an arrow at the string.

She did not answer.

Huda's hand closed on her arm, linking it firmly with his. "Come away. We have no business here."

One of the young warriors supported her other arm. It was kindly meant. The stranger watched as though it were an insult, or some kind of indecent act made in public. It was not. It was the first time in her life any stranger had wished to help her. Her own anger rose, sudden and as precariously controlled as that of the man who confronted her. She let the young man take her arm.

"Princess," he said, his youthful voice proprietorial, tight with challenge in response to that overwhelming anger, touched with the pride of a man on his own turf.

The fierce gaze narrowed, following the words, the movement, clashing with her own gaze and then fixing there, dark and complete. Violent.

"Come with us," urged her escort.

Her foot had already moved, but then she looked more closely, and she knew.

AURINIA MET HIM ALONE. The scourge of God returned the favour. They had given him a fine chamber, a difficult feat in a place as crowded as this. It was a royal compliment, but, Huda had reported, his retinue had had to be lodged elsewhere, at some distance, and rather scattered. Such inconvenience was regretted. She began to see why King Alfred was so successful.

Huda had been hard to detach; those of Macsen's men who remained had been even harder, which surprised her.

"I have come here," said her father-in-law, *he will never come here,* "for a purpose. I wished to congratulate you in person."

Aurinia watched the dark head lightly streaked with grey, the clearly proportioned face whose likeness to her husband had at first escaped her and now seemed blindingly obvious.

"Thank you." She did not say *Lord.* He was her second closest kinsman after all. "You must be disappointed your son is not here to—"

"My son is my own business." *Whatever argument I have with my father lies only between us.* "The congratulations are due to you." The tone of the compliment was fulsome. The underlying insult might have been unintentional.

Her father-in-law, Bryse, poured wine for her, his movements fast. The decisiveness of them could have been Macsen's. "How did you do it? Get my son to marry?"

She prevented herself from dropping the goblet.

He wanted to marry me. She wanted to yell the words into the fine room, into his fine sneering face, but something stopped her. That fatal, carefully glossed-over hesitation when she had asked Macsen about regrets. Her second-nearest kinsman helped her with the precious cup.

"He asked me." Aurinia touched the gold-ringed hand over the smooth smoke-blue glass because touch was often more effective at revealing secrets than what could be seen with the eyes. She wanted to feel that vicious ugly anger, and it was there. But so was the pain she had sensed from the first moment she saw him, real and unmistakable and raw.

"My son stopped long enough to ask that? Forgive me," said Bryse. "I did not think he would need to."

She withdrew her hand, the slight, not-quite-accidental brush of her fingers against his more than she could bear. She felt his gaze on her again, as it had been in the courtyard.

She had tidied her appearance, even though she had not taken the time to change her clothes because she had not wanted to keep her new father-in-law waiting. Her gown was plain. Very plain. Hardly that of a temptress. But she suddenly became aware of her unbound hair, of the fact that she had not covered it with a veil because she had never thought of such things, had not needed to.

She moved her arm back. The unfamiliar bracelet brushed against the wine flask on the table with a small metallic clink.

"I see you have your reward. No! Do not say anything. Did you think I would not have found out already about the lands he has given you for a morning gift?"

Her own temper sparked, the way it had in the courtyard, like a welcome relief, covering all the other feelings she could not look at. "I did nothing for reward. I asked for none."

"Mabon's balls, I believe you are going to tell me that you acted for love."

Her throat tightened, hot. It was as though all the other buried feelings, the ones she had not been able to look at, surfaced at that moment like a flood. Enough to annihilate.

"I did act for love." It was clear with a suddenness that

stunned her, all the bewildering, frightening, hot-edged feelings, the deep fierceness of them. More than that, the completeness.

The reaction in her father-in-law was savage.

"No. If you truly loved my son, you would not have married him. I know exactly who you are, *what* you are and what you do with your sorcerous tricks. The news has been all over this camp. Even your own cousin wanted to disown you."

She nearly stepped back, dizzied and off balance from the terrifying realization of her feelings, from the unremitting assault of her new father-in-law and the appalling truth behind it.

"It has been my son's name that has saved you and you believe it will continue to do so. But at what cost to him? Did you think of that when you decided you loved him?"

No.

"Of the cost to his family?"

She watched the cold face, striking in its offended pride, the rich clothes and the weapons, the bright glitter of the gold neck-ring so like Macsen's, and for an instant the anger inside her, dark, with its roots lying far back, obliterated the bitter pain.

"The deciding factor is the cost to you?"

The dark eyes, their fierceness so like Macsen's, glittered. "I have only one son."

He has no other son, said Macsen's voice in her head, and that glimpse of the enclosed world she was not part of.

"My other son is dead," said Bryse and the pain in him started to seep through the anger, unstoppable. "But then you know that. Since you and Macsen are so close, since he must return your love—" the warm, wood-scented air closed round her, hard to breathe "—he will have told you everything about Gorei."

He had not told her. She saw that her father-in-law knew that, had calculated it with a ruthless clarity of thought that could have been Macsen's.

She stepped back, but she was not prepared for the pain that hit her, sharp as the knife blow through her side had been, and at the same time, diffuse and overwhelming. The warm air was full of it, and it was not just her pain, but *his*, her aggressive, despairing father-in-law's. At first, she moved away from it, the way she had wanted, for that first blind self-seeking instant, to turn her back on Bertred.

"Are you unwell?" His carefully accented voice was sharp, but as though it came from a long distance.

"No." Her legs struck the wall bench. She could leave. She really could. The door was four paces away. She sat.

"Let me assist you."

No.

"Give me your arm then."

He came toward her, bringing the terrible disturbance with him, black and threaded with rage because to him it seemed so hopeless. If he touched her, there would be no barrier. He took her arm to support her and the disturbance washed through her, so deep it was impossible to manage. He was surprisingly strong.

"Drink your wine." He actually helped her with the goblet and she let him while she thought. Gorei. The brother who had died years ago. Macsen had said the name and she had not pursued it. A mistake—

He took the goblet away from her mouth. "Let me explain."

She let her hand fall on his arm before he moved away and the sudden contact told her. It was grief. Gorei's death was the cause of the pain.

"It appears my son has acted rashly. We can be an impulsive family, and whatever he may claim to the contrary, my son Macsen is not an exception to that truth."

Macsen. She understood. The terrible hurt was not only about the dead son, but about the living. Terrible because it was underlain by the bedrock strength of something she had never experienced and had always craved—a parent's love. She was so cowardly, she let go of his arm.

"As I say, my son has acted rashly with you, and I am sorry for it." He moved away, grief hidden by anger. He turned. The gilded sword in its gilded scabbard swung. "But it is no great matter. It can soon be remedied."

Never forget the warrior.

"Everyone has their price."

I know exactly who you are, what you are. It would be easy to hate her fine father-in-law with his words like battle-runes, such hostility.

"Come, you are a clever girl, there is no disputing that, and I am not unreasonable. You may keep your gold, but not the land. I cannot have a *cwene* like you anywhere near my family."

A *cwene*. It could mean a woman or a whore. Someone unused to the subtleties of English might not understand the concealed meaning.

This man did. She watched him and she sensed what she did not want to sense, the bitter anguish, felt physically like a disease, like someone dying by inches.

"A hasty marriage can be as hastily undone and cooperation can receive its just reward. I am sure you could do with a little help."

If you ever need help, he will give it. But Macsen had understood something different of his father. He had reassured her out of a husband's duty. But she had already guessed the real truth, had expected it in her hidden heart. Expected *this*.

"You want me to go."

"My son has a different destiny from this, from being tied to an outcast, a Saxon, a girl with nothing, who is not even legitimate. I want you to release him from a mistake that would ruin him. Because, believe me, you will ruin him and what you call love will not be enough to save your marriage then. A marriage like this will die in the end and nothing you can do will be able to save it. Do you think he will still want you then?"

He already knows who I am. Shall I tell you what he said to that? He said, I do not care.

The fine precious words still rang in her ears. They had sounded true. Perhaps they were. She and Macsen had a bond. But what was it meant for? How did anyone control the future?

"You are not part of his world. You will ruin his life and he will end up hating you for it. I am merely asking you to end it now rather than later, after you have brought down the man you claim so glibly to care about." There was a pause. "I will see you are provided for."

An honourable man. But she could not fault him. He loved his son.

As she did. She loved him.

"It is not just the wedding ceremony. We are bound together." She did not know she had spoken aloud until Bryse surged to his feet. The heavy wooden chair crashed back with the force of his movement, slamming against the wall. He stood, clutching the table, death-white.

"Bound? By what? By some kind of sorcery? Would you seek to drag him into that world because you have found out his bane?"

It was a very Saxon word, *bane,* that which was fated to be your undoing.

"No," yelled Bryse. "That so-called power has already brought him loss, has brought it to all of us, the kind of harm that can never be atoned. It can bring only more harm, death."

She watched the tensed figure, the familiar face of horror.

"My son knows that. He— Saint Brannoc. He has already told you."

It brings destruction. If I could choose to throw it away, I would.

"Yes."

"And you would still take that path?"

He had his hand on his sword hilt as though he would kill her. She could feel his pain, the intolerable grief and the rage that was intense, terrible and ultimately helpless. She got up. He did not move to stop her and she did not even see the warrior. She saw the father. It was more than she could bear.

There was no need of an answer. She walked out.

BUT SHE COULD NOT WALK away.

Aurinia stopped at the edge of the heathland. It spread

out before her in a single wave, empty and bright with colour. *Home—*

Such as she had known.

She sat down. She had just kept walking, four or five miles, blinded to everything. But she knew where she was. The ground at her feet bloomed with the thick purple heather that belonged to Wytch Heath, fading now with autumn. She had gone, like an animal with wounds seeking its lair, to what was familiar.

But what lived in her mind now was no longer familiar. Bryse. All the things she had done, every thought…

Something moved. Hunter. She had not seen him follow. He stretched out, ears wary, touching her. She knew he was warm and alive, but she could not feel it. The wind chilled her, blowing straight from the river flats at Wareham and the wide unseen sea. She had not brought her cloak. She pulled her dress tighter round herself. Something glinted in the light, hurting her eyes. Gold. Macsen's gift. Payment.

What had she done? Caused disaster where she had meant to bring healing?

She touched the gold on her wrist. *I am not worth you. Why did you not believe it?*

But it was her fault, not his. It was she who had seen the future more clearly, not he with the uncanny power he so despised.

She had seen the future as clearly as Bryse saw it.

Macsen.

The silence was complete and the wind cut at her, bringing the scent of Wytch Heath, and she wished passionately that she had never left it. Her home was not quite close enough to see, but in her mind she looked down on the high-pitched roof with the runes of protection across the ridge. Her eyes caught the sun reflecting off the pond that held her carefully nurtured stock of fish, all quiet and serene, untouched by the world and untouchable.

Yet even in the moment of seeing, the vision slipped, unreachable. It was as though Wytch Heath had changed the moment she had left it. Or as though she had changed, the instant she had met her husband.

She could not go back. One never could.

She stood up. The horsemen came out of nowhere, cresting the rise to her left, fast, sure of purpose. As though they had been waiting. They held throwing-spears and something else. A net? Something to trap an animal?

She ran, direct for the coppice of trees, the only possible source of cover, Hunter like a grey streak at her side. Her feet stumbled on the uneven ground and she knew the trees were too far away. Indistinct shapes weaved under the shadows like smoke. Wolves. She ran toward them. Hunter gave a full-throated howl.

Terror burst through her. There would be no escape. Her last thought was of Macsen, and the memory of him was so powerful and so clear that she thought she saw him.

"FALL BACK." THE WIND WHIPPED Macsen's words from a voice raw with shouting. But the mounted troop speeding across the river flats heard. The command was taken up with the clear note of the horn. He tried to focus his gaze. The pain from the head blow he had taken built behind his eyes, frighteningly savage and sharp-edged, growing to the point where it would become disorienting.

"It will work." Anwas, his troop captain, came up beside him as the line of horsemen spread out over the muddy ground wheeled in response to his orders, drawing together, plunging toward the sheltering line of the trees. Earl Guthrum's Vikings followed.

"Yes." It had to work. The planning had been careful, as precise as anything could be. Yet the presage of disaster still gripped him. He tried to stay upright in the saddle.

But the line of trees slipped, seemed to change shape in front of his aching eyes, almost as though consciousness had been lost after all and his thoughts had been pulled into a different place. "The ground falls away—" The crumbling bank was deadly, hidden. The grey moving shape in the tree shadows could have been Hunter, the so-called dog.

Aurinia. The danger struck through him, sudden, more acute. Crippling. But Aurinia was safe at Fearnros.

Tell me you are safe at Fearnros. But he could not see....

"The ground? It is flat near the river. Lord?" Anwas's voice brought him back.

He wiped the blood out of his eyes. The grey shape was gone. But the outline of the trees was blurred, as though double-edged, one image put over another that did not quite fit, in front of that the Vikings, closer— "Move."

In the world beside Wareham, the next part of the plan unrolled. Macsen urged his own horse back. Du Moro turned. He scanned the field, trying for focus, taking in the pattern of the men, seeking the flaw—

His own men had turned, racing forward along the edge

of the trees, toward the river bend where the rest of the king's men lay in wait. But those at the start of the line were late to the order, local levies not king's veterans, half-trained. Too slow. They would be cut off. He swore. Anwas's head turned.

"Let me go. Lord." Anwas actually grabbed at his bridle, as though Macsen would stop, send his captain where he would not go himself. They were Edwald's men of Fearnros. Bertred's. They were men who would be killed.

"Fetch the others. Bring them after." Du Moro surged forward, breaking Anwas's grip. Macsen heard him shouting orders. The small group of men surged after him, fast, the churned earth flying from hooves.

What followed was chaos, made worse for him because he could not focus, his vision blurring because another reality lay against all that he saw, a different line of trees, different contours to the ruined earth that was cut to sliding mud under the war-stallion's hooves.

They had to push the rest of Guthrum's Vikings back toward the river bend, the trap where the King's troops waited. He downed one rider whose spear was aimed at Anwas and the men who had seen such easy pickings scattered in disorder across the river-flat. Wet earth slid beneath the horse's hooves and then it was as though the clinging mud of the low-lying ground near Wareham was gone under springing heather, like the purple mantle that clothed Wytch Heath, and the bracken spreading before the trees.

In this world, the Vikings fanned out, five of them, moving fast, carrying not just spears but nets, as though they hunted.

The way to avoid the nets and the spears' flight was not to run straight, even though the cover of the woods beckoned.

But it was not a spear that nearly took him. The axe swung straight toward him, the blade bearded, heavy enough to break the iron links across his body. Awareness snapped back and he twisted, avoiding the hacking blow, the weight of the axe blade making it slower than a sword, giving him the fractional life-saving gap in time. But it was too close, his reaction impeded by the pain gathered behind his eyes, the split vision a hindrance he could not overcome.

Blood stung his aching eyes and he swayed, off balance, half-blinded. Du Moro stumbled on the cut ground, impossible to hold. The stallion plunged and he fell, kicking his feet free of the stirrups, but unable to roll, slamming into the bare mud-thick ground, the impact forcing the breath from his lungs, tearing consciousness. His last coherent thought was of Aurinia, before the darkness covered him.

But it was not dark. In his mind, he could see her and he dragged himself upright on the cushion of dry grass and bracken.

Aurinia was there.

CHAPTER

11

They could kill her. Aurinia did not understand why they had not done it. But they had cast only one spear, at Hunter. But he was almost impossible to see in the thigh-high bracken.

They had nets. She had seen them, as though they hunted prey and would catch it alive. That horrified her, the thought of being trapped as an animal, like being helpless under a violent crowd. Panic gripped her, body and mind, a hair's breadth from taking control.

But they had not caught her yet. They might not if she did not run in a straight line toward shelter as her terrified instincts drove her, but dodged through the bracken. She did not know where the knowledge came from, but it held a small measure of power that steadied her.

She swerved left as Hunter moved right. She heard the horse beside her stumble briefly. The small life-saving spark of power grew, the knowledge that was not hers because she did not hunt beasts like a warrior.

Her mind filled with Macsen.

It was as though he were with her, as though the bond held, outside time and distance and damage.

Macsen.

She nearly stumbled on the uneven ground.

Nothing between them in the real world was resolved. She wanted him so much she would die of it.

Her feet slithered under her, as though the ground near the trees must be wetter and muddy, even though it rose sharply. She could not get breath. Her mind was dizzy. As the darkness of the trees took her, she saw him. Not like a figure of her memories, fine and bright with gold, but as she imagined he must be now, in war gear, battle-hard, splattered with mud from the wet earth.

That hard-leashed power seemed to touch her and she ran, the speed of her limbs unreal, born out of that power. The determination was ruthless and fixed, the single-mindedness complete. Hunter snarled, making her nearest pursuer stumble. The wolf-dog pushed at her.

If she could hide herself among the trees—

Macsen. In her thoughts, he was there, turned toward her, running faster than her, with a speed that was break-neck, to her right, yelling, his voice raw, the sound whipped on the wind, urgent. Something broke the ruthless single-mindedness—the shape of the ground. She had to turn. She tried, but her limbs were like lead, burning, as grudging to respond as her numbed mind.

The fatigue made her stumble and the ground caved away

under her feet, vanished. She was falling, over crumbling earth, small stones, slippery leaves. She tried to swing her weight. There was a breathless terrifying sense of space, emptiness—

She was clinging to the bracken-grown slope, her feet scrabbling, finding a foothold, not enough to take her weight, loose soil and slick vegetation giving way beneath her, her body jarring, sliding, holding.

"Lean in. Take hold of my arm."

She could see his hand, the gold arm ring, the broken knuckles, the solid shape, like the embodiment of her wanting, of the wild, fierce-edged desperation of her thoughts.

"Give me your hand. Don't look down."

But she already had. The ground cut away sharply, the bracken giving out to briars, dead branches as sharp as spears. The fall would have killed her. She did not think her pursuers had intended that. She thought of the nets and her beating heart choked. They wanted to take her. She could hear them, the sound of the horses, the shouts of the men as they tried to locate her.

"They are coming—" If they found Macsen... There were five, fully armed. They would kill even him if he stayed.

"No." She struggled to get the words out of her head. "I cannot—"

"You can. Nothing else matters. Nothing apart from this."

She moved her hand. The moment she touched his flesh, she felt the pain; it mixed with hers, intense, as dark as a dream, so fierce she could not move. There was blood on his face. She thought she reached out.

The voices shouted, closer, to the left. Her heartbeat lurched and then she heard it, the worst sound possible. Answering calls from the other direction. More. On foot this time. There was no way out.

But he already knew that.

Nothing else matters.

Her hand swung, clumsy and unresponsive with exhaustion, pushed only by will. She had nothing left, no strength. But there was such power in him. Always. She pushed herself upward. The bank crumbled under her so that the deadweight of her body dragged. She felt the strength take her, the jarring pain of stretched muscle, her feet scrabbling desperately for a hold, and then there was solid ground. She collapsed, her grip still tight.

"They are coming."

"Yes."

Macsen, the experienced warrior, would make no pretence. That must be how it was in battle, the last possibility seen and then faced.

It was her nightmare, being trapped in the grip of others. But the very harshness of facing that, the ruthless acceptance, was a like a source of strength. The breath seared her lungs and the exhaustion clawed through each muscle, but the miraculous strength stayed.

She heard the sound of his voice, the roughened strain in it unfamiliar, but not the dark power. "You are alive. You will stay so." The power was like fate's thread.

There were only seconds. She tried to move, touch him,

see him, because the blood on his face and the intenseness
of the pain filled her mind. She sensed the darkness swirling
round him. But it was other hands that caught at the solid
arm, the massive shoulders, rougher and more hurried. They
dragged at him and the darkness struck like a blow, complete.

When she opened her eyes, she was sprawled out under
the dark pines, lying near the edge of a bank, her hands
fisted in earth and tree roots as though she had crawled her
way up and out. Hunter was at her side, heavy warmth
against her cold aching body. She held him briefly and then
someone came through the trees, booted feet, the butt end
of a spear slashing the crimson leaves of autumn.

Hunter stood, teeth and fur and ridged muscle. She
forced herself up, her breath still heaving, every muscle
locked with fatigue. The half wolf crouched ready to spring,
only two instinctive responses in his brain, attack or flee.
She heard the other Vikings, the horses. A wolf would be
killed with spears.

They were not going kill her. Her heart clenched in her
chest.

"Go," she ordered. "Now."

The feral head, yellow eyes, turned.

"Go." She shoved at the muscular haunches. *Do it.* Then
she moved left, luring the booted feet after her. Hunter
dived away, silent, low, gone like smoke.

Find him, but do not bring him back to me. Not this time.
It is too late.

They had said farewell.

When the Vikings found her, she was alone. They rode
for Guthrum's camp at Wareham.

LIGHT STABBED THROUGH MACSEN'S eyes. He turned his head toward it. But it was not the clear grey light of day that belonged to the battlefield. To either battlefield. It was flame through the dark. The flame was as sharp as a spear, the blackness behind it blessed, but no longer filled with dreams.

Aurinia.

He was miles from her. He forced himself to concentrate on the light.

When he moved again and opened his eyes, the pain hit him in full measure, but the fire had dwindled to lamp light, the swirling blackness to the ordinary shapes of a bower. Fearnros.

Anwas had brought him to Fearnros.

He dragged himself to the side of the bed. His shoulders were tight, like the slight drag of strained muscle. It was that, not the pain through his head, that nearly stopped his heart.

There was the sound of smashed glass. "Mabon's balls."

Heavy boots scuffed the floor, followed by isolated crunching noises. Macsen tried breathing. He could not move.

Mabon was a British hero who had once been a god, one with regenerative powers. Not someone who belonged in the Christian church.

He raised his head. "What are you doing here?" He spoke in British. His voice sounded like the stirring of dry rope.

His father, feet surrounded by crushed glass, was crossing himself rapidly to make up for what might be considered a lapse.

"Visiting you. It seems about time."

Mabon's balls indeed. He had told Garrulf his father would not come near Fearnros. He had told Aurinia— Saint Brannoc. There was not time for this. He clawed upright.

"How long have I been here?"

"An hour or so. Maybe more."

A couple of hours, perhaps, plus the ending of the battle, the time necessary to bring him here. He tried to work it out, but the pain in his head blotted out a calculation as simple as that.

"Stay there. That dried-out fool of a Saxon priest left you something."

Brother Luke.

"Where?" He was far past pride. The only thing that mattered was regaining sufficient control to get out of here. Green shards skittered across the floor. He blinked. His father had the steadiest hand in all of Devon.

"There is more in the flask." The finely decorated boots shuffled in the debris. It could have been embarrassment. But this was Bryse of Lydnan. His father poured. A wooden cup this time. Safer.

Maybe not just for his father. His hand slipped, clumsy beyond expectation. Bryse held the cup for him exactly as a solicitous parent should.

He accepted. The politeness was unbreakable.

He realized after the first mouthful that it contained poppy.

"No."

"What?"

"Enough."

"Your funeral." The wooden cup slammed down on the

bench. The suppressed fury in his father's voice notched higher. Normality restored.

Except this was not normal. He could feel the spark of his own frustrated anger, so high. He wanted to get out, now. Even though he had no certain idea where she was.

But there was no one else to ask Bryse the inevitable question without arrest followed by death for treason.

"Why did you come here?"

"A father needs a reason to see his only son?"

His only *living* son. He thought of Bryse the Briton hanging from the gibbet at the *cwealm-stow,* the Saxon execution ground. "I meant why here and not Wareham?"

"Wareham? What the devil have you heard, and how—" The words stopped at that point. "You and your black arts," said his father.

"I did not need them in this case." He held the furious gaze. "I am a king's man."

"You—" It was cut off, as always, in the appalling ritual of pretence. But the urgency was too great this time, and the anger, suddenly volatile, was out of control.

"Did you think the king does not know what happens in the west of his realm? That he does not—"

"King. That Saxon usurper—"

"That Saxon is the only protection between you and disaster." Could he not see even now why Macsen had done what he had? "If he falls, you fall next."

"Not in the west. Look at Cornwall."

"Cornwall? That was nearly forty years ago. They rebelled and they put their trust in the Vikings, just as you want to, and when the uprising failed, the Vikings left them. They are lucky the present king's grandfather did not annihilate the whole of Cornwall. You can be sure that is what their Viking masters would have done if they had managed to keep control of the west."

It was only the dizzying pain that stopped the bitter rush of words. His mind filled with the fighting just past, with all the things he had seen and known since the Vikings had seized half of Britain. The same men who had pursued Aurinia as though she were a hunter's quarry, who would hold her now. The same men who had killed Gorei.

"Is that what you think?" The black eyes that could have been his own narrowed, the fury the perfect mirror image of all that lived inside him. "Earl Guthrum tells me otherwise."

His father, who would go to any lengths when the demons pushed him. Garrulf had seen it. Only he, the only living son, had not.

"Then you should have gone straight to Wareham."

"You believe I would have done that?"

The faint edge of surprise in his father's voice made the fury break, strong as the pain, magnified by it, as though there were no barrier over the suppressed feelings, no longer any way of holding them back, so that he was blind with it. "What else should I believe?"

There was a small sound of pulverized glass. The same clumsy movement as before. The booted feet moved. Slowly, as though they were old. His father the invincible.

A man who'd had to bury his son. He tried to hold back but the control that had always been his was gone in shreds.

"What else can I believe?" Macsen shouted with what was left of his voice.

"Then perhaps that is where I should have gone," yelled his father. "Earl Guthrum will welcome me even more now. There is no other help for him since that Viking King of the North is gone to Ireland."

"Gone to Ireland?"

"Aye. So maybe your precious Saxons don't know everything after all. But we Celts have our own connections in our own world. Halfdan chose to go and fight in Ireland. The news should be reaching Guthrum right now."

He tried to grapple with the implications, but his father's voice dragged him on like a tidal flood.

"Earl Guthrum needs me," declared Bryse of Lydnan. "I was offered more than adequate terms."

"Adequate?" The impossible word was no more than a breath through the rawness of his throat. The rage drove him, the last stubborn, utterly damning threads of disbelief. "Adequate compensation for Gorei's death?"

The rage found its counterpart.

"It might be accounted so, for a death in battle. It is all I am likely to get. As for the rest, there is no compensation payment when one kinsman causes the death of another. Is there?"

The pain closed, complete, making the words sound strange, distant, the words that had been hidden for five years, known for all that time and never spoken.

The words were true.

"No," said Macsen. There was no compensation. That was the blank wall, the complete and bitter division between them, no way round it.

But the world outside still waited, strung out in a

thousand encounters like today's, balanced on a sword's edge. It had to be seen and faced, dealt with. He took a breath through the frozen sickness, trying to shape the things in his mind, the things that had to be said.

"But that matter lies only between us." He knew he had chosen the wrong word as soon as it left his lips. There was no longer any concept between him and his father that merited the word *us*. He kept speaking, ploughing on even though it was useless. "You will not find what you want with Guthrum. He will take the whole country. He already has East Anglia. If he takes Wessex there will be no Devon, no west, either Saxon or British. He will leave nothing."

The broken glass scraped. "And what do I have now? One son who is dead and another who has squandered his loyalty. I thought you might, in the end, have realized where your true loyalty was due. It seems not. Or perhaps it now lies with your Saxon wife, although I notice that you have not once thought of her, nor she, it seems, of you. I had thought to see her kneeling at your bedside."

The link became clear, more complete and more appalling in its shape than he could have imagined.

"They tell me your wife uses her own…particular arts for healing."

You and your black arts.

"What did you say to her?"

"Only the truth. That she is not fit for you."

"You told her that?" The breath scraped out past the rawness of his throat. "Do you want to know what the truth is? She deserves better. I took her from her home with a promise of protection. The truth is that I told her if she needed help and I could not give it that she could go to you. The real truth is that I told her you were trustworthy."

His father's face was bone-white, but the rage still burned, incandescent.

"A base-born Saxon with the reputation of a sorceress, repudiated even by her own kin, is not a suitable wife for my son. I had to say that. That you had made a mistake, and I can see why. It would strike any man whose balls hadn't dropped off, that look she takes no pains to hide. I can see what you want, but a wife?"

"Yes," he said. "A wife." Because as far as he was concerned it was irrevocable and for the life of him, he could not keep the danger out of his voice. "It is not a bond to be broken."

"Bond." The rage escaped. "You sound like her, that *hell-rune,* but at least she knew how to see reason. What an outcast like her wants is wealth and the security that comes with it. She can get that without you. In fact she is doubtless in her chamber now counting the good silver I sent her to get you out of this. She—"

"You do not know. You did not even wait to find out—"

"What?" The furious eyes snapped, but there was the edge of something else. It might have been uncertainty or it might simply have been the drive of rage. There was no time to work it out. No time for anything.

"Aurinia is not here."

"She is— How do you know?" And then the rage, or whatever else might have underlain it, was obliterated, by the kind of horror that had taken shape five years ago, the bitter comprehension of what he was.

UNTAMED   209

His father walked out. He did not so much as glance at the
wolf suddenly silhouetted in the doorway, so white and silent
it might not have been real. The creature let Bryse walk past.

Aurinia's wolf came to him. Its coat was matted.
Embedded in the wet fur were heads of the small purple
heather that grew on Wytch Heath, and small twigs, hollow
like reeds. The heath-walker allowed his touch. Then, after
he had finished with the rearranged use of Brother Luke's
blameless herbs and lay down again on the mattress, the
wolf stretched out beside him, its solid head on his hand
like an unbreakable point of contact.

Sleep came like a greater darkness. Even the pain could
not hold it back. Or perhaps the pain brought it. He seemed
to swim in and out of consciousness, although it was not
poppy he had taken. The step into the blackness was short,
easier than he had thought, something that in five years he
had never deliberately sought because it was a power he
could not control and he had killed someone with it.

Gorei.

His brother's soul brushed by him in the dark but he
turned away from it, as he always did because of the guilt,
and the darkness dragged him deeper. It stifled him and he
could feel the choking rejection in his lungs, in the harsh
beat of his blood. The black tide crawled over every pore
of his naked skin. He forced himself not to fight. He kept
the image of his wife's face before his closed eyes. In the end,
he could see her.

"WILL HE LIVE?"

Aurinia watched the closed face of one of Guthrum's

fighters, the sunken, dark-rimmed eyes and the white skin above the matted beard. "If his fate allows it."

But it was not likely. The guard at her elbow touched the amulet at his neck, Thor's hammer cast in cheap bronze.

She moved on to the next man, the next face, just as white, just as closed. The guard followed her, as though he thought she might escape from the middle of a fortress garrisoned by the earl's army.

"And him?"

She reached out to pour the elixir of herbs from the cold earthenware jug. She was here and as yet unmolested. But they expected her to save lives. More important than that, they expected her to stamp out the spread of sickness before it took them all. The earl had had her caught and brought here for that purpose. His men had watched around Wytch Heath, hidden and waiting for her.

I do not want you to go near Wytch Heath.

The pale face of the stranger faded before another face, death-still against linen like this, in a chamber much finer, filled with light and shadow, the chilled skin stretched tight over the strong bones, no colour, just the soot-black crescent of closed lashes. Fire and blackness. Pain—but she did not see death, not yet, she would swear that much at least.

But that was all. For the rest, there was nothing. She was utterly sundered from the man who had married her out of such rash impulsiveness, out of a desire to do what had seemed right and was not. Because of a bond that was unreal and founded on a power that was unacceptable. A power that had brought him harm, *the kind of harm that can never be atoned.*

She pushed the vision, if it was such, out of her mind.

She thought it was the shape of her own longing, a sight born out of her own mind and her selfish hunger and her need. His need was greater. She could not take from him again.

This was her fate, in the Danish camp; it would not claim him, too.

So she turned her thoughts. She forced them to turn until there was only the Viking lying before her, the Danish warrior who looked on death behind closed eyes.

"Well?" The guard at her side caught her arm.

"It is too late." The words sounded like a death knell in the fear-soaked silence.

But truths had to be faced.

She took another step. She could not save the man lying before her. The death was here, in this long timbered room filled with the sick and the dying. The guard's grip tightened, harsh, rank with fear. Fear of death, or fear of the earl? She did not know.

The task she had been given was impossible.

"NO ONE KNOWS WHERE AURINIA IS." The door to the lamp-lit chamber slammed back on its hinges. "No one," yelled Huda. "She could be dead—"

"She is at Wareham." Macsen slotted the key in the lock of the oak chest. "Shut the door." The oiled lock on the heavy casket clicked open under his fingers, the coordination of his hands flawless, probably drug-induced.

"Wareham?"

Gold caught the light, flared.

"Wareham, with—"

"Shut the door." His voice kept low, but the same fury that had broken in front of his father burned, the edge of control scarcely discernible. The door thudded into the frame.

"She walked out," shouted Huda. "She walked away. She must have. What was she doing? Running away from you?"

"Yes."

"*You.* You should never have taken her from her home. She would have tried to go back there. Her home is what she truly wants. She will never be happy elsewhere—"

Macsen did not stop the words. Because below the vicious intensity lay the guilt, the knowledge that Huda had been tasked with keeping Aurinia safe this day, and she had left. The guilt was plain to Macsen. Huda would see the same thing in him.

Aurinia's retainer sat down on the mess of the fine bed. "What do you know?"

Macsen told him. It was brief enough because he knew little. But it was what mattered.

"How do you know?" said Huda.

"How do you think?"

The close air of the fine chamber held both the aromatic traces of herbs and the aroma of slowly drying wolf. The scent of damp fur was both earthy and real. Huda would follow it.

The wolf stood abruptly. Macsen eyeballed it and Hunter permitted Huda to extract a fragment of hollow reed from behind one of its ears.

"The river mouth. You think the wolf was with her and so he would have trailed her as far as he could, all the way to Wareham." There was a pause. "That is a rather large assumption, dangerous if it is wrong, if she is elsewhere."

"Yes."

He did not expand on it. He dragged gold out of the casket at random.

"Unless there is more." Huda's words dropped into the silent chamber, the unmoving air. Beneath the scent of dampened wolf hung the sharper secret scent of unnamed herbs and the burned seeds of henbane. And doubtless the traces of other and less material secrets. Huda, of course, was not a fool.

Macsen paused, his fingers clasped round a ransom in British gold. There would be only one chance in what he contemplated, and he had had to be so sure. He had had to know that reality and half-conscious thoughts matched the pictures of Aurinia in his mind.

Wytch Heath with its heather and its trees, and the enclosed trap of Wareham.

He waited for Huda's slackened hands to form the sign of the cross, or some other and more ancient sign. Instead, the heavy fingers moved to the sword hilt. It was unconscious. So entirely practical. His lips curved in wry acknowledgment. The gold ran cold through his fingers.

He turned his head, the movement simple because pain was gone, waiting somewhere else, in some other life. He fixed his gaze on the highly polished bronze of the mirror. It reflected firelight, gold and gems burning with each movement like a firedrake across the night sky. The damage was scarcely visible.

The Saxon eyes watched him.

"And you," asked Huda, the words low, violent. "What do you intend to do? Spend your time decking yourself out like some over-wealthy British prince?"

"Yes."

The movement to the sword hilt this time was deliberate, meant to be seen.

"They will take that off you at the gate if you still wear it." He shoved rings over the fingers of his right hand. The left was too broken.

"The—"

"Of course, you can always make a present of it to Guthrum. If you come with me."

"With you?"

There was only one way. His father had shown it to him, although he had not intended this. He realized what he had put on his hand, the ring his father had once given him, which belonged to the eldest son. He would not wear it again.

"Yes. With me. To Wareham."

"You are going to present yourself at the gates of Wareham? What? Straight to Earl Guthrum? Looking like that?"

Something else caught his eye, a gilded shape among the shattered glass on the floor, wrought so finely that the outspread wings and the ravening claws seemed to move. A token. His hand closed over it. The ring that his father had given him glittered.

"How else should I look? I am offering him most of Devon."

THEY LET HER STOP ONLY AFTER it was full dark, the day's end discernible even in the crucible of the firelit room.

Aurinia touched the familiar rune shapes at her girdle. Nothing remained of the bright healing power. It was gone, like a freshwater stream swallowed by a bitter salt ocean. She could no longer hold the herb flask in her hands. She had worked with those she might be able to save and those she could not. She stepped back, the guard behind her so close her shoulder brushed the hard leather of his jerkin. There was a rush of words, Danish and incomprehensible. Her skin crawled. She did not know what would happen next.

"Take her out." It was the earl's physician who spoke in his passable English, tired and irritable, probably as afraid as she was. The tide was not stoppable, not if the earl stayed with so many men crowded into this place. The physician understood that as well as she did.

"Go." The rest lapsed into Danish. The guard laughed, his head over hers, breath touching the hot skin of her neck, thin-fingered hand hard round her arm.

The cold of the world outside hit her like a blow, so sharp after the warmth and close air of the sickroom that her senses swam. The torchlit night was filled with the men's voices borne on the wind, raised and clear, *mod-ful,* mood-proud. The sound of sudden laughter split the dark, different from her guard's, bright and sharp-edged. Dangerous as cut glass.

She walked toward it, caught by the half-heard voice, the streaming threads of darkness mixed with flame like a waking dream in the spirit-filled void between dark and light.

"Hold back." Her guard clawed at her, the fear in him suddenly palpable, the same fear that had gripped the physician. "The guests from the hall. Get back. They have to pass this way to get to the sleeping quarters."

He pulled at her, but she would not turn away, could not, as though she were caught on a spell-thread. Enchanted.

The man's grip slipped. Across the courtyard, another voice answered that dangerous laughter.

"It is the Jarl." Her guard was desperate. Never be the bringer of bad tidings to a powerful man, and the tidings from the sickroom were dire. He hauled on her arm, vicious. But it was too late. Torchlight caught them full on.

There were two men, and the servants bearing flaming brands. Earl Guthrum's power was massive. It fitted his huge fair frame like a cloak. It radiated outward, blunt and strong and filled with something she recognized at a level deeper than reason, soul-deep—the driving lash of hunger.

Not hunger for the necessary and life-giving things she wanted, for the human bond that gave existence on this earth its meaning. For a home.

That fierce will craved space for the exercise of its over-riding power. The earl would take that space by conquest and she had been blind to the coming storm, too ignorant and enclosed in her own world, to see. The burgeoning power was volatile, hard to contain because it was deeply thwarted.

The instinctive fear in her guard seemed to spread, like winter's chill, through her own flesh. Even though right now, at this moment, the earl was pleased by something.

He paused. The man beside him had already stopped walking. The earl's companion was dark, half in shadow and half in light.

Aurinia's heart stood still, all the breath in her body and the blood in her veins. All her being. He turned his head and in that moment the torchbearer moved.

Brightness spilled across the courtyard, running like flame through dry kindling, like the lamp striking light in the empty chamber at Wytch Heath, pushing back the dark, unleashing the golden brilliant warmth that brought life. She could feel it inside her despite the dark and the cold of a Danish fortress filled with the dying and the battle-hungry. For an instant it was the only thing that existed.

Nothing else matters. Nothing apart from this.

And then reality came back, the bitter world and its danger, the sacrifices that were impossible.

She looked at Macsen.

CHAPTER

12

The Viking earl had scarcely paused in his stride and now he swung back, still speaking. Aurinia thought he did not notice her where she stood half-obscured by shadows, rooted to the spot out of shock. His attention was wholly focused, locked on the glittering figure at his side.

On Macsen.

"Everything you want is in your chamber. Your servant is already there. I sent the Frankish wine. It's good. We took it from some thane's estate near Sarum. Saxon plunder. You should enjoy it."

"I shall."

She heard the hint of that deep laughter, confident and danger-laden. Like something *death-fæg*. Reckless enough to challenge fate. A gust of wind made the torch fire flare. The movement of the lithe, beautifully poised body was restless. Gold caught the uneasy light of the flame, glittered like a dragon's treasure hoard.

"Everything you want," said Guthrum easily. "I am a generous gift-giver." A lord giving patronage, the borrowed stature of a king. His English was perfect.

Macsen's dark gaze had swept past her, no pause. The heavy, eight-stranded gold moved with the sudden tilt of his head and she was watching a stranger, as hard-edged and high-hearted as the sound of his laughter had been. A thane's pride. *Over-mod.* Arrogant.

"The gifts," began the earl.

"Find me a girl," said Macsen. He used a soldier's word, one that could have applied to any of the painted faces in the shadows at Fearnros.

The shout of laughter that followed from Guthrum was immediate, as easy as his offer of other gifts had been, just as careless.

"Come and choo—"

"That one." The black gaze pinned her where she had fallen back with her guard into the shadows. The world stopped.

The huge red-bearded Viking earl did not speak and she thought at first that it was out of confusion because he had not seen her. And then she realized. He had noticed her from the start. He noticed everything the way a beast of prey does. He was a man leading an army into a hostile country with the intention of taking it. He had the confidence and the sharp intelligence to win. His cold blue eyes gave nothing. But she saw his mind work.

"She is nothing. I have better."

"I asked for her."

The earl had moved away even as he had spoken. Now he stopped, the massive shoulders straight. He turned his head.

"You would find she was not worth your while."

"Perhaps." Restless movement brought the glitter of gold into the flickering light, and with it the hard edge of power, volatile and dangerous, like a man who has taken a reckless step and now will not draw back from it.

Men fought for pride, either in battle or over the mead-bench, the potentially lethal confrontation so common-place. She could sense the hidden lash of impatience it brought in Guthrum. A weakness.

"She is what I want." The man she had chosen to marry looked at her and the invincible core, the deep danger were suddenly naked.

Her heart thudded out of time. She thought the bitter desperate sound of her breath would be heard. The power inside him was so strong, an entirely different thing from the glittering show of volatile pride. Bedrock deep. She thought Guthrum would see it. But the impatience blinded his eyes and he saw what he expected, the hard brittle edge of slighted pride.

Perhaps something communicated itself to her guard because he thrust forward, pushing himself in front of her, his eyes on the dangerous stranger. "Lord, she is not suitable. She—"

"I did not ask you." The cold disdain cut off the words. It could have been Bryse standing in the tapestried chamber at Fearnros and speaking of Britain. The wind lifted a heavy cloak, rich with thick braid. The figure paused, half-turned, wreathed in flame and thin trails of smoke.

"The jarl is the gift-giver," said Macsen. "I have his assurance." It was not phrased like a question, but like a statement of faith in a promise, twisted to mean what had not been intended. It flattered and it hung like a trap.

The impatience, the overmastering power that was Guthrum's snapped. The flat of his hand shot out so fast she could neither move nor breathe. Her guard collapsed, the thin-fingered hand still tight round her arm nearly taking her down with him. She turned toward him, the impulse to do something instinctive.

But the man was already scrambling to his feet. There was no blood. His eyes were terrified and she knew what the blow had been for. For being clumsy enough to put his leader in such a difficult position, for letting a captive be seen when the purpose she was here for had the ability to reveal a weakness that was potentially damning.

She stayed still, her breath fast, watching the Viking earl who commanded an invasion army. She did not turn her head to look on the dark figure beside him, though she was aware, through every fibre of her being, of his size and the lethal, bated sense of power, of his closeness in the cool night of the Viking yard.

She stood, motionless and apart. She would not betray by one glance or one movement all that lay at stake.

"Well?" said her husband, the dark earthy voice smooth as silk. "That is settled. Unless there is some other problem that—"

"There is none." The furious blue-grey eyes of the Viking Jarl met hers for an instant beyond time, the impact like the slash of tempered steel. "None," said Earl Guthrum. The harsh gaze passed on. "Get her ready."

Her heart thundered.

The guard stepped forward. His sharp-fingered grip, newly vicious with rage and humiliation and the aftermath of terror, fastened on her arm like claws. She made no sound. Her husband did not look.

She watched King Alfred's man walk away, the Viking torchbearers holding fire over his head, streaming flame and black, black shadows.

The guard took her back inside.

IF SHE BREATHED ONE WORD about why she was here, if she even suggested the possibility that there might be something wrong at the Viking camp, they would kill her.

Aurinia thought her guard, nursing slowly forming bruises, would rather have killed her now. But he did not dare touch her again. She had one more purpose, to pleasure the earl's guest.

The women took her.

It was a different world, one she had never entered, the hidden world that belonged behind the delicate painted faces she had seen at Fearnros, a concubine's world. It had one purpose, to provide for the pleasures of the senses.

The women's chamber was filled with firelight, heavy with scent from the myriad lamps, from the fire made with applewood and garnished with lavender heads, from warmed skin. The fire shone off bright colours, garish tapestries that stopped the draughts, odd cushions, slender-throated flasks of wine, scraps of bright cloth, clothes strewn across benches, shoes in dyed colours, a silver-backed mirror and someone's tweezers, a broken comb case, a discarded head veil, tarnished bronze lamps. In the cold light of day it would be as tawdry as a midden. In the fire and lamp light, it dazzled the senses.

The women never stopped speaking, not just Danish or English, but languages she had never heard, whispering and laughing. Their garments rustled like the plumage of dainty, many-coloured birds, a shower of sharp-eyed jackdaws about to mob their prey.

Aurinia had to fight not to step back, the old bitter hatred of crowds like bile in her throat, the shaming fear. She blocked it out. It did not matter. Nothing mattered except Macsen and why he was here and how, and what Earl Guthrum might do to a king's man.

She slapped away the first hand that reached out to pluck at her plain gown. She had already turned for the door when it opened on a woman who was different. Not because of her face, which was painted with as much skill as the rest of the women in the room, or because of her beauty or her bright clothes, but because of some inner quality that burned through like a beacon fire.

"Well? What have you done? Is the bath ready? The scented oil? The clothes?"

The volatile chaos resolved itself into order, space opened round Aurinia, the fresh trace of outside air.

It was her elemental weariness that allowed it to happen. That and the sharp restless flick of awareness inside her skin.

She knew, that woman with the assessing eyes. They all

knew. The warm dizzying air of that concubines' chamber
was rife with it—anticipation.

"Come, lady." The cool slanting eyes were not unfriendly.
"You must bathe now and we will make you ready."

Get her ready.

The thoughts in her head swirled, vivid and heated and
chaotic, Macsen's face in the torchlight, the shadowed
power of his body, the same restlessness, like fire held back.
The way he had looked at her and the hard bright edge that
was new and sharply dangerous.

The way he had looked and what he had said.

She is what I want.

The power had passed between them like flame.

The flock of women closed round her, the small unfamiliar hands stripped her clothes. They bathed her, the
water hot, scented, slick against her skin and hair, the
warmth touching everywhere, penetrating the ache in her
back, first stinging then soothing the small scratches from
her fall in the forest, the bruise on her arm.

The women sang. Their voices made a pattern in her
head. She realized what the scent in the water was, rosemary
and thyme, then orris root and lovage chanted over—the
most carnal and elemental of love spells. When her body
moved in reaction, she heard the glittering laughter of the
painted women and the spell broke.

"See…she cannot wait for what her man will take, for
his body over hers…"

Aurinia jerked away, breaking their grip, splashing
scented water over the rush-strewn floor, her eyes open.

"You must excuse them, Lady. They are jealous. Is that not so?" The clear-eyed woman helped her out of the bath.

"The earl's guest is a virile man and they would happily take him between their thighs. And he is rich. They wish he had chosen one of them to warm his bed, then they might have a double reward, in silver and gifts, and in the night's pleasure. Come, Lady. Or perhaps they will steal your place at his side." There was a question behind the frank words, a question that was dangerous.

"That place is mine." She let the words strike in the close air of the room, as frank and deliberate as the words of the women around her. She turned her head and the moment passed. The women thronged round her with drying-cloths and scented oils for her hot skin, nothing more dangerous this time than an exotic mix of roses and spice. But the carnal spell was not broken. It possessed her, a heady urge and a deep need that drove her.

The woman who looked back at her from the polished, full-length sheet of bronze was not herself. It was some fey creature whose painted eyes glittered with feverish light, whose face, dead-white, was flushed along the cheekbones with colour, the way warmth infuses the skin at the moment of pleasuring. Her skin jumped with tension at the slightest brush of her borrowed clothes when she moved. Her breath showed shallow in the fullness and the rapid rise and fall of her breasts.

The iron rune-shapes at her girdle rustled when she walked away. It was the only thing she had kept of herself.

The woman who had spoken led her outside. In the chill darkness, they paused.

"My name is Rosamund. I have a small amount of influence, sometimes even with the earl." Aurinia received an oblique glance. "I can take you to the Briton's chamber." There was a pause. "So. You will go to him?" There was the same unspoken question as before in her elegant voice with its rippling accent.

"Yes." It was all Aurinia said. There was no explanation possible and the danger writhed round them like the smoke from the torches, like the half-heard snatches of the voices of the Danish warriors in the dark.

Rosamund made no reply. But it was as though there were some bizarre sense of comradeship in the middle of a hostile masculine world. She inclined her head, as though Aurinia had answered a question that was far different. Perhaps that was so.

He was her husband and he had come here. She did not know whether their marriage could survive the damage, or even whether it should.

But she would have gone to him for a single night and a coin of silver. Nothing else was possible.

AURINIA HEARD HIS VOICE FIRST, just that, like dark magic. She paused, with her hand on the door. Her heart thundered and she could not make her body move. But there were people behind her, the other woman, warriors who would see her and wonder. Dull gold light spilled from the chamber, pinpointing her in the dark. She went in.

The light dazzled her, even in that short space of walking through the cold dark toward his room. Her husband dazzled her.

She watched the light play over the glittering display of gold, the dark gleam of his hair, the lamp glow that slid off muscular planes and angles as he moved.

The door shut. She did not know what to say, what to do, how to begin. So much crowded in her head and her heart and her heated blood, and now that he was here, and real, and with her, none of it seemed possible. She thought she was shaking.

He turned, with that restless feral abruptness, so that the candle flames guttered, and it was the dark stranger of Earl Guthrum's courtyard that she saw, hard-edged and laden with danger. His eyes glittered, fixed on her face, her body, intensely black, the pupils widely distended, almost blurred. It was as though he burned.

Aurinia moved toward him, one step across the packed-earth floor. Her bright skirts swished against her legs. Another step. The warmth of embers from a banked fire surrounded her, caressing a body already intensely, achingly aware of warmth and movement and breath. The heady, almost cloying, scent of spice and flowers rose from her skin, from the folds of her dress, from the bared line of her throat and the half-exposed curve of her breast.

The brooches on her tunic caught the light, the cheap copper bangles at her wrist where once there had been pure gold from his gift, in another lifetime, from another man, not this harsh, dazzling stranger. A fine gift to a different woman, not the mad, desperate, overwrought creature in a concubine's clothes. Different people, who had believed things that were impossible and were now gone, lost.

But she still kept walking, as though drawn on the spell-thread. Her concubine's body burned, and her heart. Her heart— There were no words for such pain. For disaster.

She stopped when he was close enough to touch her, just by breathing. Just by the slightest movement of one heavy, gold-weighted hand. She did not think he would do it and in truth, he stayed back, the terrible power locked down, yet felt through every vulnerable, tightly stretched sense.

Then her gaze meshed with his and she knew that he would touch her, that there would be no restraint.

He touched her shoulder, the brush of that crushing hand impossibly light, and the power leapt between them. She did not draw back, but watched his face until she could no longer see it and his mouth came down on hers.

The first touch of his lips shocked through her body. Her hands moved up, fisted in the black silk of his hair. Her mouth sought his, the firmness, the male taste, the hot power. His arms closed round her, trapping her, holding her so completely that the breath left her body, caught against that black demanding mouth.

He tasted of darkness and power, of an anger that was wholly new, a rage deeply hidden. He tasted of mad emotion, sex, the trace of something that wakened the healer's instincts in her, something physical, like an elusive scent she should know. She could not concentrate. She could feel nothing but him and the consuming flames, the physical contact she craved, the bitter strength in each moving muscle locked against her, the blood-gorged hardness of his manhood. Her own response was complete.

He was still careful with her. She knew that in some deep

part of her own mind. She held him, her hands kneading the tight solid mass of his shoulders, her thighs twined with his, the cheap skirts already bunched and tangled under his hands.

They got as far as the bed. She felt his weight, the solid mass of his body, its deep sense-maddening fineness. She was intensely aware of its strength, the dangerousness of its power. But she would not draw back. She was simply driven by need and guilt and all the mad depths of desire, the intoxicating power of touching him when she had thought she would never see him again. The impossible feelings in her heart.

She fell with him against the bed, her body rolling with his. She was blind to everything except need, reckless with it, mindless with the feel of his hands moulding the contours of her body, the touch of his mouth on her skin. She pressed close, absorbing the hard-locked power.

Her breath caught when his hand passed over the bruises on her arm. The almost imperceptible sound was cut off, but something made him stop. The short sleeve of her bright dress was pushed back. Her arm was bare except for the thin bracelet twisted like a copper snake with red enameled eyes. He could see.

"Who hurt you?"

He was motionless, the heavy sinuous length of his body stretched out beside her in the bed, alive with the bated power like a beast of prey, and her breath came shallow and fast from his loving. She forced speech through her tight throat.

"It is nothing." Her voice was unsteady. She fought to master it, to quell the chaotic disaster of her thoughts, the savage ache in her body. Her feverish hands dragged at her tumbled clothes. "It was only the guard. The—"

He made some movement. It was slight, but the power hit her like a wave. She went still in the tangled bedclothes. The bright garish dress was sliding off her body where he had touched her. The defensive instinct that had become so strong in her made her want to cover herself. She did not move. He did. His hand took hers. The viciously strained power did not slip. The solid fingers simply twined with hers. It was gentle. She thought something inside her heart broke.

"Say it." His voice, roughened in a way that was not his, was quite steady.

"There is nothing else." She kept her voice just as even as his, speaking slowly, as though feeling her way without light, her eyes fixed on the dark gaze that was suddenly fathoms deep and black. "It was naught."

She thought at first that he did not believe her. She pitched her voice clearly, steady and filled with a truth that was undeniable.

"It is only that he had to keep me. Just like an ordinary prisoner…"

The dark head moved in acknowledgment. He believed her. Her gaze dropped to where his fingers meshed with hers. It was the broken hand. Her sight was blurred so that she could hardly see. He said nothing and so her words rushed on.

"He did not want to let me go. You see—" She stopped.

"Yes. Like me." He let go. He stood up. She stared at her empty hand through an obscuring mist.

"What do you mean?"

"I wanted to keep you when it was wrong." He picked something up. There was a small clink. "You left me. Did you not?"

Wine splashed into a beaker made of glass, Jarl Guthrum's plundered Frankish wine. Taken from some Saxon.

She really ought to say *yes*.

"I WANT TO KNOW WHERE MY son is," yelled Bryse in English.

Of course they kept him waiting, the thrice-damned Saxon king and his retinue of paid thugs. Bastards. He paced the antechamber, his feet scuffing the rushes. They knew something. More than he did. He could tell by their lying English faces. More than a father knew about his own son.

How long did it take to unearth one devious king? The tapestry bellied out from the wall with the speed of his passage, a riot of colour and gold. Fine. He saw what it was. Some half-witted West Saxon setting foot for the first time on a British shore. Clutching a sceptre topped by a dragon. Usurper.

Peasant.

He kicked a table and a book fell off. He did not think Saxons read. He looked at it. Anything to keep his mind from running totally insane over an idiot son with the wits bashed out of his head doing heaven knew what for that…that *woman*.

He could see her face, strikingly perfect, bewitching. Reprehensibly young to him. No one was supposed to be married that young. Even if he had been himself. Once. He thought of his wife. He never thought of his wife because he had not been able to stand the loss. No reason to think of her now. She was nothing like that blonde Saxon witch.

He could see the look in the Saxon woman's eyes when she had walked out, like death.

He had believed she had taken his offer. He had believed—

He still believed it. The book was in Latin. Mabon's balls. He really looked at it. Saint Augustine. There was the beginning of a conventional translation. Some scribe's painstakingly unoriginal hand-work. A separate piece of parchment, written in a different hand, slid out.

I would know whether, it declared, *after the parting of the body and the soul...*

After the *what?*

Whether I shall know more? asked the different hand, black and thickly spiked, so loaded with power and impatience that a mere monkly scribe would have been thrown out of the monastery for it.

For I cannot find anything better in man than that he have knowledge and nothing worse than... There followed some crossings out, like a draft in the making written by someone still seeking the best phrase, and then his narrowed eyes made it out.

...nothing worse than ignorance.

He dropped the parchment as though it had burned him. The light caught something in the corner, not a word but a drawing—a dragon, the kind that belonged to only one man and was more usually carried about on an unnecessarily ostentatious battle standard.

He did not believe it. He bent down for a closer look, which was how the benighted Saxon found him crawling on all fours across the floor like a beast. He thought at first it was the dangerous, dragon-wielding, Latin-speaking king. The door shut. The lamps flared and he realized it was Garrulf, the so-called cousin. Of course, Alfred would not come himself.

"Lord?" The man's brows raised. He leaned against the door frame in a faultless assumption of ease. But it was a fighter's stance. The hostility in the chamber could have burned it down.

Hang that. Bryse did not give a curse. He stood up. A Briton had twice the wits of some brute Saxon. He was quite prepared to commit murder, but there were other ways. He would get the truth before they had even worked out that he had asked for it. Subtlety first.

"I want my son."

The naked, damning words hit the tapestried walls and bounced off again, reverberating straight through him, words he had never said since that night five years ago when Macsen had come to tell him that Gorei was dead. No, for longer than that. He could not remember how long.

Such words would kill him. They were true.

"You left me," Macsen said.

The single short word of agreement hung on the edge of Aurinia's tongue, waiting only for her will to give it form. She watched the dark-shadowed figure in its gleaming gold.

You are not part of his world. You will ruin his life and he will end up hating you for it. I am merely asking you to end it now rather than later, after you have brought down the man you claim so glibly to care about.

She thought she had already ruined him. At the very least

she had placed him in a danger that was impossible. Earl Guthrum's wine poured into the glass in his hand. He poured too much. The wine slopped, as though he could not quite control what he did. She had seen him before battle. She had seen him in Guthrum's courtyard alone. She had seen him fight. She frowned.

"You wanted to go," he said.

Yes.

Wine spilled on the floor, like spilled mead soaking the rushes before her wedding, in Judith's chamber at Fearnros with the owls beating at the window like messengers. Wisdom and hidden truth.

"I thought that I should." She had taken a step where there was no firm ground. There was no longer even right or wrong. "What I did, was walk out from Fearnros. I walked, without knowing in truth what I should do, or where I should go."

"And your steps took you toward your home."

"Yes." Except, even her home seemed no longer hers. Her mind held room only for him. "But—" She watched the glass in his large hand. Of course, he had told her not to go there, and the consequences…the consequences were what he bore now. "I am sorry."

The faint scent of wine reached her. Hidden truth.

"I wanted to find what was right," she said. "I—" What? There was no other way forward except through the bitter mire of disaster. "I spoke with your father."

He put the claw-footed beaker down. How he managed that without shattering the expensive amber glass, she did not know. But it stayed whole.

"What exactly did he say?"

She bit her lip. She thought of the fierce warrior, his dark hair streaked with grey, the prince with his fine British heritage, his rage. And the pain that lay beneath it, concealed so very carefully. She thought of what lay beyond that, the thing that was so precious, beyond her dreaming, a father's love.

"It does not matter what he said or that he was the one to speak of things I already knew. It could make no difference. I saw my own truth. I am not a fit wife." It made her shake. But she had to say the words. There was no other way he could come through this. He had given her his pledge when he had married her. An honour-word was everything to a man like him, even unto death in a Viking fortress, to ruin.

She watched him and her mind and her body ached for him. Her skin still burned from the heat of his touch, as though she felt it even now. Her body had responded to his, just as the bright, volatile fire in him had responded to her. Desire. A bond. And yet not so, even if it was everything that her empty heart craved.

"I cannot deny my desire for you, or what I have taken from you." *The hunger for you that knew no bounds from the first moment. The guilt of what I took. And I desire you still.*

I would still take. She sat straight. The borrowed dress rustled, scent rose from her heated skin. It was the tawdry trick of the love-spell, and it was her own desire.

"I wanted to be with you." She forced herself to say the painful truth because every instinct in her told her that it had to be said to him. But the other side of the truth needed saying, too.

"But I cannot be more to you than you see now. I am fit to be a concubine. I am not fit to be a wife."

13

"That is not true!" Macsen yelled.

He sought for control. The glittering creature he had married did not look at him.

I am fit to be a concubine. I am not fit to be a wife.

She was so close to him that the scent of flowers caught at him. So close. But he could not dare to touch her again, not with so little control. So he moved back.

Aurinia did not have a huge reason to believe his words. Because of the life she had led until this moment. Because of all the things his father must have said. Because of his own behaviour the instant he had had her near him again.

He could remember little except the kind of need that could kill things. His body still ached, full, driven with the bitter urgency. Her scent caught at him, the sight of her in the bright dress, her slender limbs and her pale skin. His fists were clenched and he did want to do murder. Someone like her would smell the taint of it.

He turned away. In his mind, he saw the blue bruises on her arm. He took a breath before he smashed something. There was silence between them. He wanted to break it by yelling out the words he had said before, that she was his wife.

But that was because he wanted to keep her, because she gave him something that approached magic and he wanted to possess it. The truth was that in the end there was no difference between him and Guthrum's prison guard.

Except that there had to be a difference. Otherwise, all that was locked inside him meant nothing.

He had sworn to this. She had no one else to rely on. He had to provide what she wanted, whatever it was. Marriage or none.

That was an equal truth.

There were so many aspects of truth, so many she did not know.

They were what she deserved.

"There are things you need to understand about who I am." He could not see what the outcome would be, only that she had to know. "About *what* I am." He turned round so that he could see her face. "About why my father said what he did to you."

She was watching him. He could read nothing in her eyes, not even the pain that he knew was there. She simply sat on the crushed bed in the clothes the Vikings had given her, with the danger he had pushed her into waiting outside the door, and she watched him.

"I told you of the division between my father and

myself." The past pressed on him in the brightly lit chamber and the death-shadows crowded round him, dark and unreal. Perhaps they had not had their fill yet.

"You mean because your family is British and not Saxon."

He shook his head, as much to clear it of the grasping shadows as in negation. "That is only part of it, the starting point."

He tried to marshal his thoughts, to find the right words through the murderous press of feelings, the disorienting aftermath of the herbs he had taken, the edge of pain like an abyss. He had picked up the wine beaker when he became aware that she had come toward him.

It did not seem possible. He caught the rustle of her dress first, then the over-sweet scent that had nothing to do with her fineness and everything to do with disaster. He stepped away, forced to catch the edge of the table for balance because of the disorienting blackness, transferring the glass to his left hand. She stopped well before they touched, which was fitting.

He looked up. But she did not back away. The grey eyes that held witchcraft met his.

"It is about Gorei," she said, and the pain hit him like an axe blow. He could not show it. The words came, where before there had been none.

"My father had two sons. Gorei was my younger brother. I caused his death. My father cannot forgive me. There isn't a reason why he should."

He put the glass beaker down. She watched, his hand not his face. She said nothing in reply. Her eyes were sharply focused, seemingly caught by the movement of his hand round the glass.

"Will you drink that?"

He let go, confused by what was irrelevant. He did not know why he had poured it, except for something to do with his hands.

"No," he said, and then because he was distracted, "I cannot." He was not that mad. Sheer practicality told him he would not get back to Fearnros without fighting. He could not compound what he had already—

"Because of what you have already taken." It was not a question, even though she would not be able to tell. Surely? Perhaps because of his eyes being still slightly blurred, or because of some lingering scent on his clothes or in his hair? But that was not enough.

Yet she had read whatever was or was not to be seen.

That was when he knew she really did have the kind of witchcraft that could get you killed with stones.

"Why did you take herbs that were so dangerous?" asked Aurinia and the ground opened up like a pit at his feet, one step and there would be no going back.

"The wolf came back to Fearnros without you and I...I had to be very sure where you were." It was disjointed and senseless, but Aurinia would know.

She did not say anything and neither did she look up.

"Such visions do not come for the asking," he said.

The fair head bent. No need to explain further, not to her. He heard the soft breath she took before she spoke.

"You wished to rescue me," she said, as though there could possibly have been doubt. The sharp movement he made might have betrayed him, but she was still speaking, slowly, her concentration on every word, as though unraveling the complexities of what to him was brutally simple.

"You wanted to rescue me because it was right," said her soft English voice. "Because you felt it was your responsibility to protect me from harm, however that harm came—" This time it was impossible to miss the movement, volatile and not under control, like everything that lived inside him. He beat it down, hearing the tightness in her breath. She still did not look at his face.

"In the same way, you wanted to protect Gorei."

The unexpectedness caught him, sent the pain spiraling. His body stilled for an instant that was outside time, the way it would sometimes after a battle wound, as though to absorb the force of the blow. It must have been the hesitation that allowed her to touch him.

"That is the truth. You acted for what was right." Her fingers tangled with his and he knew why she had not looked up, what had caught her attention and held it.

"That is when you must have nearly lost this hand. It was when Gorei died," said his wife and he was back in the battle at Wilton in the first year of the king's reign. He and Gorei and the rest of the king's men caught in the disaster that had followed so quickly after the first tenuous victory against the Vikings. Defeat and the dead past counting, the churned earth slick with blood beneath his body. He remembered crawling through the mud one handed, mad with pain, knowing in his heart he was too late. The freezing rain striking him, and Gorei…Gorei with the life flowing out of him in one red stream and nothing that could be done.

Nothing.

"There was no rightness." The concept did not exist. "It might have been death in battle, but the path had been set before that." He slid his hand smoothly from hers. The bones ached. "I set it."

He tried to focus on the moment, on this room, on the explanation that had to be given, to find the words.

"My brother joined the king's army because of me. I made the choice and he followed." He watched his wife's bent head and knew what the truth was.

"You see," he said, "sometimes I can persuade people." *Like Gorei. Like you.* He watched the woman who had given up her home and her way of life for him. Light suddenly shifted over the bright gleam of her hair.

"Sometimes." She looked up, catching him off guard, sending him far off balance the way only she could. Her eyes were steady. "As you have persuaded Earl Guthrum."

"That—" He stopped it. The offer with Guthrum hung by less than a thread, a matter of bluff and fortuitous circumstance. There was no trust in it and no guarantee of the outcome. The danger he had brought on his wife nearly killed him.

"It is hard to persuade people if they do not want something already." The grey eyes watched him, clear as in the moment he had first seen her. "And if they want it, they will take it anyway. People make their own decisions."

The clear gaze held him, as though there were no barrier, as though he had not taken from her. But he could not accept that. He forced his mind back on the track of truth, on what had to be said about his brother.

"Gorei was always headstrong, impulsive—" He stopped the thoughts because they sounded traitorous. Gorei was dead. Dead before his life had begun.

"There was no fair match. Gorei was my younger brother. He was no more than eighteen. He listened to everything I ever said." The bile rose in his throat, the familiar coldness. "Besides, that was not all I did. It was not a matter of simple persuasion."

You and your black arts. He had used more than the words of ordinary straightforward persuasion, just as he had with her.

With his wife, he had used all the force of a bond between them that had no existence beyond the unreal, uncontrolled power in his own mind, and if he had stopped short of claiming the future as he had once tried to claim it for Gorei, that made no difference.

He had forced Aurinia's hand in the same way. Because he was crazed. Because he had wanted her too much, so much that it was like madness in the blood with nothing left to curb it. That bitter wanting still lived in him, in each muscle of his body tightened to harshness because she was near, not even touching. It lived in his mind.

The clear eyes narrowed and she understood, in part. There was no surprise.

"It was what you saw," said Aurinia. She knew. "You saw Gorei's future."

Not all of it, but enough. More than enough.

"I saw shadows and I told him of them. What I did not see is what they meant." He made no pause and somehow he found the words for the rest of how it had been. The black shadows touched him with such coldness.

"I did not see how his death would follow. And when it did come—" He collected the well-pitched voice that could persuade people to anything and said the worst words it was possible for a man to say. "I could do nothing to prevent it. I wanted to help my brother and I could not. I could not even be near him until it was too late."

He held her gaze because there was no going back. She had to know the truth about him and what he had done.

"What you have to understand is the responsibility I have for my brother's death, for robbing my father of a son he loved. There is no way to repair such a loss, both because of the way my father cared about Gorei and because there is no compensation possible for a death within the same kindred."

She would understand that last particularly, being Saxon. No payment could be given and no vengeance could be taken that would wipe the slate clean, that would rebuild loss and satisfy honour.

"Because there is no proper ending for such loss, there is nothing that my father can do, and so the loss eats at him. I can see that and I can see that there is no way to repair whatever there was between my father and myself. But now you have suffered for it, too. That is why he feels such bitterness and how he transferred it to you."

Nothing else remained to him and he had no other way to provide for what she wanted, to stay true to what he had sworn, true to her. He said the only thing left to offer.

"When we go from here, you do not have to stay with me."

IT WAS A FAIR OFFER. AURINIA'S hands shook. She could take it. If she did, she would give him back his freedom, and one day, perhaps, it might be safe enough for her to go home. She could have Wytch Heath, her own domain, and everything in it. Safety.

She took his hand. The movement startled him. Her fingers closed round the broken hand with its flattened knuckles, the solid flesh, strength. The power flared between them like something living. She heard the sudden fast catch of his breath.

When we go from here, he had said. She stood close to him, her body tense in the bright tawdry dress meant for seduction, her flesh scented with love charms, her skin still glowing from the passionate touch of his mouth. She held onto his hand, sensing the quick breath in him and the black edge of pain that had been hidden before. So many hidden things. *When we go from here.* That left tonight. The awareness of him nearly killed her, and the mad beating of her heart.

Tonight.

She knew what her task was. She needed no thoughts of the mind. It was in her heart and it always had been. The metal shapes at her girdle rustled as she moved. She touched her lips to his.

The passion was still there, like a miracle, like a thread of pure fire that burned between the two of them, deep and intense and edged with the flame's brilliance, something that would never be extinguished.

The touch of her lips did not hold the dark erotic skill of his. It held the imprint of her desperation. But it was true, and she had shocked him, the way she had with that first bold touch on his hand. It robbed him of balance. She pressed her body against his, her mouth moulding to the curved flexible warmth of his lips and she took his breath. She forced the response he would have held back. She knew it with the instinct that was born in women and needed no concubine's training.

Her own breath caught on a deep surge of arousal and desire, of exultant power and sharp fear. He did not pull away from her, for all his strength. Her lips cleaved to the heat of his and both the fear and the harsh edge of exultation mixed.

There was all that she was in that kiss, everything that she knew how to give pressed into that fragile instant of time, the inexplicable golden power that healed souls, all that she had learned in the experience of her life. Even the unexplored shadows of what she might become.

Her touch was filled with the love she could not declare and with the edge of fire, the fire that scorched through blood and bone every time she touched him. Yet even the fiery need was new, transformed into its true shape. It was not just her need of him like a consuming hunger, but the deeper, more sharply felt need to help him, visceral and so complete that it consumed everything, its very completeness and possession of her soul a paradoxical source of strength.

Nothing mattered except this moment, now, this man whom she touched.

Her arms closed round him and her body, clean and warmed and scented, arrayed in thin linen already slipping from her skin, cleaved to his. She felt the harsh muscle and the fierce strength, the alien, ruthlessly masculine lines.

She sensed the hidden things, the crippling mass of pain,

physical and of the heart. She saw through to that and she touched it, because she was herself and no other, and surely she was meant for him? Surely... Her mouth and her body moulded to his. The moment spun out, timeless, and then she felt him draw back, the first bitter movement of that unstoppable strength.

"Macsen." Their breath still touched, the word finding its shape against the fierce erotic heat of his skin, the thick tumbled mass of his hair, as black as the raven's wing, the messenger of change, of war and bliss.

"Stay with me." Her lips grazed the smooth dense skin over his cheekbone, the rougher line of his jaw.

"Stay." She touched the curve of his throat, the smooth hollow at its base that hid the fast pulse of his blood. She still touched him and the love scent rose from her heated skin. Her body arched against the hard lines of his and she felt all the fierce volatile power of male desire.

"Bed me."

He neither moved nor spoke, even now, with the bright power in his blood and the sheen of desire on his skin. Her heart beat as though it would choke her. She had lost.

After all. After everything.

"Be with me tonight."

He had said that much—that whatever happened afterward, there would be tonight. Her fingers touched the thick muscle of his back, the solid power. She tried to hold on to whatever strength she had left. "Give me that much. Touch me as you did before. Give me..."

"What? The same kind of madness?"

She met his eyes. She forced herself to raise her head.

"Yes. If that is what there is."

She kept her gaze quite steady and the last of the strength, the steel-hard determination did not leave her. She focused on his eyes and the touch of his body and she knew quite well that the madness was there. But there were other things too.

Bryse had said that his bane, the quality that could bring him down, was the uncanny knowledge of things that did not exist. But Bryse was wrong, as he was about so many things. She understood where the only vulnerable point in him lay, just as she knew the source of his strength. They were the same.

She knew the words. If she had the courage to use them.

"I do not want to be alone," she said.

She focused on his eyes. She had seen the impossible strength from the start, from the moment he had taken a fallen comrade out of the battlefield and into her hall. And now he had just shown her that unsparing strength turned in on itself.

I wanted to help my brother and I could not.

It was the worst nightmare to be faced, but it was also the key. She had to be strong enough to use it because there was no other way.

I could not even be near him until it was too late.

"I need you to be near me," she said. "Tonight."

Her voice choked because in that moment the pain closed round her heart like death, and she could no longer tell whether it was his pain or her own. But she gained what she wanted. She saw the moment of change in the fierce black eyes when he believed her, and she knew that sharp mind and that unbreakable will believed her only because she had given a fragment of her own truth, the fragment strong enough to kill her.

She had let no one break the isolation of her life because it was far too dangerous. But she loved him, even though the future was impossible and far beyond her sight. So she said the fatal words and she knew how much she would have to give.

"Be with me now." He would have to agree. There was no other option for him. He would want to help her, just as he had wanted to help headstrong Gorei, as he still wanted to help his grief-struck and appalling father. And his wife.

Her fingers moved over smooth muscle covered by expensive linen, living flesh, heated and desperate, and trapped by its own strength. Her throat closed. She wanted to help him. If heaven granted her the power, if she had the strength and the skill and the trueness.

She knew now that she had the love.

She touched him and she felt him move. His arms closed round her and she felt one instant of the blinding strength. The precisely curved lips claimed hers. She expected the madness, but it was not that. It was all the other hidden things, the true things. She closed her eyes against the sudden stinging rush of her tears.

She had no recollection of reaching the garishly appointed bed, only that she was lying on the thickly padded mattress, her body pressed to his, so close, as though she were part of him and he were part of her. He filled her senses, the smooth movement of his body, the weight of him, the touch of his hands on her concubine's clothes, on her skin. The fire was glossed over. It was seduction, pure and uncurbed and intensely masculine.

Her response was immediate, utterly and deliberately complete. She was already open to him, her body highly wrought with anticipation. He took it higher, until she burned, lost in the touch of his fingers on her thighs beneath the fine crush of her skirts, her body half-bared, lit with flame, tingling, the bright thin dress pushed aside.

Her skin, bathed and scented and taut with desire filled his hands. The slight fast sound of her breath broke the fire-warmed silence of the room, the musical jingle of the exotic silver chains as he nuzzled her ear, the clink of the thin copper bracelets on her arms as her hands measured dense moving muscle, fineness and heat and unchecked consummate strength.

The desire inside her leaped. The tormenting, mind-dark pleasure of his mouth moved to the curve of her throat. She touched his face, then the heavy silk-smooth fall of his hair. She saw the injury that had been hidden at the hairline and a shaft of coldness stabbed through her. She had known already, when she had fled from Guthrum's men and mind and sight had darkened into dizziness, she had seen him, armed, the brilliant corselet streaked with mud, the blood on his face.

Nothing else matters, he had said, *nothing apart from this,* and he had touched her. She had held his image in her thoughts because she had wanted him so much. In the world that existed beyond the thin veils of this one, he had been there.

She said nothing of that. Not yet. Later. If the closeness

held and she was able to reach to him, if he would speak to her. If she could accomplish her task. She pressed closer, unable to stop herself, drawn to him by all that lived in her heart.

Her body moved for him in its bright disarray, taking the dark heated urgency of lips on the uncovered gleam of her skin, the curve of her breast. Her heart slammed as his mouth fastened on the aching peak. The nearness of him, the skilled touching, the flame-hot desire, had brought the anticipation so high that her reaction was uncontrolled. She did nothing to disguise it. She let him see and feel all that burned through her because of him, the desire and the need and the endless hunger for him.

She would no longer let herself be afraid of that hunger. It was no longer a weakness, the completeness and the raw nature of it that she had been at such pains to hide, fed the power between them, built the desire. She felt it in the fine fierce body of her lover as she knew it in herself.

The heavy hands caressed her skin, the touch smooth, finely intimate, knowing. His mouth… The excitement notched higher. He sensed it, held the moment for her, still, highly charged, beyond the edge of time, feverish with the gift of pleasure. She opened her painted, kohl-lined eyes. She caught his gaze, hot, intent, and for an instant she thought she saw the hunger that was her match. That must be how she looked to him, so focused, predatory.

She did not look away. If there was no proper limit to how much she wanted him, let him see that. Her heart clenched in the taut heated cage of her body. Let him see that there was nothing held back from him because he was worth more than she could give.

Her hand reached out, brushed past the secret metal shapes at her waist, touched her lover's body. The fiery, dark-shadowed weight bore down between her thighs, moved, slid lower. Lower still. The dark head bent. She knew now how he would touch her, what he would do. The anticipation flamed, unbearable, burst and shattered into impossible pleasure at the first touch of his mouth.

The soft cry of desperation tore from her throat. She arched toward him as his hands positioned her against his mouth and there was nothing but his touch, the pleasuring that caught her in magic and sent her senses spiraling into the hidden madness, darkness and light. Only the awareness of him. The pleasure shattered as he held her, and afterward she stayed, locked in his arms, and when she moved, the pleasure began again, filled with the deep magic between them.

The impossible love drove her, and she moved with him, touching more freely, reveling in the strength and the power and the dark urgency, the deep desire in him as yet unsatisfied. It was what she wanted, that and the hidden feelings behind, the fiercely held emotions. They were what she would unlock. This moment, this possibility. *Tonight.*

The hidden drive inside her, the longing to give, lent her a power she had never known or felt. It filled her—love's power and pure desire. Everything fed it, the moment snatched from nothing, the danger outside the thin walls, the lack of a future. Even the bright scraps of clothing meant for seduction gave her an alien confidence, the glint of jewelry in the lamp light, the bright uncovered fall of her curled hair and the paint on her face, the perfume rubbed into her flesh, *rosemary and thyme, orris root and lovage chanted over,* the smoothly oiled slip of her skin under the touch of his hand…

Her own hands caressed and enflamed him, through clothing, then on bronzed naked skin over dense muscle, power, the clear lines and the strength moving against her hands. His beauty confounded her, the solid shoulders, the flaring width of his chest, the tight hips, the erotic hardness of his sex, heavy and full. He fascinated sight, touch. For the first time, she let the fascination take her without reserve. She simply touched him for joy, for the fleeting moment taken from danger, for the love and the longing deep inside her and so that he would know of that longing. For desire.

It burned between them in their stolen and dangerous moment, so bright. She leaned close, her artfully curled hair framing her face, the crushed and trailing brightness of her clothing half concealing, half revealing her body.

He pulled her closer and her hands fed on him, tracing the harsh strength, the power, the fluid movement. The hot urgency surrounded and possessed her until she was part of it, part of *him,* the drive and the need and the hunger, the heat and the feel of him close, the intensely intimate caress of his hands and his lips, the deep invasion of his body between her thighs.

She took and she incited, her fingers digging into the thick flesh of his shoulders, her hips tight with his, moving with him, taking the deep thrust of his flesh, both the strength and the intensely erotic restraint, the pleasure that he gave and the wildness beneath that restraint, the visible, palpable edge of the hunger and the madness.

Her mind and her body filled with the bright awareness of him, her heightened senses dizzied, were possessed and filled by him. The sheer power of the physical pleasure broke, overwhelming, experienced with him. It all merged in the heady tumult of her senses, in the insubstantial realm of her thoughts where she could believe that her mind touched with his, that the bond was real and beyond breaking in this world or any other.

AURINIA LAY WRAPPED in his arms, the closeness seemingly still there like a miracle. She lay with him, her body entwined with his, cradled in strength and heady warmth, hearing the fast beat of his heart slow to its natural steadiness, feeling the night deepen outside the island of light round the bed, the first whisper of cool air against her skin, scarcely discernible, on the edge of sensation, but there. She concentrated on the warmth.

He touched her hair. She felt the gentle brush of his solid, gold-ringed hand on the artful curls, her head, the delicate line of her ear, and the sweet tingling sensation running across her skin. The thin silver chains with their tiny filigree spheres rustled like music. She thought of his mouth, the warmth of his breath.

"Earrings are a Swedish fashion." Her voice filled the shadows and the solid hand went still. She thought her heart did, too.

She did not know whether she could do this, whether for

all her healing powers, she had the skill. She was not used to other people's thoughts, to intimacy.

"They say earrings came to Sweden from the east, that the women there wear them all the time," said her voice, as cool and steady as spring rain. "Of course, they look fine, but they are noisy and the little jingling sound goes through your head like a vibration that will send you mad."

She felt him take breath, rapid, harsh.

"But then I suppose that is the point." *Such precious erotic madness and all it hid.* She smoothed a fold of gaudy material.

"The dress is supposed to be royal-purple. But I fear—" the heavy muscle beneath her moved "—that they could not afford the right dyestuffs and so it turned out like this."

There was a small savage tightening under her touch.

"But I suppose it would do well enough in the dark."

"Aurinia."

She had her hand on the deep heaviness of his chest, over his heart. There seemed only one single dangerous beat in which she could speak.

"I lost the bracelet you gave me, the true gold." Her captors had taken it. "Can you forgive me?"

"Such a thing does not matter."

She said into the rapid pause, "Can you forgive me, for dragging you into such danger?"

"You? It was not you. It was my fault."

She had touched on the hidden things and she had forced him to speak. It was success. Of a kind. She lay still and waited for what he would say.

"I took you away from your home and I did not look

after you." He had moved. There was a torn breath like a savage beast's. "And then my father said such things to you. He can be such a mad fool, so impetuous he only hurts himself. And others—" He stopped speaking.

Oh God. How much that desperate tormented father hurt his remaining son.

She did not know how far to push it. But her husband was so tough. There were no half measures with him. And she had been given no more time. This night, and then there might be nothing.

"Gorei was the same, was he not? So impetuous?"

The silence crept from the walls of the small chamber in the Viking camp like something living. The very breath choked in her throat. She did not allow it to make a sound.

He was no longer touching her. She told herself the unvarnished truth, that the unconscious withdrawal of that warmth did not matter. What mattered was freeing him of the burden. She watched the shadows, the dark shape beside her in the borrowed bed.

"Gorei was my brother."

It was the world of absolutes she had never known, of kin ties. Of family love. Her heart ached with a bitter emptiness, with the sense of loss, with worse things—with all the potentially destructive bitterness of envy. Envy even for the pain. She spoke through it.

"You loved him well. Just as you love your father." She could not seek the destruction of such ties that held him. There were things that were right and things that were not.

And sometimes there were things that had neither time nor place.

"That kind of love endures," she said. "It makes no difference if they are two mad fools, and impetuous."

Aurinia heard his breath, caught the sense of hot power. The force of impetuousness lived in him, too, family bond. But there was also the clarity, the ruthless judgment that had sent him to fight for a Saxon king. The next breath was slower. She had her hand clamped round the iron shapes at her waist, bind-runes, *os* with *rad* and *peordh,* the combination that held the power to unlock knowledge that was hidden or forgotten. The metal edge dug into her palm.

"It was beyond foolishness with Gorei," said Macsen. "It was disaster. It truly was madness."

The words came out like something forced, something long suppressed that perhaps only now found its shape.

"My brother did not understand. It was as though—"

She watched the small, skillfully glossed pause, the ruthless way it was mastered. *Always go on, face the next challenge because it had to be done.* The pain hit her across the distance that separated them, even though they did not touch. They no longer needed to. For her, the barrier between them was gone.

Yet there was no visible sign of that hidden pain and even she, with her finely attuned senses, might not once have understood what was now so clear to her. She thought, *he has never shown Bryse this. He could not.* He kept speaking, as though it were easy, as though all that she sensed in him was not crippling.

"It was as though Gorei believed he was invincible.

I had told him that I had already seen him as a king's man. I was the older brother." The smooth, perfectly balanced voice filled the shadows. No hesitation. "Gorei believed me."

The sense of pain choked her.

"My brother behaved as though the things that affected others could not affect him, as though he were—" The glossed hesitation this time was over the right word. The brilliant dark eyes narrowed and she was reminded that English was not his first choice. "You would say *unfæg,* unfated, undoomed. As though death could not touch him."

She forced herself to speak, to match that terrible, hard-won courage.

"You would have explained to him, told him what—"

"Of course I told him, as far as I understood anything myself then. But once he had that belief in his head, I could not persua—"

She did not finish that word for him, *persuade.* It was enough that he could think it. She did not give him time to form the habitual counter to that thought, but said something else instead.

"Gorei was eighteen." *As far as I understood anything myself then.* "How old were you?"

"Twenty. I—"

The difference in a man's life between twenty and twenty-five was vast, that between a youth and a warrior who had been tested.

"I was responsible."

That was the other side of ruthless thinking. It spared nothing of itself. She stared at the starkly shadowed form in the rumpled bed, the bright glimpses and the darkly hidden strength. She could not break that strength. She could see no way round it. Her fingers slid over the rune shapes, *os,* the inspiration of knowledge that came through

language, the rune of persuasion. And *peordh,* knowledge
that was deeply hidden.

The way was unseen.

CHAPTER
14

"You told your brother something you saw," said Aurinia. Her husband made no answer. It was not a question, and the firelit air was suddenly tight with all those unseen things, with the awareness of all that had passed between them in the realm that surrounded this one.

She lay still in the bed still warmed from lovemaking and forced breath.

"You witnessed all that you had said as it unfolded, just as you had seen it in your mind, because what you had seen was already true."

She watched Macsen's eyes. Time was not straightforward like a simple line. It rested on *wyrd,* fate, and fate was a web. Past, present and future sometimes touched.

She waited, scarcely breathing. She thought he would deny that truth, but then she knew he would not, could not. Clear sight.

"Yes." There was a small pause. "But I did not see where it would lead."

He said nothing about that small word *already*. His eyes did not change. She wanted to reach out and touch him, if there existed one small measure of comfort that her healing power could give. But even as she reached out, he moved away. The lamp light flared, less gold, less bright, than his skin. Flame and black shadow poured over living muscle, fine lines, quickened movement and power.

She thought he would go to the window. He did not, though she thought he wanted air to breathe, the sense of space, more than he wanted life itself. But his was not that kind of recklessness. He stayed, drawn back in Guthrum's closed room.

"I did not see Gorei's death."

The wolf trapped in its pit.

"Would it have made any difference if you had?"

The brutal directness of the question sparked pain, like a mirrored reflection. The dark head on its graceful neck, the heavy shoulders, turned. She made herself go on.

"You could not alter anything. His fate was a pattern—" She stopped over the words. She did not know whether he saw what a Saxon like her saw.

"Fate, the future, is a web in the weaving, a pattern made of deeds. You saw the pattern when it was nearly complete, but even if you had seen the very end, the death-day, you could not have unwoven the pattern that had been made. You saw deeds already finished. No one can alter them."

"You would say I was fated to be Gorei's bane."

The pain flared, dizzying. *No. It is your father who would say that. Or perhaps he did not need to. You would say it for yourself.* She watched the brilliant fire and the shadows.

"I would say that Gorei was fated to be Gorei. He faced the risks a warrior faces." *The same risks you face every day. The merciless risks that press on you now.* "Even though he died, he kept *weorth*—a warrior's honour, a good reputation."

It was so fundamental, British or Saxon. He could not dispute it. The tough fighter's body turned.

"Your father sees that, even through grief." She watched the implacable, vividly passionate face that could have belonged to Bryse. "Even through self-blame."

The powerful movement was arrested. "*Self*-blame."

She saw the uneven breath swell the gold-black deeply muscled wall of his chest, the long line of his throat. He did not speak again. She saw the ruthless mind work.

"I talked to your father and I saw all that was there. He betrayed himself to a person like me with every word."

He did not question it. Neither did he look at her as though she were a *hell-rune.* He was the only person in the world who would not look at her in that way. She glanced down because she could not bear to look at him, her throat tight, her heart desperate with longing for all that she could not have. She made herself speak, the last effort.

Her hand sought the rune that would give her wisdom. But her fingers ran over a shape that was different, unexpected. *Wynn,* bliss, the magical point of harmony and balance, where alienation disappeared.

She raised her head again and looked on the inner strength and the fire-shadow, the brilliant body that had shown her what life meant, the bright glitter of the prince's gold.

"The other thing he cannot conceal is his love for you."

The dark eyes were impenetrable.

"That endures." She watched him. "Nothing makes any difference to such a feeling." *Nothing, not even if I never see you again.* Nothing could change the feeling that now lived in her heart, that had been born like a spark of magic in the moment she'd first seen him, before then, when she had known him in her mind. It had taken its true place now, and if she was worth that breath of life, she would be able to help him.

"It is true." For a moment, she held his eyes and naught else existed, everything was there, real and unreal, known and unknown, the past and the present and the future. She thought she moved toward him. She thought the shared power was so strong that no resistance was possible. But he looked away.

"I am sorry it came to this," he said. "For you."

"But I do not—"

"I have shown as much impulsiveness as Gorei or my father could have done. Since the moment I saw you."

I do not care. I would rather be here in this chamber at Wareham with you than untouched at Wytch Heath before the Viking storm came. I would rather be at your side than anywhere else in the world. I would rather be your wife… Selfishness. It must be so. Her mind was suddenly filled with that small instant of hesitation when she had asked him whether he regretted marrying her and the cold memory stopped the words. She thought the press of feelings would kill her. She tried to think, to find the words that were right.

"It was my own steps that brought me here."

She watched the dark exotic beauty of her husband, more than that, the bitter strength.

"All of my decisions have been my own." She could not say less of the truth than that.

He neither moved nor spoke and she thought of all that waited outside the walls of the firelit chamber. She had done what she could with words, but there were other ways of healing.

"But I would not be alone."

He came to her, as she knew he would; the warmth and the fineness and the costly strength were hers. She simply let that loving strength take her, at first, lost in his touch, mindless and desperate with longing, filled with the need she could not express. She beat the terrible force of her own need back.

She held him lightly, her body twined with his. She concentrated thought and mind and every heightened, aching sense, and the golden warmth filled her. She was so close. Her awareness of him was intense, so utterly complete, more than she had ever allowed herself to feel for anyone. There was no limit. No defence. She felt herself dizzy with the power of it, at once real and unreal, a thing of the body and of the spirit.

"Macsen…" His name scarcely made a sound, but he heard.

"It will be all right." His lips formed the words against her hair. The dark whisper of his breath touched her throat. The golden warmth suffused her body where it lay wrapped in his. The living closeness surrounded her. It seemed natural for her to touch his head.

"Sleep with me." The warmth seeped through her skin, the palm of her hand, her fingertips. "Stay." She could feel all that was hidden by formidable strength of will, the exhaustion, the dizzying, crippling edge of pain, the bitter disorienting aftermath of the dangerous herbs he had taken to bring the dream state that would show him where she was.

"For a short while. Then we must go. When it is full dark. When the guard changes and we have the best chance. Before dawn comes."

"Go?" The word shocked her into consciousness. "Tonight? I thought that Earl Guthrum— That you had—" The sudden lethal tightening of the fierce body stopped her.

"That I had persuaded him?"

She did not draw back. She simply held him. "Yes." There was a moment of intense stillness while her body lay against his and her hand cradled his head. She deliberately did not move.

"Then you had better tell me," she said without the slightest inflection.

"I hardly needed to persuade him." His voice was as blank and free of expression as hers. "He was persuaded already. He had sent a messenger to my father seeking his support. There is a spectacular reward on offer for an appropriately timed rebellion against a hard-pressed king locked into war. Earl Guthrum is generous man, an open-handed lord and gift-giver. When he is desperate."

Saint Beren.

"A reward on offer?"

"I have just given acceptance on my father's behalf."

She shut her eyes and she was back in another chamber with him, lying close, much like this. At Fearnros.

I have given the king my oath. If he fails there will be nothing, neither English nor British.

"You will not keep that acceptance." She thought of the expression he used when it came to a matter of choice, of honour, never simply *will not.* "You cannot."

"No."

A ruse with Guthrum. Another betrayal in Bryse's eyes. One more in a line that had begun with Gorei and would never end. And she had forced him into it. By taking marriage and walking away so heedlessly into danger; danger she had been warned of, but had paid no heed. Fate's weaving. She made a small desperate movement and then stilled it. She stayed with him, her body pressed to his, now that it was too late.

"I see." She moved her hand softly from her lover's head, down over fine warm skin to the steady beat of his heart.

She thought of the danger that lay outside the well-appointed chamber, of the Viking earl and his greed that had plunged a country into a war that demanded sacrifices that were impossible. Her own heart swelled with pain and grief, with a sudden and unquenchable fury, so that she wished she could kill them all, every last Dane who had set foot on this soil. She wished she had murdered the men who were ill in Guthrum's sickroom, not tried to save them.

She bit her lip and held her hand steady over the beating heart and the living skin and she knew that such a thing was not possible. She did what she had to do. Just as Macsen did, and Bryse, and the last surviving Saxon king.

"Does the king know?"

"It depends what you mean by *know*. I could not tell him. If I did, it would not matter what my intentions are, the king would have to arrest Bryse, take all he owns and either hang or behead him. He cannot do otherwise."

Cannot. She lay still, feeling the beat of his heart under her hand, the effort required to speak, to tell her. The terrible control.

"So I spoke to Garrulf. In some ways it is the same thing."

The king's cousin, the first person she had seen at Fearnros. The first person who had greeted Macsen.

"Garrulf had suspected already. He tried to warn me and I, God help me, did not believe him. But it seems it was true after all and he knew it, and he waited for my father to make a move. Or perhaps for me to."

She saw the golden-haired warrior in the courtyard at Fearnros, the way Macsen had spoken to him, the familiarity that only came with long friendship.

"But he would not think…" Her voice stopped. *Hang or behead him…*

"I have no idea what Garrulf thinks. Only that no one stopped me from coming here."

She thought of friendship and oaths, of the unsparing demands of honour and duty, of surviving in a state of war. Of kin ties and love. She had been mad to think that she could reorder such things, mad and naive. She had said that love endured and it was true, both true and at the same time impossible. The awareness was terrible, maiming.

"And your father?"

"I saw him after you did. He wanted me to join him in what he planned. He should have known that I—" He stopped speaking and whatever it was was withheld from her.

Oaths and duty.

She lay still, her body still touching his.

"He does not know what I have done. Not yet." He moved.

The suddenness shocked her, the suppressed force that even she had not fully sensed. His gaze caught her, intensely dark, filled with that deep, bitterly held force, with a thousand things in the shadows and the firelight that she could not follow. Trapped things.

Her heart lurched. She caught his arm, dense muscle, fine skin with the blue design deeply etched into the living flesh. Her fingers traced the curving shape, exotic, British. His hand moved to touch her face, the gesture oddly gentle, at such marked variance with the hot force that seeped through his fingers. The power passed between them like a lightning bolt.

Her breathing stopped. She heard the tight catch of his own breath, felt it. The moment stayed, absolute. Then his hand dropped away from her face.

"You have to understand why I am telling you this. Even if things here turn out well and my father survives this, even if there is no open breach of his loyalty, there is no way past what has happened between him and me."

The black eyes held hers. "I thought there might be, but there is not. I thought there might be a family for you, a life free of taint. I thought…things that were wrong, now."

"No—" But his voice stopped hers.

"Let me say the truth. I cannot give you all that you should have as my wife," said the brother who had wanted to help Gorei, the son faced with a father bent on rebellion, the prince trapped in an unsuitable marriage. "I wish it could have been otherwise."

She wanted to say that all she wanted was to be his wife, that nothing else mattered. But all those other things did matter. She knew that love endured, that her own love would endure for her as long as she lived. But she did not know whether it was right to stay with him. She did not know what would happen tonight, at Wareham, whether he would live through the disaster that had been wrought, whether Bryse would live, or what would come afterward.

"Sleep with me."

She lay in his arms, her skin touching his, her body pressed against the strong fine planes that had given her magic and life and that she had loved. She stayed with her husband, perhaps for the last time, and the warmth came, like a miracle. It held them.

It WAS THE WARRIOR who woke her.

Aurinia came out of the trancelike state, halfway between sleep and waking, the state that allowed healing.

"It is time to go."

The shadowed shape leaned over her in the bed, heavy and smooth and filled with power. There was no hesitation, nothing visible of the pain and dislocation of the senses that she had felt in the dreamlike awareness of him and that she had sought to heal. He moved away and began to pull on his clothes.

"Come."

The damage was hidden, buried under the willpower and the strength that seemed inexhaustible but was not. Light and shadow raced across bronzed skin, the long densely flexed muscles of his back, the linen bandage. She slid out from the bedcovers. He held out his hand. She took it, intensely aware of his half-naked state, the feel of his hand, the closeness of him filling sight and sense, the broad wall of his chest with the scattered dark hair, the compressed muscle of his thigh beneath the fine dark trousers.

The power leached through her and she was aware of the way his body had touched her, the hot intimate touch of a lover. Her breath was tight and it seemed as though the wide-palmed hand held hers too long, that the shared night spilled over again into now, something endless. But it was not so. The cold of the borrowed chamber struck at her, empty and deadening after the warmth of the bed. He let go and she reached for her cloak.

The fire in the hearth-pit had burned down and the shadows were intense. He did not make more light. She watched him dress, the darkness of the richly braided tunic extinguishing the clear lines of his body, the smoothly bronzed skin. The competent hands fastened the jeweled belt at his hip, the movement quick, economical, flawless. It was not the lover of her bed, but the warrior whose ruthless focus had so unnerved her that first morning after their wedding at Fearnros. The king's man. Dangerous. Cold.

The sense of distance, the complete concentration, and the danger unnerved her still. But she could see so much else now. All the other qualities were still there, the honour and the duty and the essential rightness. The same person. The lover who held her heart.

She fastened the cloak with the cheap brooch made of copper. There was little she could do with the crushed, garish dress underneath, but most of it was hidden and the cloak was dark.

"We will go out beside the river to the south where the wall ends."

The Frome. She knew the river flats, even though she had come to avoid towns such as Wareham.

"My own men will be outside, waiting."

She nodded and he had turned for the door when she realized what the power and the edge of danger had blinded her to.

"You have no weapons—"

"It does not matter. The guard will."

"The—?"

"There is a limit to the level of trust, even between a desperate Viking and an oath breaker. Some helpful servant will be loitering outside the door. There will be another outside the window."

"Of course." She remembered the way he had held back from the closed shutters blocking off the night air. She swallowed.

"Are you ready?" The dark warrior's eyes regarded her steadily and she knew what the question meant, more than whether she had fastened the borrowed cloak. *Could she do this?*

She thought of the desperate earl and his army, the sheer numbers she had seen, the swirling volatile feelings that filled a camp of fighting men in a hostile land whose lives hung by a thread. She thought of the more particular disaster that faced Macsen and herself. He waited for that split instant and there was not just the ruthlessness and the single-mindedness, but courage. Courage and the awareness of risk. Duty.

"Yes." She had smiled at him before she even knew she had done it. She saw the reaction in his eyes and only then did she remember Judith's words about trust, and the shadowed beating wings of the owls.

She had never trusted anyone. It had been something beyond her ability, burned out of her, and now it was there. Complete.

"It will be all right," she said, taking the words he had used in the night to stop her fears. "You will make it so." The impulsive smile widened, became as high-hearted as his courage, the faith she could rely on, return. "You are supposed to give me a silver coin first. For last night."

The fast, dazzling brightness in his eyes changed, flared, was absorbed into the other dangerous fire that burned in his gaze, was part of it.

"If you think you were worth it."

She raised her head and her gaze held his, timeless, re-flected flame.

"Go." He unbarred the door, the trained warrior's hands sure, firm. "Go."

Without hesitation she passed through the narrow gap into the cold air. Her cloak brushed his foot. Something moved ahead of her in the half dark. The loitering servant with the weapons. She had hardly time to see him, to register tallness, unkempt fair hair, a solid form, before the dark-rich voice called her back.

"You forgot this."

The silver coins arced through the air, catching the flickering torchlight like sparks of flame. She half turned, her attention caught by that abrupt, unexpected flicker of movement, her startled reaction faultless because it was true.

The same reaction caught the man with the unkempt hair like an unavoidable echo. He watched the bright flash of her lurid dress in torchlight, the fall of the coins. He did not look up again.

Aurinia's gaze locked on her husband. There did not appear to be any blood or obvious bruises. She looked at the Viking sprawled full length at Macsen's feet.

"Did y—"

"Hardly. He is not dead. No. You are not going to touch him."

She had stepped forward instinctively. She halted.

Macsen dragged the body into the chamber. It took seconds. She glanced at the shadows and there was no one, no sound. Her head turned.

She swallowed.

"Did you get what you wanted?"

He had a throwing axe thrust through the jeweled belt, and a hunting knife in his hand, no sword, but suspended from the belt, lying against one solid thigh was that most skin-chilling of Viking weapons, a *long-sax,* a single bladed knife three feet long.

He was not even out of breath.

He gave her the hunting knife, just as he had once before. She took it.

"This way."

There was definitely no blood. "How did you—"

"I am a king's man," he said, as though that explained everything. They turned south, toward the River Frome. It was terrifying.

Macsen seemed to know his way through the maze of dark buildings and the even more menacing open spaces. Once, she found a shortcut she remembered from her journey to Guthrum's sickroom.

Her most enduring feeling was the kind of primitive gut-wrenching fear that must afflict a hunted beast, that and the sense of power close beside her, the grip of Macsen's hand on her arm, hard and uncompromising, too hard. She did not care. It was unfailing.

He stayed with her and they clung to shadows, once waiting, held breathless with no more shelter than the lee of a hay barn that belonged to the farm serving what had once been the nunnery of Saint Mary. The Danish voices faded at last.

They pushed on through what had been the complex of the church and the abbey buildings. She could see the river, smooth and black, the vegetation and the reeds that provided blessed cover. It was there. She saw the guards.

Holy mother. She heard a deep earthy voice with the same accent as Earl Guthrum's, confident and full, laced with an edge of impatience. She felt the jolt through Macsen's hand where it gripped her arm, but he did not hesitate, just pushed through. There were three of them. No, four. She took breath.

"How—" But he pulled her to a stop on the edge of shadow and made a gesture for silence. It was full dark, close to dawn but with no lightness yet in the sky. They made neither sound nor movement but the Danish speaker knew they were there. She would swear it.

Her hand moved to the knife hilt. She would use it, despite inward terror and all the horror she had of bloodshed. She knew she would use whatever weapon she had if someone touched him, if four people attacked him.

She stayed, close to Macsen, every sense stretched, waiting. But the speaker gave no sign, nothing betrayed his knowledge of their presence, so that she thought that her trained senses had betrayed her.

The man laughed, but still with that edge of impatience. He seemed to be persuading one of the four to go back into the camp. He made an abrupt movement and Earl Guthrum's insignia, the clawed bird, showed faint blood-red in the starlight. Not persuading, ordering. One of the four left.

Macsen did not move, so she kept still. Three. The knife hilt was in her fingers. The fourth Viking had vanished. The hard hand round her arm moved. He let go. She had the blade out.

"By all the saints," said Earl Guthrum's man out of the starlight, "I fear your wife is about to kill me."

Macsen's gaze moved from the speaker to the dull metallic gleam of the blade in her tight fingers and there was a moment of stillness when she could not read his eyes in the darkness. Then his head turned toward the man who had spoken. His hand closed over hers.

"Ashbeorn. I did not think you were at Fearnros."

The man shrugged massive shoulders. His eyes were on her, quick, assessing. The pale blur of his face, the deep brown hair caught the light as he glanced at the knife. She shifted, instinct, but Macsen's hand stayed where it was, locked on hers. Perhaps they thought she might use the blade anyway. The blood still pounded in her veins.

"I got back tonight," said the man called Ashbeorn. "Most of us should be here now."

Macsen only nodded, as though few words encompassed much, and she realized the man belonged to the same company as Garrulf, the world of oath-service to the king, duty and honour, Macsen's world, the world she and Bryse had nearly destroyed for him.

The urge to step back gripped her, but the touch of his fingers meshed with hers round the knife hilt stopped her, a huge warrior's hand covering hers, the heavy palm only faintly warm in the predawn air. The touch was different, like comfort. She stayed her ground.

"Just as well," said Ashbeorn. "You could do with someone who can speak Danish."

"Aye. It seems I could. Let's go."

There was a split instant before Ashbeorn moved.

"Down the riverbank. It is clear enough. For us." The king's man in his borrowed Danish armour turned smoothly. His hand touched Macsen's shoulder. It was a gesture that arose from blood brotherhood, strong. But she had seen the look in his eyes.

"We had best go," he said. "Before your Saxon friend here works himself into a seizure from impatience."

Aurinia saw through the darkness who the waiting Saxon friend in Viking livery was. Huda. He came toward her. Macsen let go of her hand.

15

They were stopped twice, each time more nerve-racking than the last. Aurinia was almost maddened with it, with the spine-crawling fear of waiting locked in shadows, Macsen in front of her with the long-sax and the axe, Huda bristling at her side.

But each time, Ashbeorn in his Viking earl's livery pushed forward and talked them through it, with Danish that was smoothly arrogant, giving out either commands or the crude jokes of comrades as the situation needed, always perfect. He moved and spoke with the same confidence that had hung round Macsen in Guthrum's courtyard.

Then it was emptiness and a silence that was complete, so intense that her light frame made more noise than the massive bulk of Macsen beside her, and after that, speed.

They found Macsen's men with the horses, out of sight and earshot of the camp, even of the advance guards. She breathed out, her lungs heaving. She could sense the nearness of Fearnros, she would swear it. Safety. It was within reach. She had not caused death.

The relief, the release of the tension from the last day and night swelled inside her, suffocating in its intensity. She tried to breathe. She watched the men round her, the Danish-speaking stranger, Huda, Macsen unstrapping the *long-sax* from his hip. Someone handed him his own sword. She saw the familiar gleam of gold and gems. He was talking to the king's man, the shield-companion, the dark head and the brown close together. She could not hear the words.

Coldness cut the burgeoning relief under her heart. She stepped closer.

"...have to take the trackway...King Ubbe..."

Ubbe, who was the brother of King Halfdan of the North. They had their own army. Such an army, in addition to discontented Britons, might be a more efficient source of help to a trapped and dangerous Viking earl.

"King Ubbe?"

Both heads turned as one. The rapid voices stopped. She saw Macsen's eyes and the coldness possessed her, bitter and terrible, more potent because she had thought— What? That it was possible to outrun disaster?

He spoke to her in that calm voice, the smooth, deep, perfectly pitched voice that hid everything. "Huda is going to take you back to Fearnros." And when she said nothing, he added, "Aurinia? It will work out all right."

It can't, not if you are not with me. She watched the concentration in his face and did not say it. She forced speech.

"I see. And you?"

Ashbeorn made some gesture of negation, but after one glance at Macsen, he did not speak.

"Halfdan, the King of the North, has crossed to Ireland. Guthrum has to find help, so he will also send to King Ubbe for aid," said Macsen. The stranger did not question that word *also,* which meant he knew what Bryse had planned in secret. Her spine chilled.

"The messengers will leave Wareham with the dawn and go north from here."

"And you?" she said again, but she no longer needed to ask that question. Her eyes were locked with his, dark as the cold night that surrounded them. But not cold. Not his eyes. The pain closed round her heart, choked its fast, frantic beating.

"You are going north."

"Yes."

That was all he said. No explanation, no bitterness. No turning away.

If things here turn out well.

That was the task that had to be accomplished in recompense for Bryse's broken loyalty and his life, the price. Her husband was going to pay it.

Don't. She swallowed the word. Even if there had been no Bryse, no bitter disaster, her husband was oath-sworn and the reality of the world that must be lived in lay below them, in the fort at Wareham. You faced that or you did not.

"Wæs hal." She did not know how to say it in British. But Macsen lived in two worlds. He understood.

Farewell. Be safe.

She did not know whether he understood all that was behind the words, the force of love. She knew it was best if he did not. But her gaze was fastened on his, on the night-dark eyes filled with unspoken things. The bond was still there, everything that had seemed to exist for them in some other place. Separate. Shared.

"*Wæs thu* Aurinia *hal.*"

They did not touch, not in the physical world that others could see. He turned away, swinging himself lightly onto Du Moro's back. The horses wheeled and vanished in a thunder of hooves.

"Lady?" Huda's voice broke into her abstraction. She could have been back in the sunlit hall at Wytch Heath with the dream-shreds still half in her mind—the sight of Macsen in another place than this, surrounded with the sound of fighting and the smell of blood.

"Lady. We must go."

But this was different. This was now and wholly real—the black shapes of the horses disappearing across the heathland, their riders leaning low, the dark cloaks flying in the icy dawn air. A tight group round her husband, except—

"Aurinia." Huda's hand shook her, as though she were still lost in dreams, which she was not. "Are you listening to me?"

"Of course."

"We have to get back to Fearnros. Now." But, like her, he stared after the riders.

The group split apart, some of the horses wheeling left

across the heath and the rising ground. There was a grey shape ahead of them. Macsen kept straight north.

"Why did the others ride that way?" She glanced at the lightening horizon. "Northwest."

"What?"

"You saw them," she said, racked by the tension inside her, the impatience. "You were watching, too. The Danish speaker led them."

"The— Ashbeorn. Ash. The king's man. He— What did you see?"

She suddenly realized, in the growing light, the way Huda was looking at her. It was the way he looked at her when he was frightened of the golden power that lived inside her. But it was she who felt the leap of fear, who crossed herself. She did not have the sight of things unseen like Macsen. But...only in things that concerned him had she felt such a power.

"You did not see it."

Huda's gaze slid away from her. The fear tightened. But there was no longer any place for that. No time. If there was power she would take it. For him.

"Tell me the truth."

He looked up and there was something in his gaze that was different.

"I did not see that. I watched the horses move in a single group until they were beyond sight."

Then he said with none of the hesitation she expected, "But you saw."

"Yes."

It was the key and it had been given into her hands. She

turned to her own mount. The thinning darkness of the heathland was lifted by a slight breeze. Light-change. The time when the veils between worlds were at their thinnest. The metal shapes at her girdle whispered.

"There are two possible routes Earl Guthrum's messengers could take," said Huda unexpectedly, "the northern road and the trackway. They must have decided to split to cover both. The king's man, Ashbeorn, has taken the trackway. It is closest to the Saxon lines so he will also try to find the West Saxon patrol from Fearnros to help them. It is a risk whatever they do."

Huda shifted in the dark, as though the same impatience, the same tension, gripped him, too. "They do not have enough men to stop the troop Guthrum will have sent."

She touched the cold iron of the stirrup.

"Macsen knew that." It was no question and she expected no answer from Huda who had disapproved of her marriage from the start. But she heard the sharp hiss of his breath behind her.

"Yes. He knew."

God's mercy. "I am going to help him." Her decision was irrevocable. She would go with or without Huda's assistance. But she stopped long enough to hold that tough, long-familiar gaze.

"I think he deserves that."

It was the war veteran, the man who understood fighting, whose gaze dropped.

"Aye."

Huda did not say anything else. He was not the kind of

man who was inclined to. Besides, after a shared lifetime, nothing else was necessary.

He helped her mount.

THE GREY SHAPE WAS VISIBLE. Aurinia did not follow her husband's path, or even that of the other king's man, Ash, not directly. She followed the silver wraith.

It waited for her.

The treacherous, uneven ground of the heathland, the shifting dark swallowed them. She kept waiting for Huda to say something, to tell her that the direction she was setting on the tireless, patient horse Macsen had given her was too far west, almost southerly, like a circle.

She did not know whether Huda could see the shape she saw, moving low along the ground like smoke, or even whether it was real. In the end, it did not matter. There were different definitions in any case for what was real. It was a brave man who was exclusive in such matters.

The wraith-like form, the new sureness in her own heart, told her the way. She came back to the place where she had started, under a stand of wind-twisted oak and pine, within sight of the path that led to Guthrum's fortress. It was the place where her Viking captors had caught her on the heath. She stopped.

"Well?"

It was the first question Huda had asked, even though she had brought him back within sight of death. All that loyalty that had begun with her mother and perhaps still belonged to that memory. But he was her responsibility now. Her heart caught.

"We—" She did not know what to say, why it had to be here, at this point. Now. There was no longer any sign of the gray shape, nothing but darkness relentlessly thinning toward betraying light.

Her cloak lifted in the cool breeze. Huda's great roan stamped and was curbed, the tension caught from its rider. The harness fittings jingled and at the edge of sight something moved. Horses, men. Heaven's mercy, how did she answer for this? Huda already had the sword out, the heavier horse pushing in front of her, so close Huda's knee touched hers. His voice brushed past her in the wind.

"Go...."

It was like watching his death before it happened. Her fault and there was nothing she could do to prevent it. Pale light gleamed off steel. She thought of Macsen with Gorei, of disaster.

"*Wait.*" Then she said into the small fractured moment of time before death. "Bryse—"

"THERE." MACSEN PULLED THE sweating horse to a stop. Nothing moved except the faint breath of the dawn wind. It carried the scent of the sea. It flattened the dark cloak against his back. Southeast. With luck it would carry the sound and the scent of their quarry when they came.

They would need more than luck.

"The ash grove." He set Du Moro at the slope beside the roadway, the great hoofs slipping on the mossy ground starred with fungi. The earth was wetter under the trees but not impossible. The view from the tree cover was as lengthy the twisting road would give. The light was already increasing.

There was not time to try further.

He steadied the stallion with knees and one hand. Anwas stopped beside him.

"Take your half of the men." It seemed ridiculous to divide a force as small as this. But it was what they had planned. No other choice.

So he made some jest of it, despite the pain that at times had the power to blind him, despite the knowledge of what was to come and the consequences if they failed. The encouragement, the glib words rolled effortlessly off his tongue until he had them laughing. The best he could make out of nothing. They all faced death.

"Go, then."

Anwas did not move. "I did not ask for anything better. Neither did any man here."

The words, even the dubious jests dried up and, he could not speak, the person who could talk a clutch-fisted moneyer out of the contents of his coin mint. He did not know why Anwas had said it. Anwas outstared him, which must have been the only time anyone had done that to him in his life. The rest of them watched.

They were the men who had come from Devon. They could have gone back there without loss of face five years ago or at any time since. He had made that quite clear. But these had stayed. He had known it was because they thought as he did.

He simply had not believed it until this moment.

"Lord," they said.

Some of them had come with Gorei. But the faces that stared back at him held war veterans' eyes, the eyes of men who had seen many fights, who knew what it meant, the value of each decision. Truth.

"Across the road then?" said Anwas.

Something changed in his expression. He hardly knew what. An acknowledgment he had not understood and which was necessary. "Yes."

"Lord."

He focused back on what had to be done. "You know the signal…." The harbinger of disaster.

It all went smoothly. They spoke in British, as they always did on those rare occasions when there were no West Saxons present. Because they were *combrogi*, fellow countrymen, and it was their world. His father would not have believed it.

Anwas vanished across the muddy roadway with his impossibly inadequate force. The rest stayed with him. He had them deployed as well as it was possible and they waited in silence, not even the sough of the wind. He wondered whether the ash grove had once been sacred, as such trees often were.

The silence was old, older than Briton or Saxon or Dane, the air beneath the trees still, unreal, sense stealing; until the unrealness seemed no longer in the silent air, but in the leather reins under his hands, the tense stillness of the stallion, the tension in his own body.

Appearance and reality. Aurinia's face filled his mind, as it was in truth and in dreams, her light voice and the touch of her hair, the warmth that was hers and the way her body had taken him in. The brief time they had had, so short, but to him it could not be contained in the counted time of this world.

She had not asked him about the future. He would not have been able to tell her. There was naught he could see, only blankness, the lightless dark that stopped everything.

No one could hold the future.

The waiting stopped.

He gave the order. The faint whirr of arrows split the stillness and the yelling started from Guthrum's men on the road below. He judged the moment. The trained stallion moved to his urging, plunging down the slope, hoofs sliding on the mossy ground. He shouted only when they hit the roadway. He struck out.

It was worse than he had thought. Far worse. It was not a stealthy message the desperate earl had sent to a fellow king. It was an embassy complete. Far too many. He thought his own men would break under the shock, even the most loyal from Lydnan. They did not. They had the advantage of surprise, speed, but it was thin. The savageness of desperation existed on both sides.

Anwas, hidden down the road, held back. Macsen kept pushing and his men followed. He thought something might be possible. But then the worst happened. The Viking force split. They were Guthrum's men. It might have been the most ruthless option, but it was the intelligent one. The message was more important than the lives of those left behind.

He had planned for that, as far as it was possible. But there were too many. Anwas, held in reserve at the next narrow bend of the road would never hold them. The same decision that had faced Guthrum's commander pressed on him. There was no mercy in it. Just as there had been no mercy in the oath he had sworn at an imperiled king's crowning.

The fighting had lessened, but what he did was still every bit as ruthless as the action of Guthrum's man. He sought to turn the labouring horse, slashing out with the sword, getting free, somehow, his sight half-gone with the pain and the blood, like a blank darkness closing. But it did not shut out the sound, the yells of his own men and the clash and the desperation behind him. He left them and he thought it would kill him.

He focused on the bend in the road, on the impossible, unfurling disaster. Du Moro surged forward. At his urging. But behind him came the real impossibility, the voices yelling him on in British.

"WHERE IS MY SON?"

They had moved away from the dangerous closeness of the path that led to Wareham and were deep in the sheltering trees. It was just as well, since Bryse, even low-voiced, carried the effect of a blood-chilling bellow.

Aurinia steadied the patient horse. She made sure they had moved northward and now the two of them had gone apart from the rest. She watched the volatile collection of shadows that was Macsen's father.

"I am not sure that I should tell you." She thought he would like to murder her, which was good. Provided he did not actually do it. "Since your interests seem to lie with Earl Guthrum."

"*Guthrum.*" He nearly spat it. "My *interests* lie with my own kin. Something you would not—"

"Understand?" The sudden unstoppable stab of bitterness in her chest unnerved her, so strong. Inappropriate. She cut it off. "No. I have no kin."

The infuriated black eyes raked her and she was suddenly aware of the things she had hardly spared a thought for, not even under the assessing gaze of the king's man. The tawdry jewelry and the crushed dress in its violent imitation of royal-purple. She thrust it out of her head. Nothing mattered except what happened in the next few moments, the decision she could wring out of a heart locked in anger and bitter grief. A clever mind.

"No," she said, deliberately. "I have never had kin. No one whose life would be endangered if I changed sides." She took a breath. "Until now."

There was a deadly silence. She took another breath that scored the dryness of her throat.

"Of course, I understand that—" Her voice gave out. It was like dealing with a flame-snake.

"Macsen is my son," said Bryse with the kind of hammer-blow finality that ran in the family. The great stallion in front of her pawed at the ground with one heavy hoof. Its master's impatience. Crushed grass flew. "You understand nothing."

"Oh, but I do understand," she said and it was no longer possible to hold anything back. She simply dealt with him with the same strength she had used for Macsen. But with Macsen, the raw power she faced was tempered with thought, always. She forced speech.

"I understand exactly why you would have sold out to Earl Guthrum."

Her words struck home, more fiercely and more quickly than she could have expected and whatever drove Bryse was now beyond control. The shell cracked before her eyes, shocking, deep, until she could see down to all that lay beneath, the same pain she had sensed at Fearnros, bitter and real. A father's desperation.

"Guthrum can hang himself," yelled Bryse. "So can that Saxon king. I have come for my son. I will know where he is."

It had survived, the bedrock love that endured everything. She told him. All that she knew and everything she guessed out of Macsen's mind—the careful calculation, the edge of recklessness, the determination. Even the nonexistent chances. It was the truth or naught. There was no time and there might be death.

She thought, in the growing light, that Bryse's face was dead-white, and the pity that threaded every other feeling, even the fear, clawed at her. She could not show it.

Her heart beat fast, out of rhythm, the force of it savage.

"He did that? For this Saxon king of his?"

"Yes." She chose the next words. "He wished to do that to stop the Vikings from taking all that they want, regardless of whether it is West Saxon or British." Her eyes were fixed on the white face. "But that was not all that was in his mind."

"Oh? And you know, do you? You can see into my son's mind?" The fury was palpable, intense as a beast of prey. "Is that because you think you love him?"

Her gaze held his, all the fury and the baffled grief and the destructive force.

"I do not *think* I love him. I know it."

"Know?" There was no abatement in the fury. It increased. "What can you know after half a dozen days?" The strong face, the dark hair threaded with grey were clear in the first light.

"*Love,*" spat the British voice. "Try the responsibility of living through it for twenty-five years, try keeping it through death and disaster and then you can speak—"

She watched the truth in him and everything took its place, the bitter danger of this moment she had helped to cause, her unacceptability, the task she had set herself, even the unacceptability of her love.

She could not match twenty-five years.

"I believe," she said gently, "that what Macsen thought is that if this turns out well, and if you did not join with Guthrum after all, then what he is now trying to achieve might serve as a proof of loyalty. The suspicion was already on you. He knew that. And if he could help you by what he does—"

"If he could *what?*"

"You are his father," she said. She did not mention Gorei, not in words. But Bryse would see, surely. He would understand. "And you no longer have another son to stand with you."

THE ROADWAY AHEAD BURST INTO chaos in front of Macsen's eyes. The second ambush caused a shock wave in Guthrum's men that broke the headlong charge into disorder. But the success, as ever, was wire thin. If the Viking troops regrouped, Anwas and his men would be overwhelmed.

He pressed the stallion forward, at a speed that was insane on the slippery roadway, making the horse scream its battle-rage, yelling himself until his voice tore. Any advantage of surprise was less important than that his own men should know he was there, that the impossible plan had a chance of success. That the first moment of initiative might hold.

He rode through the first slashing rays of sunlight instinctively, so that the fire-bright light caught him and it was impossible to tell that the shadows behind him were empty.

He knew Anwas caught the trick. He saw his captain move in response, urging the men. He struck out with a force that was mad because he was the target for Guthrum's men. He heard the savage shouting from his own troops like triumph. The thin circle of British warriors closed, forcing the Vikings inward, crushing them together, robbing them of the space to move, to fight.

He felt the balance change. But the difference in strength was great, the weight of numbers on the side of Guthrum's men, and it was no straightforward battle. If one person escaped them to take Guthrum's message north, all they had done, the rest of the struggle between life and death had no meaning.

So he fought on. The rising sun held him, but he could not feel it. The warmth of it, the more bitter heat of exertion on his skin, the sickening scarceness of breath, the savage beating of his heart, were nothing. As though his mind were detached, elsewhere and on the edge another realm, watching the ceaseless driving movement of his body, the moment pressing ever and relentlessly nearer when even that would fail.

He could no longer feel the pain through the head wound, through each aching muscle. The dislocation allowed the kind of movement, of strength, that was unreal. But it was becoming harder to see the light. The blank darkness that waited for him was closing.

Not yet.

He could see the Viking captain turn with the same fast ruthlessness as before, the perfect battle-instinct. The Danish voice shouted orders, trying to form the push that would break the Vikings free. Macsen drove forward before it could happen, hacking with the sword, using the weight of the stallion, all finesse gone. The greater numbers closed round him, unstoppable. He did not think there was hope, not unless Ashbeorn had found more men, could send them here. But that was impossible.

The unreal part of his mind thought of Aurinia, of all that remained undone and unsaid because it could not be spoken. Because there was no place and no time. Not in this world.

Something struck at him, a blow he had not even seen in the moving chaos. There was no pain. Just the sense of falling. He tried to stop it, desperate. If he fell, the others might be lost. He caught balance where it was not possible, the tortured lungs in the thin shell of his body sought the life-giving air and something made his head turn.

There was movement at the bend in the road. He saw Aurinia's form outlined against the dark trees, the grey shape of the wolf at her side. His conscious mind heard the hoofbeats, horses, men yelling.

MABON'S BALLS. IT WAS EXACTLY the kind of mess the dangerous wench had described. Bryse did not know how his son could have got himself into it. He closed his mind to what the uncanny girl had said, to his son's reasoning.

The mess unraveled below them. It was something he could fix. But not a moment too soon. He led the charge down the churned slope, no time to waste. He shouted his orders as he went. Chaos. Touch and go at first. But he managed. The warriors already fighting responded. One thing about Macsen, he knew how to train men.

The intervention worked. Success. He swallowed the almost annihilating relief. When he found his stupid witsick son, what he would do, say…

The confusion cleared. He found the men he knew. Macsen's. No sign of Anwas. But that one with the broken teeth who could fight like the devil. He pushed the great stallion through, downing the Viking he had chosen, turning—the men were yelling at him, shouting like people demented.

Farther on. Down the road.

There was no sign of his son. Suppose Macsen was dead already? Before he had even got here. His heart beat as though it would choke him. *Dead.* He could not move. There was no control over his breath or his limbs, his hand on the reins. He wanted to turn back and look at the fallen but the men kept yelling, pointing forward.

He turned.

Movement caught his eye, along the slope above the road, someone running, a light figure in flying draperies. The girl. And something with her, like grey smoke against the dark trees. Already running as though she knew all that in his pride and his strength had escaped him. Where his son was. What had happened. She simply ran, swift as the light along the grass. Unhesitating.

The Saxon, Huda, turned to follow her. Bryse set spurs to the horse. It carried him, fast, well-trained, brilliantly responsive to the urgency. He shouted his own men to come after. They were quick, disciplined, the response perfect, impossible to better. He rounded the bend in the road and he saw.

He saw Macsen, yards away, in the heart of the moving press of fighting men, surrounded. There was not a chance of survival. He measured the strength of the Viking force, the strength of his own, even added to those of Macsen's men already fighting. His breath choked and his blood seemed to freeze, then to run the more fiercely in his veins. He had to get to his son. It was that simple.

He pressed forward, mad, all the fury of the past days, of the past countless, pain-filled years ignited, driving him, along with the desperation and the fear. The bitter love he had boasted about to the girl.

The ranks of the Viking Guthrum's men closed in response to some unfathomable signal from their leader. They fought as though they believed themselves invincible, as though they possessed the same savage desperation that lived in him. He could not get through. The disbelief numbed him, stole the breath from his lungs, everything, even the rage.

He kept looking ahead and he could see in glimpses the lathered black stallion pushed back toward the trees, the tirelessly moving figure in its bright chain mail, the flash of the sword. He shouted for his own men, anyone. The press of fighters only thickened, relentless.

He saw what his son was aiming for, the man who was the earl's commander even though he wore no insignia for this mission. The leader was the source of the fierce drive that had taken Guthrum's men so far. Stop him and the driving cohesion disintegrated. He was unmistakable, surrounded by his men. There was no way Macsen would reach through that.

His son moved, like someone possessed, unreal. The shining figure struck, the sword blinding in the dawn light, and at his side, a shape that was like a grey shadow, not human. It was a true blow, but even as his heart leapt, he saw the bright figure fall, trapped by the press of men. He could do nothing.

Nothing.

A wolf's howl split the air, and the sudden, fast thunder of hooves from the west. Too late. Too late even if the riders were West Saxon. He saw the lithe figure of the girl and then he lost her.

16

Aurinia stopped at the edge of the damp bracken.

The voice of the wolf had terrified them. The deep howl, beginning low and then rising to the edge of human hearing, brought horrors, the deep nightmares that lived hidden in people's minds. It touched on what was primitive, on dark places that were uncanny.

Hunter screamed. She held still. The rippling shock of that full-throated sound at the time of light-change might be enough to tip the balance in men who were already desperate, pushed to the limit of what mind and body could achieve.

Aurinia stood, breath uneven, caught at the edge of the slope and the advantage tipped for her. But her awareness, the strong inexplicable thread that bound her to Macsen, was gone.

She could see the body on the wet ground and the deadly circle round it. The wolf crouched low over the unmoving form of her husband, jaws open, howling. It was the way her wolves at Wytch Heath howled when one of their number was dead.

The blankness, the lack of any connection to that still form, terrified her. She'd believed he had known she was coming. She had believed in that, just as she had before she had ever seen him with physical eyes. It was the way she had seen him on that earlier battlefield near Wareham.

She had come to him. She had tried to convey that absolute certainty. But this time it had been different, the bond of awareness had been resisted.

He had not wanted her to come.

The knowledge panicked her. The coldness of despair welled underneath, but could not change what she had to do.

She followed the trail taken by her smoke-grey messenger. She walked. She had dropped her cloak so that there was only the slashing, shimmering dress and the silvered girdle reflecting the first fire of the sun. The rune shapes shifted with each small step, their metal voices singing in the still air.

The Vikings saw her.

Not one of Guthrum's warriors recognized her. They would not, even if they had glimpsed her before at Wareham. She knew how she looked to them in the half light of dawn, unearthly, with her hair loose and unkempt, and the signs of power visible, a *vargamor* who commanded wolves. She kept moving out of the dappled tree shadows and into the light and back again, so they could not see her clearly, only shifting darkness and glimpses of burning light.

She kept walking toward the momentary stillness of the warriors surrounding the body. She could see it clearly now, the heavy lines graceful even in lifelessness, the dark hair spread back from the bloodied profile with its closed, densely lashed eyes, the strong, high-bridged nose and the clear lines. She could see his hand curled in the mud, two inches from the sword.

He caught the sun—the gilding on the sword's hilt, the rings on his hand, the heavy arm ring, the dense, complex net of forged steel that covered his shoulders and the straight line of his back.

The Vikings did not move. Their eyes flicked from the glittering riches to the feral shape of the wolf, ears back, head tipped, howling. To her. Back to the unmoving shape with its outstretched hand. They wanted to make quite, quite sure he was dead. They wanted vengeance for their fallen leader. They wanted whatever they could take.

She took care how she walked, her gait smooth, as though it were unreal, no hesitation. She could not show by one movement, or one breath, the fear and the surge of horror inside her.

The sense of nothingness, the dark blank, terrified her. If it was death—

She could not think on it. She kept walking, in and out of light and shadow, her gaze fixed on the body. But she watched the Viking warriors under her lashes. It took only one to break and the rest would follow.

In the same way, it took only one to attack. She knew how crowds worked. The protective sign on her breast, the shape of the *eolhx* rune drawn over her heart, seemed to burn. She focused past the annihilating rush of fear. She was so close, now, near the lifeless form that had loved her in the dark hours at Wareham, to the curved fingers.

Almost close enough to touch and yet her heart felt as though it would die, as though there was no bond, as though the connection to another person that she had never sought, had shunned all her life, was broken. And now it was gone, she could not live without it.

One of the Vikings stepped back, the war axe slack in his hand. It made the others shift. *Now. Please heaven.* She thought it would happen. The booted feet shuffled backward, but not far. They might believe in the old ways, but they were war trained, Guthrum's men. Someone's spear grounded in the dirt. They had the advantage.

She hardly dared move closer, into the full light. They would see not that otherwordly being, a Viking *vargamor,* the wise woman of the woods commanding her familiar wolf, but a desperate unarmed woman.

The bluff was called.

Her feet touched the treacherous sliding unevenness of fallen branches held in mud. She stopped, unable to move.

She had failed the person she loved. She saw defeat and the same pattern of loss.

She thought of death. She thought of all her husband had sacrificed, for her, for Bryse, for the land and for the king who held it. She could hear his voice, *If the king fails there will be nothing, neither English nor British.*

She did not step back. Her hand sought the hunting knife. There was nothing else left.

Her wolf growled, as though he sensed from her that it was now or never. He stood, like a ghost, the uncertain light bleaching the colour out of his pale fur and then coating it in flame. Hunter, faithful to the last.

There was a collective gasp of shock from the Norsemen. But it was not just for the wolf. She could not understand it. She did not dare meet their eyes with an all-too-human gaze. She gripped the knife. Her foot pushed forward on the crossed branches, but the indrawn breaths stopped her. Crossed branches, one straight, the other intersecting it in a diagonal slash. She realized what her painted shoes beneath the bright skirts touched. She saw not with her eyes, but with theirs—the shape of *nyd, naudhr.* The need-rune.

It was a war-fetter.

She stepped forward, her confidence as immediate as it was complete. Through the clash of battle around them, she heard sudden shouting, a sound like the drumming of horses' hooves, many and wild, moving recklessly fast. As though at some unseen signal, the great fallen war-horse that was Macsen's surged to its feet.

An expensive war-horse could be trained to protect its fallen master. More than that, horses had always held power. They symbolized the intention to carry something through to the bitter end, a bond that was unbreakable.

The first of Guthrum's men turned—

Seconds later, the new sound obliterated everything. There was a renewed yelling through the trees and the king's man, with the West Saxon troop, rode out of the dawn.

It was cold, dense, impenetrably dark. The blankness held him, so deep he would never get out. It separated him from everything, from the rich Wessex earth, from awareness and breath, from the painful force of life itself.

From Aurinia.

It was the blinding darkness Macsen had foreseen, that he had feared. Yet now that the dark had come, the overwhelming nature of it encompassed its own attraction, as though it held a promise and a different kind of light, as yet unseen, the trace of something else beyond his reach that his soul craved.

Peace.

Of a kind that was deeper than his comprehension, existing beyond time or knowledge, a kind that did not have a place in this world but which stayed somewhere beyond its boundaries.

He thought he could reach it.

If he did, it would hold him, in the separate realm beyond the reach of this world and its impossible demands, beyond even the pain.

The pain and the demands would have no power against the peace and there was nothing that could not be reconciled.

It was what he longed for. Gorei was there. Aurinia—

Warmth seared through him, bright like melted gold, the deep brightness that belonged only to Aurinia, warm as the touch of her hand, her skin, the smooth supple grace of her body when it melded with his. It was as though his very thought had conjured her, the way he had glimpsed her form against the trees.

She touched him now, even in the complete and overwhelming dark, as though she were with him, unfettered by all the impossibilities that divided them. As though she were part of the place beyond the boundary and she would stay.

The golden brightness pulled at him, insistent, disturbing even in the flow of its warmth, breaking the encompassing shroud of the dark. He sensed distress mixed with it, bitter, filled with the hopelessness that belonged to the locked world, and part of his fractured mind knew that Aurinia was not truly with him, but was trapped in the other world of stumbling limits and wrong chances and pain.

He thought he heard her weeping. She had never wept since he had known her. It was the sound of someone who was alone. He could not leave her to be alone. He told her—what, he did not know. It was something that had no words, part of the bond that had sprung up in this way, outside existence. His mind seemed attuned with hers and the brightness dazzled him. But even as it happened, the sense of her presence moved away.

The pain he knew would be waiting hit him. He heard the sound of Aurinia's voice, real, something that belonged to the physical world, as though she were speaking to someone over his head. He could not make out what she said. A separate voice answered. It could have been his father's except that that was impossible. The voice was filled with the same bitter depth of distress. He opened his eyes.

MACSEN WOKE WITH HIS HEAD jammed against a chain mail sleeve, the sound of furious cursing pouring over him. He tried moving.

"What—" His voice gave out. It sounded like the scraping of gravel under old boots.

"What—"

"Mabon's balls."

It couldn't be. He could not think about it. Not now. He could not even breathe.

Third time. *"What—"*

"I thought you were dead," said his father, which did not precisely push the conversation forward. "I thought—"

What happened with Guthrum's men? He could not get the words past the dryness of his throat.

There was a suppressed sound, then, "It is finished," said Bryse. Thought transference of a different kind. Something had got through. "They are all dead or taken. Every one, it seems, though that Viking who claims to be Alfred's man—" *Ash* "—has taken his men out scouting to make sure."

He started breathing again. If Ash had come and cleaned up the mess, it was all right.

"You might as well know…" It was impossible to do anything but listen and for once his father's thoughts followed the path taken by his own. It was all laid out more succinctly than Anwas could have said it, how the fighting had ended with his father's help. How his father came to be here—

"It was that girl."

The hard-won breath seemed to stop.

"It was she who found me. You might as well know…." The voice continued with the same precision, outlining both what he already knew and what he did not. Aurinia against the shadow of the trees. The wolf.

Aurinia.

"…and then you going after the Viking commander like

some half-witted berserker. I could see why, because they would lose direction without him. But of all the moon-mad pieces of idiocy…I could not get near you. I thought you were…"

He lifted his face out of the net of steel. He could not see for the pain. *I thought you were dead.* The unlikely words and the bizarre choked sound that followed them cut the air. Like breaking glass. He did not think his father would speak again. The tension reverberated, a sword after the blow.

"I could not get near you," said his father, as though driven by some force he could not stop. "I thought it would be simple. I do not lose fights. I am one of the best. But I could not do what I had to." And then the aggressive voice cracked on a strangled pause.

"It was like that for you in the battle when Gorei died."

The pain closed over him, not just from the wound to his head, but inside, the pain and the dizzying sense of dis-location. Disbelief. He did not say *yes.* But this time he thought it was understood without words. He stayed still on the damp Wessex earth streaked with his own blood and because there was nothing else left, he admitted the failure.

"I could not help Gorei," he said in the voice that sounded as dry as wood shavings. "I could not do it."

"It was not your fault," said his father.

Those were not, of course, his father's words. They could not be. It was something imagined, the effect of the blow on whatever moon-mad, berserker half wits he possessed.

"I was too impatient," said Bryse. "Too angry. Too— It was easier to blame you and all this Saxon-king business and pointless oath-swearing and battles like—"

Today's.

"It was easier than blaming myself for keeping Gorei too close and expecting too much, so that he had to do something just to get away." His father was choking.

Macsen tried to force words out. "You cannot think—" The scraped-wood quality of his voice gave out.

"No? Gorei was never as clever as you were. At least you believed in what you did. Gorei was too impatient. We both know where he got that from. So you might as well blame me for—"

"I don't." This time his exhausted voice cracked like a lash. There was an instant's silence while his mind struggled for the rest of the words, but it was his father who filled the void.

"I thought that you did blame me. I thought that you must. Five years of being faced with that inscrutable wall you put up, not even the relief of an argument after that first day you came back after Gorei's death."

"You wanted *me* to argue with you over Gorei's death?"

"Yes. No. I don't know. At least I would have known what was in your head instead of imagining so many things. And perhaps I would have realized—" There was a sharp breath of impatience. "But then again, perhaps not. I am what I am, after all."

Macsen's mouth quirked despite the pain.

"We both have that problem." An inscrutable wall. He had not known, in the kind of mad grief that had afflicted him, what he had done. Or perhaps he had.

"I believed all that time that you blamed me," said Bryse, the holder of equally unknown thoughts. "But you don't, do you? Otherwise you would not be here, like this." The words stopped on a cut-off, inarticulate sound.

There was nothing about the past that could be changed. Except what you did with the results, or tried to. The inarticulate sound came again. He spoke across it and the divergent paths they followed met like a circle.

"Where else would I be but here? You are my father."

The solid weight beside him shifted. "So, it is true, then. She told me. About my own son, and it was she who had to tell me."

There was only one *she*. The half-witted mess that was his mind tried to grapple with what his wife had achieved, a miracle that seemed to extend beyond even the limits of sorcery, the strange beginning of a reconciliation where none had been possible.

"You might as well know," said his father, "that Saxon you married, that sorceress…"

Macsen made some uncontrolled movement that nearly sent him back into the headlong dark. The mail-clad arm picked him out of the mud.

"Aurinia," continued his father. "Since you have not bothered to ask whether the wench was alive or dead. But then, I suppose you already know."

What was the point of wrapping it up? "Yes."

They heard the sound of hoofbeats. Ash. It had to be since no one had challenged him.

"Ah. That must be king's most loyal Viking coming back. I had better go and see whether he wants to arrest me."

"Aye." Reality. The saints alone knew what would happen at Fearnros.

Macsen stood. He could not figure out why his father kept hold of him until he got to his feet. The mail-clad shoulder suddenly jammed against his stopped him from falling. Bryse's fingers caught his arm, his hand. Something hard and unfamiliar dug into the edge of his finger. He looked, and the rising sunlight showed him what it was—Gorei's ring, the token he had taken back to his father all those years ago.

Bryse must have placed it on his hand while he had still been unconscious, on the smallest finger because Gorei had been slighter than him, than either of them, and his own hand was now so distorted.

"Mabon's balls."

"So at least you can still swear in British," observed his father.

They did not say another word, but walked together toward where the Saxon king's man was standing beside the fallen Viking leader, the ruthless thinker, the man he had taken down, he and Aurinia's wolf. Even as he looked, the sprawled figure moved.

"Don't," he yelled at Ash because there had been the flash of a blade, the defensive reaction to the movement of the man on the ground instinctive. There was no reason to spare such a man. "Let him be."

His father made an exasperated noise, but the king's man turned.

It was not Ash, but Garrulf. And beside him, wrapped in light, was the figure of the miracle-worker, his wife. The sorceress. She had her arm round a wolf.

"You might as well know," began his father for the

hundred and fiftieth time. "It was Aurinia who saved you from death when you fell."

HE WHO PLOTS AGAINST THE LIFE of the king shall forfeit his own life and all he possesses. If he wishes to clear himself he shall do it by an oath equal to the king's wergild.

Those were the dooms of King Alfred. Aurinia was not sure that even someone as rich as Bryse could produce enough to cover the life price of the King of the West Saxons. The fact that his impressive head was still attached to his arrogant neck was due to other reasons.

To the fact that he was a prince with many followers and the king needed every man he could get. To the fact that Bryse was more bitter and desperate than actively treacherous and it had all come to nothing. To the supreme irony that he was British.

And then there was what Macsen had done.

Aurinia watched the sunlight through the half-opened shutters. In some other chamber at Fearnros, a richly decorated chamber that held an angry king, the prideful gold-ringed neck that belonged to the man who had become her father-in-law must be well and truly bent. An almost-broken oath renewed. It would be irrevocable this time. But she did not think it would be so bitter. Macsen was with him. They were both part of the same world at last, a world much bigger than that finely appointed chamber with the king.

Gorei would be there.

She turned in the sun-filled bower where her marriage had begun. Sweetly smelling rushes scattered at her feet. Her muscles ached, fatigue washing over her the way it did when a task was finished.

Because it was truly finished. Over. Done. And Macsen was alive. That was what mattered. Her heart still beat hard with the knowledge. She would do nothing to harm all that had been gained. There had been so many sacrifices. His.

Something fluttered at the window frame, making her halt. Muninn. The raven. She watched it settle on the oakwood, messenger of battle and bliss, the light gleaming on its blue-black wings, the colour of her husband's hair.

"He is alive," she said. "He is with the king, now." That mattered, too, the demands of the real world, war and survival, loyalties and keeping honour. All the things that allowed her no place.

"He is alive," she said to the bird. "But I am not fit for him. I have no position and no honour. No family, not even a dangerous one."

The dark head moved. The fierce round eye fixed on something behind her. The feathers on the arched neck ruffled out like a warning. A moment later, she heard it, a faint scratching at the door. A beast's claws. Hunter.

But she knew it was not.

She did not want to move. The bird looked at her. Memory and thought. Fate's power. The glossy wings beat and then settled. The raven stared.

She crossed the room.

It was Bruna, ears back, ribs starting to show as though the dog had not eaten for three days.

She followed.

"I did not think you would come," said Bertred.

Aurinia closed the door of the sickroom. The messenger leaped onto the bed and coiled up, nose buried under the covers. Bertred winced.

She felt shock. It was not only Bruna who was not eating. Her trained eyes took it in. It made little sense. Brother Luke knew what to do. She assessed the herbs laid out neatly on the bench, the healing draught that, among the expected herbs, smelled of lemon balm, which soothed restlessness and fretting.

"I hoped you might come for your hound if not for me," said Bertred.

She looked at the wreck on the bed. The pain hit her across the distance of six paces, the same pain she had sensed and taken inside herself at Wytch Heath.

"Bruna is your dog now."

The shadowed, mood-proud, uncertain face went rigid. "How can you possibly forgive me after what I have said to you?"

She opened and shut her mouth. She had hardly realized that was what he wanted. She thought of the moment at Wytch Heath when he had tried to repudiate her before the king and Macsen had stopped him.

Bruna made a small contented noise and pushed her nose deeper under Bertred's arm as though nothing were wrong, now. Perhaps it was not. The frightened boy she had healed at Wytch Heath stared at her.

"Macsen tried to tell me once about doing things you regret and then having to live with them. I didn't want to listen. I was just incredibly rude, boorish, and then I thought afterward about that thing with his dead brother and what he meant."

The thing with his dead brother. Gorei. She could not speak.

"I did not think," said the boy of seventeen winters. "I just threw it back at him when he was going off to fight, only he never told me that and I didn't know. Just left him to go, with everything unsaid and then he got hurt and could have died, and all the rest happened and you…"

Well, that was clear. The brown eyes beseeched her, speechless. The dog yawned under a childishly bony elbow and settled itself.

"Can you forgive me?" said Bertred. "Fearnros ought to be yours. You are Edwald's daughter, and I was no more than his nephew. It is the only thing I can do."

There were gilded rings on his hands. There was a sword on the bench beside the bed. It had silver wires on the hilt, a badge of rank. Bertred's gaze followed hers.

"I will swear on the sword if you like."

He had used that sword in battle. He was not a child. He meant what he said.

"I can find witnesses." The light brown gaze was very direct.

"No. Fearnros is yours. I do not want it. No," she repeated, over his quick breath. "That is the truth. I…I could not be happy here."

His gaze held hers until she found a smile. What was the point of holding a grudge? Too much had happened. She was a different person from the wary self-protective girl of Wytch Heath and it was better so. Because of Macsen.

"What you can do for me is eat something. You and the dog."

He nodded his head. She watched the colour come back into his face and thought it would be well.

"Thank you," she said gently.

"I know Macsen will give you everything you want and he is better at making things right than I am. He got everyone he knew to go to your wedding and then he asked Brother Luke if he would talk to you."

The wedding feast she had walked out of without thinking and the mess with the sick colt. Brother Luke helping her the next day, lending her the protection of that benign approval.

"But if you ever needed anything, I would give it," said Bertred. "You are my cousin."

She could not say anything, only nod her head as he had.

Bruna's warm silken body shifted, half in sleep. Her master's ringed hand settled her comfortably.

"You would not actually leave Macsen, would you? Only he does not seem to know for sure."

She clutched at the door frame, dizzied, too fatigued and too confused to stand.

"He does not want you to leave him," said Bertred, who was no longer a child.

HE CAME BACK.

Hunter walked with him like a shadow, a *fetch* for that fiercely courageous spirit. He left the wolf at the threshold, the hand with its unfamiliar gold ring briefly buried in smoke-grey fur. The door shut and she was alone with him, Macsen.

He does not want you to leave him.

There were a thousand reasons why she should. He was not looking at her. And then he turned his head. The blue-black hair reflected sunlight like the raven's wings and he spoke.

"I did not know whether you would be here."

She crossed the floor, the rushes and ordinary dried meadowsweet rustled under her feet. They might have been the Nine Herbs scattered on her floor at Wytch Heath, breathing the natural power people called magic. Yet power did not lie only in one place, but in many, not all of them tangible. Like courage.

Her mouth settled over his.

17

It was like the first time Macsen had touched her, breathless and intoxicating. Aurinia's heart beat hard, caught by the same sense of magic, of falling into something depthless and unknown because it was so powerful.

His arms closed round her. He did not push her away and she was drawn into the dark excitement of that embrace, the seductive power that was so familiar.

Yet it was changed, forever different, deepened because of all that had happened to them, all that had been shared. Please heaven it was because of that. Because they had shared.

Her mouth clung to his, melted under that deep magic, so that the sensation washed through her, the sharp kick of desire; more than that, what she felt encompassed everything that lived in her heart and everything she knew how to give.

She did not know whether Macsen could sense all that lay behind what she did, only that when she touched him, the world, her world, was complete. She had fought against that complete involvement, but in this moment it was strength, whole and pure.

It was what she wanted to give and only now did she begin to understand how. Because he had taught her.

Her body turned into the smooth power of his embrace, meeting his touch so that the sense of completeness poured through them both. Through the kiss. Her hands closed round his back, her fingers kneading the tight muscle, the heavy supple lines through the linen tunic. The physical closeness a driving desire, intense and overwhelming. But that was only part of the whole.

It was as though she could feel the touch of his mind. That deeper touch was what she craved, the longing something she could no longer deny and did not want to. She spared no thought for whether that connection was real or imagined, she simply followed it. Nothing else mattered. Nothing existed.

His hands on her body, the caress of his mouth, the touch of her own hands on clothed flesh, on skin, were only the outward expression of that inner life, quick as a flame, true and deep. She pulled him down onto the bed. They knew how to touch each other in the physical world, how to evoke pleasure and hunger and the shivering anticipation of delight, the pure and blinding desire and its deep, deep release.

She felt the weight of his body beside hers, the moment of stillness, then like a miracle, the caress of his hands, the solid warmth, the closeness of heavy flesh, the smooth supple movement of his body. Alive.

The sacrifices he had made poured through her mind, the

risks he had been prepared to take, even to death. As long as she lived, she would never free her memory of the way he had looked, sprawled at her feet in the forest dawn, dead-white and unmoving, the Viking warriors packed round him.

She held him, her arms suddenly tight and clumsy round his body, unable to match the smooth caress of his hands, unable to breathe. But he did not stop touching her. The warmth never faltered, filling her and carrying her with it, unlocking the power of senses and mind until she saw what he would show her, the same quality that had captured her from the first moment she had seen him, the power of life that burned deep within.

Pure fire. On that first day she had watched him kindle flame out of nothing, calling the primal fire that sustained life out of the dark emptiness of her sickroom. She remembered how it had felt, how she had watched him, unable to look away because he created what she needed. He had called the flame out of her. He would do that now, always, and she would respond in the same way, as though she were meant for him, the other half of a soul. His mouth covered hers, possessed it. His hands smoothed her skin beneath her clothes, the touch desire-filled, the sensuality complete, intensely arousing.

The heat flared inside her. She held all that force of life in her arms, the virile strength and the male power. Her lips traced the firm curve of his. Her fingers traced the shape of his body, finding the warmth of skin beneath the already loosened clothes, testing each muscle, feeling it react.

Her own desire surged, she was aware of the fast heightening of her power. She had never truly welcomed that power before. But now the inexplicability of it did not matter, the mysterious power, the golden warmth of it, was a strength, something uniquely hers. She touched the heavy, fine, olive-tinted skin and the taut muscle beneath, and every sense was filled by what she did, intensely and passionately alive.

The power grew and that awareness was totally focused on her lover, on the warmth of his skin, each separate hidden muscle, the smoothness and the small tears, the scratches and the bruising, the harshly suppressed edge of pain. She did not touch his face, his head, not yet. There was too much pain. It frightened her still. Wounds to the head always touched her with fear, for all her skill.

She moved with him and she was aware, with a sharp uncanny clearness that she had never known before, of the deeper need, the drive for a release that was both physical and so much more.

The hidden things touched her, less substantial things that belonged to the realm of the mind. They swirled past her like coloured shapes, strong and intense, as elusive as shadows. She sensed the vital, deep, overmastering strength of desire and behind it, the pain and the edge of exhaustion, sharp like a beast's claws. Sadness and anger and something bitter that she could not read that was black like despair, and the merciless need.

Such things flew past her with the pain. She caught them and held them along with the brighter notes of the desire and the hot outpouring of life, and the touch of the strong spirit that had followed her into the hell of Wareham and had endured.

She took all of that because she knew how. Only *she* knew, because of her power. The fluid movement of her hands on living flesh was so sure, complete, filled with the golden warmth of healing, sharpened by the intense power of desire. Because she wanted him so much, because of the love in her heart. The wild desire and the wish to heal were one, the way they had been when she had first touched him. She had not understood then. She did now. She could give, wholly and without restraint, the way he did.

She held him, moving with him in love, hardly aware of how the last barrier of clothing was removed, only reveling in the greater freedom, touching his body, the strong lines of his back, the sleek supple beauty and the strained marring of the wound across his shoulder, the bruising and the raw unconquered strength. Nothing existed but the way he moved under her touch, the catch in his breath, the hidden fierceness, the erotic swell of muscle in his upper arm, the way his heart beat, the tightening of the heavy muscle of his thigh, the touch of her fingers there and then the hot hard jut of his sex.

She felt his hand touch her intimately and she was so bound in him, in closeness and wanting and arousal, that there was no control. Her body responded to him, to the power and the skilled touch of a lover who knew every secret she had, each source of desire. Her feelings were so intense that the touch of his hand between her thighs as she leaned over him, the slow glide of his finger inside her, penetrating her heat, sent her mad, so that she bore down on his hand, moving so that he touched her as she wanted, needed, at the point of desire until she was blind with it, filled with need and the power of wanting.

The deep pleasure shattered, pouring though her in waves and there was a moment like oblivion. Even then, they stayed close. She knew he held her, hard against his body, as though they were one and always would be. Her heart caught on an intense stab of longing, lethally complete, but she beat it back. She would not think of the future and what it might or might not bring. She would think of now.

The awareness of her husband still coursed through her, body and soul, its power so intense, a thing beyond her knowledge that might never come to her again. Fate's gift. One chance. The golden warmth flooded her veins like rare magic outside time, a gift that was hers and yet a gift that struck power from the force of life in him.

She touched him. There was the same dangerous moment of stillness there had been at the start, the moment of thought in him that existed alongside the fierce impetuous force, the quality that must be partly born out of his character and partly imposed by everything he had had to endure, the result of intelligence and courage and bitterly strong will. She waited, breathless, unmoving, the golden warmth pouring from her in waves, power mixed with desire. And love. He must see the wanting, surely. *Please.*

And the response took life. The power between them caught flame, incandescent.

The feel of Macsen's hands on her skin pushed her heightened senses headlong down the mad path of desire, of love. Of longing and reckless want.

She could see the same desire reflected in his eyes, and a different power that was the match to her own, complete in itself, quite dangerously full.

Impossibly exciting.

His mouth touched hers, the touching brief because the hidden pain racked him. But the deep merciless need drove him past that, drove them both. She had the sense of no limits that she always had with him, of falling into a world that had no ending, something that the damaged part of her spirit had always sought to draw back from. But not this time. She let the unknown depths take her because that meant she would be with him.

She was prepared for the cost, the surrender of that precious guard over herself. But the loss did not come. The power filled her, strong and unbreakable, a shared bond.

Her heart beat fast, intoxicated, drunk on the power, the movement of their bodies, the heated slide of skin. The feel of his hands, the mad pulse-pounding freedom of touching him, everything allowed, accepted, taken and given. And for the first time in her life, there was so much that she could give. She touched the fierce lines beneath her, the fine heated flesh and the desire-taut muscle, heavy and solid and filled with strength, war-damaged.

She watched the reaction, deep and primitive, intense as fire. More than that, because of the bond, she felt it— through her own heightened senses and the surge of her own blood. The shared arousal grew and there was nothing but that, one path and one conclusion. But when she would have moved, he held her above him, his hands at her hips.

She gasped, her slighter body positioned over the raw aroused power of his. Her heart beat and she watched him, every line and shadow of his body, his face, the feverish brilliance of his eyes, wide and spellbinding with desire, the black centres blurred into darkness, like the coming of visions. There was no fear in her, only the intense aware-ness and the bond.

His strong hands guided her and she moved to him, with him, feeling the taut full-ripened thrust of his flesh, taking the heat and the hardness of him deep inside her body, taking everything, the need and the madness of desire, the fierce edge of tenderness.

All the hidden things she sensed in him swirled past her in the shadows, like part of her own soul, the despair and pain and all the bitter sum of the last days, destruction and risk and the fine courage, the possibilities that existed with him always. The hope of something new. Strength, even now, mixed with pain and the relentless dizzying edge of exhaustion. That was what she could heal, the deep pain.

She moved with him, finding the rhythm of that intense passion, the deep desire that increased, even with the bitter pain, fed by need, by the fierce primitive demands of life over death.

She gave herself to it, utterly, and the fire passed from his flesh into hers where they were joined, first through the smooth vital movement of his body, then, as he moved position, taking her with him, through the dark unre-strained ardour of that harshly curved mouth on hers, through the bright heat of his skin. Her consciousness slipped, changed, expanded as though the vision she had sensed in the darkness of his eyes now closed over her.

Shock ripped through her, not fear, but the bone-deep recognition of another fragment of time, a moment already burned into her mind because of all that it meant.

It was the vision she had seen of him on that first night in the chamber of healing at Wytch Heath. She had knelt beside him on the rush-strewn floor with her hand on his fully clothed arm and in her mind, they had already been lovers.

She had not understood, then, what it meant to love, to give. The emptiness and the bitter isolation had been so strong.

Now she did. Everything had led her to this moment, this place, this man.

Her hands touched his body. She sensed the passion fuse, beyond control, the hidden need and the pain behind it were so clear. Her body moved to the fierce urgency of his. The golden warmth glowed through her flesh like a reservoir of light dammed inside her, a wellspring of healing and power and loving. She touched his head, the bruised and damaged skin at his temple.

The outpouring of power burst the dam, its strength unbroken and pure, vitally new in its measure. The warmth suffused her whole being, moving through her skin into his, heat like flame. Love. She felt his body move, her own shattering response in the plane that was real, the physical sensation potent, visceral in need fulfilled, brightly exquisite in joy. It was only part of their world.

AURINIA LAY QUITE STILL, IN light and shadow, her body twined with her dream lover's, Macsen's. She could feel the push of his breath, the fast strained beat of his heart.

Her right hand was buried in the wild black richness of his hair. Her fingertips touched bruising and crushed skin. A wordless sound choked her. There was a faint movement in the heavy weight beside her.

"I am sorry. Your head will pain you."

"No. Not now. I thought you knew."

She withdrew her fingers. The echoes of the unknown power hung round them both, obvious in the shadows, undisguisible, especially to someone like him. His hand on her side moved slowly, gentle as a caress. He took a breath to speak. It was too shallow and she thought of all that she had done, the power he had seen.

"I am going to take you outside and see whether Bertred can arrange for someone to stone you to death." But he did not move away. He tightened his hand on her, a glimpse of the strength she did not think he was aware of. Her heart leaped.

"What do you think?" he asked.

He kept holding her, very close. Her heartbeat increased, the tentative joy painful. She felt her lips curve into a smile that felt like tears.

"I think that Bertred would not do it."

"Really?"

"Really," she said to that perfect aristocratic sneer. "He is a friend and kinsman, a *wine-mæg*. A close kinsman always starts a blood feud if someone slights their relatives." She sensed the change in his breathing, the small unstoppable movement of that harshly curved mouth. He turned his head.

"You did speak to Bertred, then. He did not know whether you would."

She could see his eyes. Her heart beat fast as wildfire.

"I wanted to."

The bright and invincible power that had been so strong in her now seemed so very far away. Its echoes vibrated in the shadows, but the rest was very human. This was the world they had to come to terms in, if such a thing were possible. *If.* Such a small word for so many possibilities.

"Bertred offered me Fearnros, even though he is probably still under the impression I am not Edwald's legitimate daughter."

"You are his *legitimate* daughter? You did not tell me."

"No. There seemed no point in harming Bertred, in trying to prove something so difficult. I thought—" All the reasons vanished beside the blinding truth that she had hurt him.

"But I should have told you. I am sorry."

"I would have made Bertred acknowledge the truth, give you what was yours."

She watched his eyes and knew that he would, not for pride but for her sake.

"Yes. You would."

She heard him swear, not just for Bertred and for Fearnros, but for all the secrets that had lain between them both, unspoken. She shook her head.

"It does not matter. I like Bertred's kinship but I do not want his property, even though he offers it. I might have a claim to Fearnros, because despite the rumours my father encouraged, I am his and he never formally divorced my mother. But I do not want it. Fearnros belongs to the past."

She took an unsteady breath.

He does not want you to leave, Bertred had said.

She glanced away, but her gaze caught on Macsen's damaged hand where it rested against her flesh. She thought of the things he had said to her in Guthrum's chamber at Wareham. She thought of the things he had done. How he had touched her now. Of the deep things said not by persuasive words, but by what he did, trying to tame headstrong Gorei, standing by his father after such a deadly breach, standing beside the king. By her.

She watched the power in his fingers, the ring that was new. Her gaze saw the distortion of the bones beneath the strong flesh, damage that was the legacy of Gorei's death, in body and mind.

I cannot give you all that you should have as my wife, he had said at Wareham. He was not a man to say what he did not believe, neither would he constrain her to something she did not want.

She had only to believe in all that she had seen, in all that she knew of him. She had only to say what she wanted.

Risk and faith.

"I want the future," she said. "With you." She did not qualify the words or soften them. As a statement of intent, it fitted the House of Bryse, and all those long-dead Roman patricians and British chiefs who did not know the meaning of compromise.

"What do you think?" She repeated his earlier question with a carefully turned irony that was entirely Saxon. She lay still, her heart pounding, touching him, the warm living skin and the hard bright gold at his neck, and waited to see whether she was right.

She heard the small intake of his breath, felt the movement of muscle.

"I think what I did before I met you, that if I had to live without you, I could not do it."

God's mercy. "Then—"

The next breath was harsher. The deep, fine voice stopped her words.

"But that was only what *I* felt. My decision was made, but you had no chance to make a true choice. You were alone, your home as good as lost. There was nothing but danger round you, and nothing you could do."

"No. You were my choice."

"You had no other and I...I was lost from the moment I saw you because I wanted you so much."

She lay, still holding him, unable for that moment to move or speak, absorbing the words. *I wanted you so much.*

"Huda tried to tell me how much it would hurt you to take you from your home, but I did not listen. So many things drove me, wanting you, knowing already that there was danger waiting for you at Wytch Heath even if I could not see what it was. Just finding you, after knowing you in my mind like a dream." The solid sheet of muscle shifted in her arms.

"I was crazed enough—" he took a sharp breath "—selfish enough to use even that bond to make you come with me."

He turned, so that she could see his face, all its stark beauty, all the passionate feeling that lived in it, everything that she should have known how to recognize and had not.

"You asked me once in this room, in this bed, whether I regretted what I had done marrying you."

Her heart stood still.

The night-black eyes held hers. "I did not know how to answer that."

She made a small choked sound, not a word. She could not manage that. She watched her husband's finely etched mouth shape the sounds.

"I could not regret it, not for myself. But I did regret what I had taken you away from, your home, and I did not know whether I could compensate for that."

"Then—"

But the fine voice swept past her. "I once said to someone that I could not see the difficulty with marriage. It seemed so simple. Make the decision and act on it. But I did not see the true consequences for you." The dark eyes were steady, unsparing. "I would have used anything to have you."

Her heart swelled as though it would choke her breath.

"You did not need to." Her own gaze held his. "I already wanted you."

The black eyes narrowed, their focus intense, locked on her. "You knew nothing of the outside world when I met you."

She held his gaze, the raw strength and, behind it, the hidden magic. "No, I did not." She caught the bright flare of heat. "If I had, I would have known sooner how things were. I would have understood what love was."

There was a moment between them that was pure fire. Her breath seemed to stop altogether. "I would have known and understood from that first night at Wytch Heath, from before then, how much I love you, even though I am not your equal." She took the last leap of faith. "I would have known enough to recognize the worth of what you gave me—love."

She lost sight of his eyes because he was too close. The kiss was fierce, heart-stopping.

"You are my wife," he said as though that answered all questions of unequal status and a background that would always be less than pristine, despite Bertred's support and acknowledgment. He had said such words to her in this room before and she had not understood the force behind them. She had thought only of duty and obligation. In her blinded distrust of everyone, she had given no room to the love that had been staring her in the face.

She could feel the smile slip through tears. "It is what I want, everything that I want." Something moved outside the shutters, like the flutter of owls' wings. Owls, of course, did not fly in broad day. But they had flown at night, outside Judith's chamber, speaking wisdom she had been too ignorant to catch while Judith's voice said, *What Macsen needs is someone to have faith in him.*

The truth had been there, even when she had not been able to acknowledge it. "In my heart I always knew you would never let me down." She felt the sharp reaction, something that cut him like a spear's blow. "That is how it was. I was only afraid of the damage I might do—

"It was not his fault," she said to all that suddenly tight force. "It was what I thought, all the doubts that lived in my mind before I met Bryse."

"My father is a savage."

"Yes. In some ways."

She heard the tight breath of frustration, but the fierce tension abated slightly. He stilled in her arms.

"How did he survive renewing his oath?" She thought of Bryse kneeling, hand and bowed head laid on the sword of the Saxon king.

"Better than I expected. He can look forward."

She digested what seemed like a miracle.

"But nothing will ever be simple. You know my father."

As long as he could see his son clearly, that was what mattered, for the peace of both of them.

"Aye. I know what he is." Bryse, the meaning of whose name in British had a lot to do with hastiness.

There was a muffled sound between exasperation and laughter. "You have the advantage of him, then, and I believe he recognizes that at last. He wishes to tell you that you have more perspicacity than him."

"He— Did he say that?"

"He is going to apologize."

She had the sense not to ask which stubborn-minded Briton that idea belonged to.

"Yes," added her husband unexpectedly. "He did say that about you. Beside the fact that it happens to be true, you are his daughter-in-law and you should know by now that everyone in this family is twice as good as the rest of the world."

"Indeed I—I suppose I should." *Saint Beren.*

"He gave me the ring that belonged to Gorei."

"That?" She touched the heavily patterned gold on the smallest finger of his left hand and understood. "Peace."

"Aye." He did not say that was an odd word for her to use. She held his hand and the bond of understanding spilled out.

"I can think about him, now. Gorei. I could not before. It was wrong not even being able to think about him. I turned away."

His hand tightened on hers, the gesture unconscious. It did not hold reserve. Her eyes stung with tears. Her gaze focused on the small movement of those strong fingers, the kind of gift she had never thought to be worth.

"You have him back," she said.

"Thanks to you." And then before she could speak, "I wish you could have seen him the way he was, possessed with life. Gorei comes from the word that means *best* in our language."

She could see the point beyond which no words were possible for him, and so she left the pain that was transforming itself into acceptance. He had spoken of Gorei and he would again when he wished.

"I wish I could speak British."

"I can teach you." The voice was steady, like the warm touch of his hand.

"What? A Saxon like me could learn to speak British?"

"Aye. It is possible." Light flashed through the dark eyes like sunlight at the edge of a storm. "The king took Bryse's oath in British. My father was not expecting that. It nearly killed him. He does not know much about Alfred."

Good grief. Aurinia rather thought that Bryse was going to find out.

"Afterward, my father actually spoke about Gorei. About me. Things I had never expected. Meek as a lamb. What did you do to him? Enchant his balls off?"

She choked on laughter. "Aye. I have the spell. You had better watch yourself or—

"All right," she said later. "You can keep them." She tried to get her breath back, to think, to say the last things that had to be said with her lips still heated from such kissing and her body tight against his.

"When I... When I walked out from Fearnros—" She

sensed the sudden tension in her lover's body, but she did not stop. She could not lack the courage, just as he had not. Everything had to be said if they were to be able to go on.

"It is true what I told you at Wareham. I simply walked without knowing what I should do, or where I should go. I did think about what marrying me had cost you, what it would always mean. I begin to understand, now, the true value of what you did, supporting me when Bertred could not, giving me marriage, everything that went with your name, all those people you had at the wedding feast, and I walked out... Brother Luke—"

She touched the tense muscle. "No, you must let me say it. I could see enough of the truth from the start, and I cannot blame your father because I felt the truth of it. But even so, I felt torn in two. I did not want to leave you and even when I found my steps had taken me toward Wytch Heath and I could see my home in my mind's eye, it had changed. *I* had changed and so had what I wanted. My home had been safety to me, but sometimes, it seemed like a prison. And then you came to Wytch Heath."

She took a breath. "I wanted that. I wanted you to change things. You must have known that even before we met. I believed I should turn you away from Wytch Heath because of the way I lived and who I was. I even made myself try to do it, that trick with the air moving in the hall that you saw straight through, and Huda. I thought you might kill him."

"You mean much to him. He wanted to protect you."

"He wanted to protect me from everything, from life."

"From me."

"At first. You brought change. But afterward, when we escaped from Wareham and I turned back to follow you, he came with me. Not just for me. I told him I wanted to find you because it was right and he agreed."

She caught the small negative movement. "It is so. He saw what you had done, all of it, why. He also saw exactly what you risked. How could he not? He is a *duguth,* a war-veteran. He understood exactly, and he told me."

The solid wall of muscle beneath her flexed. Lethal strength.

"You could have been killed following me—"

"You followed me into Wareham and—"

"My father told me exactly what you did."

Never argue with a word-happy Briton. It was impossible to win. "Then he would also have told you no one harmed me." She gave him a cool glance, the perfect match to that passionate heat. "They did not dare harm me. In case you have forgotten, I am a *hell-rune.*" She had never been so fiercely glad of it in her life.

"Aye. They will have to pin your corpse down in the grave to stop it moving."

She let him hold her far too tightly and then said, "Yes."

The slightly uncontrolled pressure eased off. He touched her face. "I could not believe you were real when I glimpsed you along that roadway. I did not want you to be real, to be there as though I had conjured you out of my own wanting, in such danger. I tried to tell you to go."

The blank wall and the sense of distance that had so terrified her. She caught her breath.

"I would always want to be with you, just as you would

want to come to me. When I was so afraid when the Vikings pursued me at Wytch Heath, it was you I saw."

Her eyes sought the dream darkness of his.

"When there seemed no hope, when I fell on the treacherous ground, I saw you in my mind and that was what gave me the strength."

Her gaze meshed with his. There was no denial, only the kind of acceptance she had received from no one, the care, deep and boundless.

"But what you risked to follow me from Wareham. I cannot believe what Huda did."

"Why? Because he is there to protect me? He knows that. But he also understands now how things are between you and me."

The lethal strength seemed to tighten again, but she kept speaking, her voice even.

"Huda understands because those were his own feelings for my mother. He loved her. That is why he stayed with her when she left my father. Huda was my father's retainer, a warrior already making a fair name. He gave up everything to go with her and she never noticed what he felt. She never knew." *Unable to see love when it was given. Like me.*

"Huda wants to protect me so carefully, because I am all that is left of her."

"Huda stayed where he loved." It was one of his uncompromising statements, but the fierce tension in him had lessened.

Yet it was still there.

"Wytch Heath was part of you. When this is over, if—" He caught the word. "*When* Guthrum is forced out of

Wareham," he said with that enviably blithe Celtic war-spirit, "you will be able to go back there, for as long as you want to stay. You have a wolf pack to look after."

Her throat closed up.

"You can do anything you want to. You can rebuild the hall if you wish and have your runes carved over your new door."

Ethel, which marked legitimately owned property, something held by right. How she had wanted that, had held that thought to herself, told herself that this place, out of all the world, belonged to her. He knew.

"Wytch Heath is yours. It always will be."

Marked as hers. Restored and her own. She could *see* it.

"I would not go there without you." Her fingers touched the warm flesh.

"Wytch Heath was my refuge and the only home I had ever had. It was mine and I wanted it. The woods and the heath that kept out every threat, but also so much else. I wanted more." Her fingers spread out over the smoothly heated skin under her hand, over his heart.

"I wanted you, from the moment I saw you in dreams, and that was stronger than anything. I wanted you to find the path through the wood and the heath, and the wolves guided you, the wolves and your own strength." Her hand moved, her breath caught high in her throat. "That is how things were and how they still are. If you think your decisions could be selfish, consider mine."

Her fingers tangled in his hair. "I took from you."

"No." Just that, the single word. Then, "I wasn't a whole person without you."

He meant it. She digested the truth of it while the shared

warmth flowed between them and the shreds of power floated in the air, and his sense of life filled her.

"It is the same for me," she said, "wherever I am, Wytch Heath or Devon, here or in that terrible room at Wareham."

"Then will you stay with me?"

It was a choice, fairly offered. She had her own position, now, acknowledged even if she would never contest Fearnros from Bertred. She could have Wytch Heath and she had wealth. Her husband would not take her marriage settlements from her even if she left him. They were a morning gift. The gift she had not seen was the most precious—love.

She touched him. Her fingers found the damaged hand with Gorei's ring. Her head rested on the strong width of his shoulder.

"Yes," she said. "I am your wife."

Author's Note

In the 870's the English kingdoms had been largely overrun by the conquering Vikings from Scandinavia. Only Wessex remained free, but in 876, what must have been the deepest fear of its ruler, King Alfred the Great, came to pass—invasion.

The people of Alfred's Wessex were already a mix. The Anglo-Saxons had arrived from the area around northern Germany 400 years before to settle amongst the existing inhabitants as the Romans withdrew. Historians no longer agree on whether these existing inhabitants were "Celts". The Saxons called these people *British* and this is the name I have used to describe them in my story.

By 876, Anglo-Saxons and British were closely intermingled in Wessex, although the "British" strand was stronger in those areas west of Selwood Forest, where Macsen and Bryse's beloved Devon lies. The people of Wessex together valiantly resisted the Viking invasion force led by Earl Guthrum.

Those wily opponents, King Alfred and Earl Guthrum, truly existed, but so little is known of them for sure that the interpretation in my story has to be my own. All the other characters are fictitious.

The fabulously named Wytch Heath also exists, although not Fearnros. But again, how this area looked in Anglo-Saxon times is not known and so the Wytch Heath of the story has a large helping of imagination.

* * * * *

*Turn the page for an exciting preview of
Helen Kirkman's dramatic novel DESTINY.
A sweeping tale of love, honor and redemption
set in Dark Age Britain.
To be released for the first time in Mass Market
June 2007 From HQN Books.*

Kent, England—The Andredesweald, AD 875

Elene had two advantages—desperation and a spear. The man had a sword. Light glittered off his chain mail, off the deep gold fall of his hair. It sparked from him as he moved.

The warrior's sword, gold-hilted, rune-carved, was as yet undrawn, as though he thought he did not need it. She balanced the seven-foot shaft of grey ashwood in her hand. The leafed blade at the tip was strong enough to pierce the hand-linked steel across his chest.

He was shouting. Elene did not heed it. She would deal death rather than be in another man's power.

He ran, closing the gap between them, lithe as a grey wolf, fast. He was huge, a shape of strength and threat. His shadow was black. Behind him was the open space in the half-built wall of the fortress. Behind that was the forest.

She tightened her grip on the smooth wood. The distance between her and the warrior narrowed at a speed that defied thought, closed. Striking range.

He did not unsheathe the sword. *Why?*

No weapon. She would have to spear a man unarmed. The world closed to the glittering moving shape, the death-black shadow. But she was close enough to sense fast breath, heat, living muscle, the courage to face killing steel. For a critical instant she held back.

Her breath choked. She would have to strike him or she was gone. Back into hell. A captive. She could not bear that again.

He swerved. Left… She tried to follow with the spear point. He yelled, his voice harsh, so strong like him.

He lunged.

The madness made her strike, the point of the spear aimed true, straight at where his heart would be, locked to his movement—it was a feint. She realized too late. The twist of his body, supple despite his size, was too swift to follow.

He took her feet from under her. The spear scraped metal, ripped out of her hand. The point pitched into the dust. He caught her before she could follow. His arms imprisoned her, a solid leg pinned hers.

The feel of his body was pure heat, hard metal, heavy muscle, size. Such size. Weight. It was the way Kraka used to hold her. She struggled, insane. "…keep still, woman…" The words came through, Danish mangled by West Saxon. She hit, her fist jarring on metal, on flesh hot with sun and exertion, fine skin. *"…hell-rune…"* Hell-fiend, sorceress. It came out in English, equally mangled. She realized what his accent was and went still. She swore. The language she used was the same, only the dialect was different, the pure Mercian that belonged farther north, in the broad midlands.

"You are English, then." The deep, richly accented voice held a thread of amusement, exasperation, the fierce intensity of the shared struggle. He was breathing hard.

"Will you stop now?" he enquired. She swallowed with a dry throat. The spellbinding shape of his voice had no significance. East Anglians were dead meat anyway, their rich open landscape lost forever to the Viking army, to raiders like the ones she had lived with.

"Well?" demanded the dead East Anglian.

She did not know why he was interested in her word. He could kill her one-handed. He knew it. Her chance was gone.

For now.

"Aye."

He loosened his grip. The fingers of her left hand were tangled in the bright mass of his hair beneath his war-helm. She had pulled bits of it out. She unclenched her fingers. Threads of pure gold stuck to her flesh. When he breathed, the solid wall of his chest pressed into her, metal and padding, and beneath it strong life. His hands, huge, heavy, eminently capable, burned her skin through the bedizened, inadequate gown.

He shifted a dense, thickly muscled thigh. His hands moved briefly across her back, the curve of her ribs, under her arms. Shivers coursed over her skin. Her half-clothed body slid down the metal-clad length of his, hardness and heated flesh. Her skirt caught between their tightly pressed legs, lifting. She yanked it down, vicious with fright. He moved. The material came free, dropped, covering the revealing flash of skin, the bright red shoes.

But he had seen the strumpet's dyed shoes of cheap leather, the curving shape of hidden flesh bared to the knee. He had touched her. She read the flare of heat in his grey eyes, beyond anger of vengefulness, deep as instinct. Male. Her breath hitched.

He caught her arm, his hand warm, alive, the touch direct, shockingly intimate, more so because of the brief, naked moments when they had fought between life and death. Close. Deep inside her, sharp feeling uncoiled like a snake waiting to strike.

It was anger, the bitter melding of rage and fear like a killing frost. Rejection. He kept his hand where it was. The heat of the feeling, the solid living touch of him mocked her.

Her feet lighted on the ground and the dizziness hit her. She felt ill with exhaustion, with mad, fey strength of the struggle gone beyond recall, spent. Her belly clenched. No food, no money, no hope of anything. All lost like her freedom. She made herself stand up straight. Not the freedom, that was not lost, not that. She would do whatever it took.

"Lord, you have caught her—"

She stiffened with shock. She had not seen the others, or even realized they were there, that anything existed beyond the man who held her. She turned her neck on tight muscles.

The garrison of the unfinished Kentish fort surrounded

her and the East Anglian warrior like a circle of carrion birds after the battle. Near her feet on the dusty ground lay the lost throwing-spear. Beside her captor's large boots lay the scratched linen bag of pilfered food, the leather bottle of clean precious springwater. Someone's ration of dried meat spilled onto the ground.

"She is dangerous, Lord. We could have shot her, but…"

She saw the man with the arrow ready on string. The bow was still bent. *But the East Anglian with the flashing armour, the one referred to as the leader, had flung himself at her with a wolf's speed, shouting.* Her foot grazed the deadly spear shaft. The *lord* held on to her, a tightening of iron fingers on her bare arm, like a warning.

Like a sign of outright possession.

"She is a thief," insisted the man who could only be the garrison commander. The speech, thickly Kentish, alien to the richness of East Anglia, brought sullen murmurs of agreement.

"Of the armoury?" The lord's voice was flat. The captain of the garrison flushed. Elene should not have found the throwing-spear. They had been unforgivably careless.

"She speaks Danish."

This time her belly clenched with fear. The accusation was true. She spoke across them, shouting. "I am not Danish." She nearly spat it. She sought for calm, reason, for her voice to ring with conviction. "I was living in the forest. The Andredesweald."

"An outlaw, then. And—"

A *hor-cwen*. The appalling scarlet dress clung to every curve of her body like a second skin. Her flesh spilled out of it, her arms bare past the elbow, the curve of her shoulder exposed, the tops of her breasts. The material was thin, now travel-stained, ripped at the hem and—heaven knew what she looked like after fighting a warrior built like Beowulf the monster-slayer. It was only the iron grip of his hand on her arm that held her still. The strength seemed to pour from him in hot waves. He did not speak, but her accuser suddenly stepped back, bowing his head.

But it did not stop his vengeful gaze, the mixture of anger and thwarted lust. The same look, the same resentful fire lived in the eyes of every man in the tight circle that hemmed her in, trapped her from escape. She had made fools out of them all. She was a Danish whore. She consorted with those who had raided their land and killed their kindred and taken their families as slaves. Kent had suffered badly, ravaged by horrors.

It was nothing to what had happened in East Anglia.

The relentless pressure of the massive hand on her arm increased. The fierce strong body with its merciless courage moved.

"I will deal with this."

She could feel the unslaked anger in the company of men around them, the resentment of her. There were a score of weapons. But the unexplained right over them the East Anglian lord possessed, the command, the unbreakable strength of his will was enough.

"My lord Berg."

Berg.

The packed ranks of men opened in a sunlit path that led straight into the heart of the fortress. "Come," said the man called Berg.

Question, command or offer. It did not matter. The choice was clear—him or the pack of angry bated hounds on the scent. The lord in the brilliant armour did not spell it out. No need.

She tossed her head. The whore's dress rustled as she walked.

helen kirkman

Helen Kirkman's love affair with Anglo-Saxon
and Viking history began when she was a schoolgirl
standing on the mysterious grassy remains of a hill
fort and dreaming of what might have been. She
completed a degree in languages and worked at
various jobs before beginning to write.

Helen's powerful romances are charged with an
emotional intensity fueled by a love of history
and all things romantic.

Born in Cheshire, England, she now lives in
New Zealand in a house by the sea.

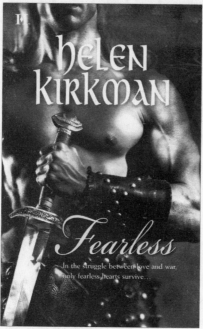

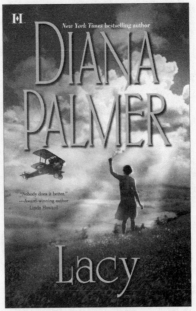